Detective Inspector 1

THE LIAR

A stunning psychological thriller full of breathtaking twists

JANE ADAMS

JOFFE BOOKS

First published in Great Britain 2019
Joffe Books, London
www.joffebooks.com

© Jane Adams

ISBN 978-1-78931-267-6

To my lovely friend, Nikki Kennedy.
Thank you for all your support over the years.

ACKNOWLEDGEMENTS

My thanks to Greg Algar for showing me around his micro-brewery at The Dambusters Inn, Scampton, Lincolnshre and for taking the time out of his busy schedule to answer all my rookie questions about the mysterious process of brewing beer.

My thanks also to Darren Bell of Lincoln Yurts for sharing with me his knowledge of running a glamping business.

CHAPTER 1

Along this stretch of the beach, broken revetments jutted out like jagged teeth, giving the appearance of a war zone rather than a place of leisure. He supposed that was what it was, really, a war, increasingly one-sided as the man-made barriers were outflanked, time and time again, by the fierce actions of tide and wind.

The day had begun misty and though the pale threads of fog had burned away inland, here on the beach the mist remained. It clung stubbornly to the breakwaters, settling in heavy pools beneath them and drifting lazily across the beach. At times he lost sight of his dog and at others he could no longer distinguish the wooden teeth jutting so threateningly from the sand.

"Ca–arson," he called and heard the dog bark in reply. Carson's heavy, wolf-like form emerged briefly from the fog. He bounded around him and rubbed his thick flank, beaded with dew, against his hand, before running off to explore. Man and dog knew the score: each had his own agenda on their morning route, checking in with one another between forays and adventures, though Carson's adventures, despite encroaching old age and stiffness, were probably more energetic than his owner's. This early in the morning, he was content to stroll and take his ease, relishing the absence of people and noise.

There was no warning then, no sense of unease, of being watched or of any wrongness, until he heard his dog bark once and then whimper as though in pain.

"Carson?" The man began to run towards the sound, imagining sharp tidal debris which the inquisitive animal might have explored too thoroughly, but Carson was unhurt. Instead, he was crouched in the lee of a breakwater, close to the steps that allowed passage from one section of beach to the next, staring up at something high on the clifftop. The man bent to examine the dog, still looking for a physical cause but there was no blood, no flinching from his touch, no sign . . .

The man looked up, peering through the drifting fog to discern what it was his dog had seen. The sense of unease, absent until he'd heard the dog cry out, now took hold. He gazed toward the clifftop, in the grip of a primal, unreasoning fear. Hackles rising, he was no more in control of his impulses than was his dog.

The great black hound peered down at them, crouched as though about to pounce, though the man knew that the cliff was some thirty feet high and there was no way any creature could hope to make such a leap. Though he supposed it could scramble down . . .

The local newspapers had been full of it over the past two weeks — reports of a large black dog that had killed three cats and had a go at an equal number of dogs.

Just in case . . .

"Carson, come. Come now." He scrambled up the wooden steps and then down the other side, losing sight of the animal on the cliff top as he dropped behind the breakwater. His anxiety seemed to have infected his dog — not that his imposing-looking animal was particularly brave at the best of times. Soft as tripe, that was Carson. As though to prove his point, Carson yelped again, clattering on the steps and then running ahead, desperate to get back to where they had parked their car, his owner giving chase, feet slipping on dry sand as he headed up the beach, heart pounding and breath ragged in a burning chest.

Clear of the breakwater and able to see the way they had come, he risked taking a look back. No sign of anything on the cliff. The mist had almost lifted and he had a good view of where the hound had been.

Relief flooded through him, draining the energy from his limbs. He almost managed to convince himself that he'd been mistaken, that some strange mirage had fooled them both. But then he saw it again, now standing at the top of the breakwater steps, seemingly magnified by the light of the sun behind it. This time it was the man who yelped. He made the final dash up the low break in the cliff, through the cut and to his car. Carson was already there, whimpering impatiently. The moment the door was opened, the dog threw himself inside and crouched on the back seat.

Gratefully, his owner slammed the door and locked it, fumbling the key as he tried to find the ignition. He swung the car around on the rutted path, glancing in the rear-view, afraid of what he might see . . .

Nothing. Nothing there.

And then, in his wing mirror, the slightest glimpse of movement. He screamed, no longer caring how idiotic he might feel later when he was safe and could tell himself it was just a bloody dog. Right now, in this moment, he was as scared as he had ever been. He slammed the car into gear and took off far too fast down the potholed lane. And each time he risked a glance, the dog was running parallel to them, tall and powerful, keeping pace without effort, and it crossed the man's mind that it was aiming to get in front of the car to cut him off.

The engine shrieked in protest as he redlined before remembering to change gear. He accelerated towards the gap that led back onto the main road, praying there would be no traffic, not daring to slow down. It was only when he hit the road that the dog dropped back. He found himself laughing in sheer relief at having escaped, and at his own overreaction to an oversized hound. Even a vicious oversized hound.

Carson lay silent. The man risked looking over his shoulder at the big, hairy wolfhound whose heavy body took up most of the rear seat.

"Carson?"

No answering lift of the head, no lazy, contented flick of the tail. He knew, long before he reached home and dared to stop the car, that Carson, old friend and faithful companion, was dead.

CHAPTER 2

They had gone into Norwich for dinner and eaten at a restaurant that his friend Mike had recommended on the grounds that Maria liked it. Mike, unlike his wife, was inclined to eat anywhere that the food was not actually bad, and was therefore not to be relied upon to judge.

"Will you come in?" Martha asked as John halted the car in front of the Two Bells B&B.

John smiled. "Better not, it's very late, but I'll be here bright and early tomorrow." He hesitated. "I enjoyed tonight. Very much. It's been . . ." What had it been? Strange for a start, bewildering really, that he should suddenly be experiencing those sorts of feelings again. Since Grace, his childhood sweetheart and wife of almost forty years, had died some twelve years before, John had put all thoughts of romance aside. At first because it had been unthinkable — it would have seemed like a betrayal of his love for Grace — and later because he had convinced himself that he was far too old. Then Martha had arrived.

"I'm glad," she said. Her smile was warm, eyes crinkling at the corners, her mouth twitching in amusement at his awkwardness. "It's been nice. No, more than nice. In fact it's all been rather wonderful, meeting you and, well, you know . . ."

She had celebrated her birthday just the week before, and was eighteen years his junior. John was under no illusions — eighteen years was a considerable stretch of time — but for now he was hopeful. "You could come back to my place," he suggested tentatively, regretting the impulse almost as soon as the words were out.

She looked away, turned back, the smile in place but this time not quite reaching the eyes.

"I'm sorry," he said. "I shouldn't have . . ."

"No, I'm flattered that you did. Believe me, John, I want to say yes. I do like you, a great deal. I'm just not sure if . . . if I'm ready for anything more, not yet." She leaned across and kissed him on the cheek, then, when he moved to kiss her properly, she accepted the pressure of his mouth on hers.

Disappointed, he drew back, cursing the stupid impulse that had shifted their relationship onto the back foot.

"Well," she said, "I'll see you in the morning. Thanks again for a lovely evening."

He watched her step inside the B&B, turning to wave as she opened the heavy wooden door. The adjoining pub bar was still open and he toyed with the idea of going in, but the scant ten minutes until closing time and the fact that he'd already drunk his allowance for the evening made it seem like superfluous punishment. After all, she was just next door. It might feel as though he was stalking her, hoping she might suddenly change her mind.

Just what had he been thinking? He knew she liked him, but she'd given no sign, no real indication of wanting to get to know him *that* way.

"Out of practice, you old fool," he told himself. "Too heavy-handed by half." But then, the only woman he had ever had to woo had been Grace, and that was so many years ago he doubted the same rules applied.

He turned the car around in the narrow road and set out for home. The salt tang of the ocean drifted in through the window that Martha had left open and, glancing to his left, he caught a glimpse of moonlight on still water. Emerging from the village, he flicked his headlights onto full beam. At this time of the night, the coast road would be empty, the flat landscape giving him plenty of warning of vehicles headed his way.

Twice, he thought he saw something running along the verge but he could not be sure. Something larger than a fox. But his thoughts were still with Martha and the conundrum that was 'woman', and he paid the shadow scant attention until suddenly it was there, leaping out into the middle of the road, blocking his path and forcing him to brake to a skidding halt that left the car in the wrong lane, square on to the creature.

John stared in disbelief, the hairs on his neck rising.

The animal gazed back at him.

It was tall, Great Dane-like in height but more powerfully built, its neck thick like that of a mastiff but the head lacking the heavy jowls and the ears pricked and sharp so that it looked like a wolfhound on steroids.

The creature snarled at him, baring its teeth and lowering its head. Its eyes gleamed red in the headlamps and some small corner of his brain told him that only a fox's eyes reflected red. John slipped the car into reverse. He was unnerved now, his mind wandering to the old stories of Black Shuck, cursed hound of local legend that roamed these fields. The papers had been full of sightings this summer, mainly from tourists willing to be spooked, or locals playing on the regional folklore to drum up custom. John pushed such ideas aside, concerned with the more prosaic worries about potential garage bills and insurance claims.

The dog circled the car, coming round the front towards the passenger side. John reversed slowly, easing the vehicle back to the right lane and preparing to speed off the moment his path was clear. Preternaturally frightening though it was, he had no doubt that this animal was flesh and blood. But it was large enough to do serious damage to his car should he hit it trying to get away.

It was now at the passenger side and he could hear its padding feet, its deep snarl, the slow regularity of its breathing. Too late, it occurred to him that the reason he could hear these things so clearly was that the passenger side window was still open. It lurched forward to thrust its massive head inside. John stamped on the accelerator. Forgetting for an instant that he was still in reverse, he zigzagged backwards down the lane. Precious seconds were wasted while he stopped, slammed into first while fumbling for the button to raise the passenger window. He didn't have enough hands! He charged at the dog, hoping against hope that it would be the one to give way, but was forced to swerve violently when it did not, mounting the grass verge and praying he didn't end up in the ditch. He accelerated hard, cursing himself for giving in to panic . . . over a dog, for goodness' sake. Just a dog.

Looking back, he could see nothing on the road and nothing when he scanned the fields on either side, half expecting the apparition to reappear ahead of him.

It was another mile or two before he decided he could slow to a more normal speed. He decided too that he had a duty to alert someone before the dog caused an accident, or bit a child . . . or scared someone properly witless instead of just halfway there. He was aware of reports that cats had been savaged, dogs attacked in their own gardens and the body of a badger found ripped apart by something with very big teeth. Now he'd seen it, he could well believe that this animal might take on a badger and not come off worst.

He pulled into the entrance to a field and found his mobile phone. Long retired he might be, but ex-DI John Tynan was still well remembered, and he had no difficulty getting through to an officer he knew.

"It's about that black dog you keep getting reports of," he told the amused desk sergeant.

"Oh aye. Don't tell me you've succumbed to the mass hysteria too?"

John laughed, but it sounded a little shaky. He hoped his former colleague wouldn't notice. (He would, of course.) "As a matter of fact, I think I have," he said. "On the coast

8

road about a mile outside of Happisburgh, heading Cromer way. It's a big bugger, came bounding out of the field and across the road. I nearly hit the bloody thing."

It felt good to swear about it, albeit mildly. Though the words he'd really have liked to use might well have placed him in the hysterical category and he wasn't prepared to be considered that.

"Scared the pants off me for a moment," he admitted. "It's got a temper on it and a lot of sharp-looking teeth."

"Oh aye, dogs do go in for them. All right, John, I'll see if I can rustle up a dog van, maybe a patrol car. You're the second today, by the by."

"Oh? Who else has sighted the bugger?"

"Businessman, Norwich bloke, taking his German shepherd for a walk. Reckons he saw it on the beach. Reckons as how it chased him, and his Alsatian ran away faster than he did." He laughed. "So much for man's best friend."

John laughed with him, feeling more relaxed now he had shared the experience. He hung up and set off again for home, knowing that he'd done all he could. He was still disturbed by the events of the evening and, even while he chided himself for his foolishness — dogs not generally being gifted with the ability to use bolts and keys — he double-locked the door and kept his downstairs windows closed.

CHAPTER 3

It was early Monday morning, too early to go and collect Martha, but John had been unable to sleep and had risen early. He had parked his car on the clifftop, beside the as-yet-unopened tea rooms, and walked back into the village. Outside the village shop an A-frame advertised the local paper. Black Dog had the front pages yet again. John reckoned it must be the third or fourth time this month. Still, it made a change from the bad weather, the economic downturn, the cliff falls and the very real threats to the lighthouse, which had dominated the landscape for years, but was now uncomfortably close to the cliff edge.

Oh, and not to forget the toing and froing of local — and occasionally national — government officials sent to assess the damage and argue about what, if anything, they could do. There was talk about abandoning the village to the sea, but the locals had mobilised and John knew they would not give up the fight just because the distant government thought they should.

The early sun, already hot, glared startlingly bright off the whitewashed walls of the shop. Inside it was shadowed and dark and small, the shelves stacked high and deep with tins and packets and notepads and toilet rolls. John bought the morning paper, intending to sit on the beach and read, and picked up some mints and a roll of wine gums, the jewel colours suddenly attracting him.

He walked back to the beach along the cliff path, past the lighthouse and down the steep flight of steps built to avoid a precipitous scramble down a section of crumbling cliff. He stood on the steps and studied the landscape, examining the latest devastation — the mudslides and the remnants of what had once been homes leaving their tell-tale trail of brick and tile wedged in the marl and sand.

Slowly, he made his way down onto the beach and, finding a gap in the revetments, wandered onto the sand, damp from the receding tide. He poked about with the toe of his shoe, looking for shells and belemnites. Occasionally he had struck lucky and found odd pieces of amber too. Grace had started the collection years before, depositing her finds into a wicker basket beside the fireplace. Once the basket was full she kept the most precious things and used the rest to mulch the pots on her kitchen windowsill or the containers in the garden. She'd done it ever since they first moved here and John had teased her — blaming her, playfully, for contributing to the beach erosion. Now, in the long years since her death, he continued to search.

He had loved his wife with a passion he found hard to put into words and he was still in love with her, always would be, even if someone else took her place at his side or in his bed. It was this, far more than his awkwardness or the lack of opportunity, that kept him from looking for a new companion.

He wondered, somewhat darkly, what he would have done if Martha had accepted his offer and gone home with him last night. Would the morning have been difficult? Or would it, somehow, have felt all right after all?

The sea dragged lazily at the darkened sand. It was a rare calm day but looking up at the sky, John noted the bloated clouds, hanging low above the horizon. An hour or so of sunshine before the storm, he guessed. The far-off line where sea met sky was already stained by a creeping bruise where the distant rain was falling. With the sound of gulls and the soft susurration of water on sand the only sounds to break the silence, John closed his eyes for a moment and absorbed the sun, the silence and the peace. But it failed to soothe him. This village, this beach, held other memories, sad and painful ones. A child dead and a woman too, and another little girl almost lost. A case John had been unable to solve until his friend DI Mike Croft had come along and together they had found solutions. The friendship forged during that unsettling time had proved to be a lasting one. Lasting, too, was the discomfort John still felt on returning to the scene of such loss.

Glancing at his watch, he judged that he could safely make his way to the B&B where Martha was staying. They planned to go out to yet another church today, pursuing Martha's family history project. His, too, he supposed, as it turned out Martha was a very distant relative.

A little reluctantly, he turned his back on the ocean and began to walk back up the beach. He thought about his *faux pas* of the night before and wondered if there would be any awkwardness today because of it. He hoped not. He genuinely liked Martha, though he also had to admit he couldn't quite make her out sometimes.

A sound, both familiar and unwelcome, shattered his reverie. Police sirens were not often heard out here. John turned his head to try and get a bearing on the source of the sound as first one and then a second car hurtled into the village and out past the church before stopping dead.

There was only one dwelling that John could think of up there — the Two Bells. And something told him that the cause was—

"Martha!"

He tried to run. The sand that had been such a source of pleasure dragged at his feet now, slowing him unconscionably. To go back to the steps would take far too long. He turned and headed towards the lowest point of the cliff, which offered the semblance of a cut-through into the field beyond. By the time he reached the little hotel, an ambulance had joined the pair of now silent police vehicles. The owner of the bed and breakfast stood in the doorway. She was crying, trying to tell a female officer what she wanted to know.

"Mrs Beal," John hurried over, aware of the sand still pouring from his shoes and the sweat stains on his shirt. "Mrs Beal, what happened here?"

"Sir." The police officer didn't know him — too young and too new. "Please, sir, I'm afraid you'll have to—"

"Oh, Mr Tynan. It's so terrible." She shrugged off the tentative attentions of the young officer and almost hurled herself at John. "She's dead, Mr Tynan. Someone stabbed her. In her room. I went in and there she was — dead."

CHAPTER 4

John waited for close on an hour before at last seeing a familiar face. An ageing, battered Volvo V60 estate pulled up in front of the little hotel and DI Mike Croft eased himself out, pausing to stretch his long legs before glancing around and assessing the scene. His gaze fell upon John.

"John? What are you doing here? Are you all right?" Mike strode over to him and laid gentle hands on his arms. "You look grey. Come and sit in the car."

"I'm all right. Please, don't fuss. It's the shock, that's all. The dead woman . . . Martha, she was a friend of mine. I mentioned her to you?"

"The one researching your family? Oh Lord, John, I'm so sorry."

"Inspector Croft," an officer stuck his head around the front door and called out. "CSI say we can go in now."

"Thanks, Terry. John, I'm afraid . . ."

"I know. Civilian that I am now." He tried to smile. "If it's all right with you, though, I *will* sit in your car."

Mike patted his arm, handed over the keys and followed the young officer inside. Reluctantly, John settled in the passenger seat of Mike's old Volvo, playing the waiting game again. He stared up at the closed curtains of Martha's room, his vision blurred by tears, trying not to visualise what those inside the room could see.

Stabbed, Mrs Beal had said. She had described a single wound and a lot of blood.

Stab wounds he had seen. Murders he had seen. Violent death, though not common in these parts, was nonetheless familiar, but for it to happen to someone he had kissed the night before . . .

John, ex-DI Tynan, finally gave in. He put his head in his hands and cried.

*   *   *

Constable Terry Gleeson had been the first officer attending, and as FOA had been at pains to preserve the scene before the CSI and the investigative team arrived.

"Mrs Beal was in bits," he said. "I asked her what she'd touched and she looked at me like I was daft in the head. 'Like I'd have touched anything.' That's what she told me. 'Like I'd have touched anything.'" He shrugged. "It must have been obvious the poor woman was dead. According to Mr Beal and Harry Pickson, who works in the bar and was helping Mr B change the lines in the cellar, she come down the stairs shrieking like the killer was after 'er."

"So how did she come to find the body?" Mike Croft asked.

"Apparently she went to check the next bedroom and the shared bathroom. They're expecting a family tomorrow afternoon and she wanted to remind this Mrs Toolin that she wouldn't have the bathroom to herself after that, so she knocks on the door, door swings open, she sees the body on the floor."

"So the killer fled and left the door open?"

"Pulled to, Mrs Beal reckons. It looked closed but wasn't latched. Soon as she touched the door, it opened. She says she didn't go inside, and the state she was in I'm inclined to believe she had one look at the body and took to her heels."

Mike nodded. "Anyone else go up to the room?"

"Harry Pickson, the barman. He's a first-aider and he was worried in case the woman was hurt but not dead, so Mr Beal calls us and the ambulance and Harry goes to have a look. He says he never went further than the doorway. It was clear the victim was beyond any help he could give, so he came back down and took care of Mrs B. She was still all of a dudder, shaking like a leaf."

"And how long before you were on scene?" Mike asked.

"No more than five minutes. I live just along the North Walsham road. I drink here, and I've been emergency key-holder for the village hall and the Beach café since they had a break-in last spring. The Beals have my number."

So, thought Mike, this was very local and very personal to Gleeson.

"It's supposed to be my day off," Gleeson said. "Hence the civvies. I didn't take the time to change."

He didn't sound apologetic, so Mike didn't bother with unnecessary forgiveness. "If you drink here, had you seen the victim before today?"

"I think I may have done. Night before last I was in here for the darts match. I try and make the pub quiz night when I can. I generally notice the outsiders and the Beals often point out their guests — introduce us, like."

They had been talking on the first landing. The stairs dog-legged up from between the lounge bar and the door that led off to the kitchen and the annexe where the Beals lived. Mike allowed Terry Gleeson to lead him up the second, short flight of stairs. Off a small landing, a door opened to the right, into a bedroom fitted out with a double bed and bunk beds. Off to the left, facing towards the front of the pub, was a door marked 'Bathroom' and a second bedroom. Aged and well patinated floorboards, covered with a bright and rather too modern runner, creaked beneath Mike and Terry's tread. Terry stepped aside to allow Mike a view into the room.

The bedroom was typical of its kind. Cleaner than most, Mike thought, but with the standard divan bed and slightly mismatched furniture, most of it nineteen-thirties brown, except for a flat-pack-style bedside table on which stood a lamp with a red shade. Rose chintz curtains that didn't quite meet in the middle hung at the windows and an equally busy rug covered most of the floor, leaving a border of dark stained boards. The fireplace was blocked off, heating now provided by a radiator beneath the window, but tiles from the old hearth remained and a jug of flowers had been set in the centre, like an offering to the displaced gods of hearth and home.

A magazine lay open on the bed and there was a cup of cold tea on the chest of drawers next to a tray with an electric kettle and a little dish containing individual sachets of tea and coffee, two kinds of sugar and non-dairy creamer — a pet hate of Mike's. Some things even *he* was fussy about.

There was no en suite. The bathroom, as he had seen, was next door, shared with the currently unoccupied second bedroom.

Nothing seemed to have been disturbed. Everything was as it should be, except for the body stretched out on the floor beside the bed. The victim lay on her back. She was wearing light blue pyjamas, cotton, with a tiny floral print. No dressing gown, and her feet were bare. Shoulder-length blonde hair had fallen back from her face and revealed white skin, lightly freckled, blue eyes still open but already sunk back into their sockets. A knife with a varnished wooden handle protruded at an odd angle from just beneath her ribs. Mike knelt beside the CSI, the paper of his disposable crime scene bunny suit straining and almost tearing as his long legs stretched it to its limit. The elasticated cuffs at the ankles hitched up his trouser leg, exposing an expanse of calf and mismatched socks. The CSI glanced at them and laughed.

"Maria away, is she?"

"Yes. Why?"

"Oh. Nothing."

Mike glowered, or tried to, but it was not an expression that came naturally to his rather placid face. "What do we have?" he asked.

17

"Right, well, single stab wound. From the angle of the knife the direction appears to have been upward from below the ribcage and, I'm thinking, entered the heart. At least we don't have to look for the murder weapon. Doc reckons time of death somewhere between midnight and three, but the usual provisos apply."

"Have you turned the body yet?"

"No, we were waiting for you." He beckoned to one of his colleagues and Mike straightened up, pressing himself against the wall to give them more room. Blood had soaked into the woman's clothing and seeped into the rug beneath her body but the centre of her back was clean of both injury and staining.

"Looks like she was stabbed and just fell," Mike said. "Would it have been instantaneous?"

"Death, you mean? Could have been if the knife went in right. No defence wounds, no sign of her moving after the attack, so yes, likely. As you say, she was stabbed, she fell back, the body landed where Mrs Beal found it."

"So," Mike speculated, "someone she knew, someone she allowed up close. Presumably she didn't see the knife or she'd have cried out, tried to escape." He glanced once more around the room. Nothing seemed to have been touched, nothing disturbed. "Anything taken, so far as we know?"

"Nothing obvious. Her handbag's in the bedside cabinet. We took a quick look but her purse is still there, with money and cards. Her watch and bits of jewellery are in the drawer. No mobile phone."

"Dressing gown?" Mike wasn't sure why this was important, but felt that it was.

"Hanging behind the bathroom door. There's some toiletries and such on the sink in there. The landlady says she thinks she heard the bath running at about half eleven. OK to move the body now?"

Mike nodded.

"Sir?" The female officer who'd been talking to Mrs Beal stood in the corridor. "She's up for talking to you now. If you're ready?"

"I'm on my way. Jude, if you were in your pyjamas and, say, someone knocked on the door, would you put your dressing gown on?"

She laughed. "Is that a chat-up line? I'll tell on you."

"No one would believe I had that much nerve. But would you?"

"Yeah, probably. I mean, I lounge around at home in a T-shirt and trackie bottoms, probably show more in that than I would in my pyjamas, but it's a night thing. Kind of intimate, you know? Depends if I knew who it was, I guess. How *well* I knew them, if you see what I mean, though if it was *that* kind of knock on the door, I wouldn't be in my grubby old PJs."

Mike nodded. That was what was bothering him, he supposed. The pyjamas worn by the woman, Martha, were comfortable, functional, not the kind of thing you'd wear for entertaining bedroom guests. But would she want to cover up if she had visitors? He knew that his wife, Maria, would either don her dressing gown or, if the visitor happened to be someone she didn't know very well, might even get dressed.

Not that their out-of-the-way cottage attracted many nocturnal visitors.

Did it matter? Or was he playing silly buggers with random facts? He paused on the landing, and then took a quick look inside the bathroom next door. A second CSI was already there, bagging the items left on the shelf above the sink.

"Anything of interest?"

The CSI shrugged. "Towelling bathrobe behind the door. I've not bagged that yet but nothing in the pockets except a used tissue and some fluff."

Mike peered in around the door. The bathrobe was faded blue terry cloth. It looked well-used and worn, rather like the pyjamas. These were items of clothing Martha would use at home, nothing bought especially for the trip. It was as if she'd just picked out what she needed, shoved it in a bag and come here. An impulse? Or was he, again, making too much of nothing?

"Shampoo and such on the sink," the CSI said. He pointed at the items already bagged. "Half used. I'd say they're what she always used, not bought especially for the trip."

It was as though she'd been following Mike's thoughts, and the fact that she too had noticed Martha's either frugal, sensible or ad hoc packing made Mike feel slightly better about his musings.

"Anything unusual? Anything that might tell us—?"

"Popular brands, as advertised on TV." The CSI smiled at Mike. "She coloured her hair, used a shampoo that was supposed to make the colour last longer. Whitening toothpaste, and a soap meant to be fragrance-free and kind to older skin. Make of that what you will. Oh, and an anti-wrinkle night cream." She waved the pot at Mike. "All standard, widely available brands."

Mike nodded, satisfied there was nothing more to see. He took a final glance around the tiny bathroom. Clean and functional, just as the bedroom had been. He backed out onto the landing, where ds Burnett was waiting for him.

"OK, lead on," he said. "Let's see what the landlady has to say."

CHAPTER 5

Mrs Beal sat in a plump, red easy chair in their private living room. Mr Beal perched on the arm with his hand resting on his wife's shoulder. He looked uncomfortable and uncertain, as though he was neither used to perching while his wife sat or offering this kind of physical comfort. Mike knew them both — the bar in the Two Bells did a selection of real ales that John was partial to and a rather good Sunday lunch menu, so he and Maria and John were semi-regular visitors. He was used to seeing the Beals in motion, serving behind the bar or waiting table, or glimpsed helping out in the kitchen when the staff were under pressure. Short and stout, they were far more suited to bustling and doing than they were to perching and sitting. He reckoned Mr Beal would be better employed making everyone a cup of tea.

The uniformed officer pulled up a wooden chair and sat down close to the couple, pulling out her pen and readying herself to take notes. She looked altogether too eager, but Mike made allowance for the fact that Cathy Stephens was new, young, just out of training and inexperienced enough for her first murder to be exciting. He was relieved when the door opened and Jude entered quietly, flashing him a brief smile. Mercifully, ds Jude Burnett was long past that stage.

She took in the scene with a swift glance and said, "Mr Beal, would you mind very much if I get everyone a cup of tea, or some water or something? It's a hot day and I think—"

He was on his feet in an instant, a look of profound relief on his face. "Of course, my sweet, I should have offered. I'll come and give you a hand."

Mike nodded in appreciation, while Mrs Beal half rose from her chair and cast a longing look after her husband as though envying him his sudden freedom.

Jude would get anything useful that there was to get out of Mr Beal. Mike turned his attention back to the wife.

"Tell me about Martha Toolin," he said gently. "What were your impressions of her?"

"My impressions of her?" Mrs Beal looked momentarily taken aback and then settled down to think, her eyes drifting around the room as though inspiration could be gained from the thick, textured wallpaper and the framed floral prints.

"Was she friendly? Chatty?" Mike let the question hang and waited until the focus of her gaze returned to him.

"Chatty? No, she didn't say a lot. She said she needed a break, that she came out here because a friend had told her about it. I assumed it must have been John. Mr Tynan, you know."

"And she'd been here for . . . ?"

"Ten days. You know, she was lucky. Usually, we'd have been booked solid this time of year, but what with the weather and such it's been real slow. I told her when she came I could only do her three days, then we had a cancellation so I told her she could stay on. I think she was pleased, but she weren't the sort of woman as you could really tell."

She looked at Mike for approval and he nodded encouragingly. Constable Cathy Stephens did not look up. Head down, she was busy taking notes. Mike decided he'd have to have a gentle word about interaction during interviews.

"How long has the second room been unoccupied?"

"There was a young couple on the same landing for two nights, left yesterday morning first thing. I'm due another couple arriving at the weekend, they're booked into the downstairs self-catering and a family in the family room upstairs . . ." Her voice trailed off as she realised that custom might now be lost. Mike, aware of how tough these last two summers had been, knew this reaction was not down to lack of feeling. "I'll need the names and address of the couple that left," he said. "It could be that they heard something, or Ms Toolin mentioned something to them. I'm sorry, Mrs Beal, but that whole wing has to be regarded as a crime scene for the moment, until we work out how and when the murderer came and went."

Mrs Beal paled, but nodded. "What about our rooms?" she said. "Do we have to leave?"

Mike thought about it. The annexe housing the landlady and her husband was effectively a separate building. It could be accessed from the pub, but the door had been locked the night before and there was a completely separate entrance that led to a private car park at the back of the pub. It was, or so Harry the barman told them, used only by the Beals and by whoever might be staying in the self-catering flat that made up the third side of the building. Having walked the scene, Mike was pretty certain that Martha Toolin's killer would have accessed her room from the bar, up the stairs, and would have had no reason to go around to the back of the pub.

"You should be able to stay," he assured Mrs Beal, "so long as you use the back entrance. CSI have cleared an access route."

She nodded. "Yes, the girl showed me. Said I had to come and go just where she said. Anyway, I doubt the guests'll want to come now," Mrs Beal said sadly. "Not with a dead woman next door."

Mike didn't bother reminding her that Martha Toolin would be gone later that day. "Did she have any visitors while she was here?"

"Well, there was John, of course. Mr Tynan." She frowned. "And then there was that boy. He wouldn't stay away. Right nuisance he was."

23

"Boy?"

Mrs Beal was excited now. "Yes, boy. No more'n a teenager, I'd say. Came here a time or two to see her. They had an awful row and she told him to . . . well, to go away. I had to tell her I didn't want that kind of upset nor that language. We get families staying here." She glared defiantly at Mike, who nodded sympathetically.

"Did she say who he was? Where he came from?"

"No, but he did. He told me he was her son."

"Her son?"

"Yes, that's right," she said, "but I ask you, the way the two of them were fighting there was no love lost even so."

"And you don't have a name for this son?" Mike asked.

She shook her head. "No. I thought, well, some people do carry on, but it isn't my business. Mrs Toolin was a guest and she'd be gone soon enough. It wasn't my concern." She paused, frowning sadly. "It isn't right though, is it? To lose your mum at that age. Nothing but a boy, even if she didn't want him."

* * *

"What time did you leave last night?" Mike asked as he and John Tynan drove away. For the time being, at least, Mike would act as Senior Investigating Officer. He had appointed Jude as his DSIO, with the proviso that he might have to bump her sideways into another role should their boss decide that the case required a more experienced deputy. Jude, with local officer Terry Gleeson assisting, was in the process of setting up an incident room in the village hall. It was the second time, Mike thought ruefully, that it had been commandeered for this purpose. A decade before, when Mike was new to the area, this village had witnessed the disappearance of a child, and they'd set up the incident room in the same place then. The child had been found — though there had been deaths enough — but the inhabitants of this little village would no doubt be nursing the memory.

"Was the bar still open?" He rephrased his question as though hoping to jog his friend's memory.

John nodded. "I think we got there at eleven, eleven fifteen, something like that," then, "No, I'm wrong. It was a bit before, because the pub was still open and I thought about getting a swift drink, but changed my mind. About ten to, then."

Mike nodded and glanced at his friend, sitting tense and uncomfortable in the passenger seat.

They had called at the Beach café and arranged to leave John's car there, while John drove back to police HQ with Mike. He'd made a brief formal statement before leaving the Two Bells but that already looked as if it would need revising. Even witnesses experienced in criminal investigations, like John was, could have trouble recalling events once they were the focus of them.

"You'd been out for dinner."

"Yes, like I told that sergeant of yours. We had dinner in Norwich and then I drove Martha back here. I'd had one small glass of wine, if you're interested. She asked if I wanted to come in and I said no."

Mike noted the slight hesitation. "But?"

John Tynan sighed. "You think you're past the age of making a bloody fool of yourself, don't you?"

"With women? I don't think the average man ever reaches that stage. What did you do?"

"I suggested she came back to my place. Stupid. I knew as I was saying it that the answer would be no and I was ruining things."

"Was there much to ruin?" Mike glanced at him again, his concern deepening.

"Truthfully? No, I don't suppose there was, and I'd probably have run a mile if she'd said yes. But, you know, it's the first time since Grace died that I've even considered . . . well, anything. And it felt nice, just to feel the impulse. You know?"

Mike nodded. He was as awkward with women as John was. Maria, now his wife of ten years, had made all the running in their courtship, while Mike had largely made inept noises from the sidelines. He was profoundly grateful that she'd found him worth the effort, and even more profoundly grateful that she'd understood that it wasn't lack of interest on his part that made him hesitate, just utter terror. He'd considered Maria way out of his league.

"You told me she was a distant cousin or something. Is that right?"

"Yes, come to track down the family tree."

Something in John's voice gave him away — to Mike, at least. "That bothered you?"

"At first, yes. She'd got my name from one of the few relatives I'd kept in any kind of touch with. My cousin Billy and I were close as kids and young men. We drifted, rather, in later years but we exchange Christmas and birthday cards and we speak on the phone regularly. He phoned one day about two months ago, said he had this woman asking questions about the Matthews side of the family — that's my mother's side. Billy was from the Tynan branch and asked if I would mind having a word. Next thing I know, she's turned up here, and I don't mind telling you, I was not pleased."

"So, what changed?"

"Oh, I don't know. I got to like her, I suppose. She was fun to be with and attractive and I think she made me realise that I was lonely. Don't get me wrong, Mike, you and Maria — all my friends, in fact —are very precious to me, but it isn't like having that special someone, is it?"

"No. No, it's not."

They fell silent for a moment or two. Mike thought about his wife, away visiting her sister who'd just had another baby. Five, that made it. Nieces and nephews to spoil and enjoy. Mike was due to join them in a few days and was thoroughly looking forward to it. That they had no children of their own was the one less than perfect element in their lives. Mike had been married before and had a son, Steven. He had been killed in a hit-and-run accident and the marriage had not long survived his death. Mike and his first wife had both grieved desperately for their loss but the trouble was, they'd never managed to grieve for Stevie together. His death had been the final wedge that had broken their already shaky marriage apart. Both he and Maria had wanted children but, for one reason or another, it hadn't happened, and they had become quietly resigned to the fact, transferring their affections instead to the growing clan of nieces and nephews that Maria's sister, Josie, kept providing.

Mike dragged his thoughts away, back to the problem at hand. "What was Martha trying to find out about your mother's family?"

"Ah, well, there's the problem, you see. She had all the questions, but the truth was, I didn't know what the answers were. My mother died just before Grace and I were married and my grandmother shortly after that. They were the only relatives from that side I really cared about, and I've had little to do with any of the Matthews since. And, frankly, Mike, I'd be happy if it stayed that way. That's what I told her too, but she was not a woman you could put off. She'd got it into her head that her branch of the Matthews family came from round here and that we could track our shared ancestors down."

"And did you?"

John shrugged. "There seem to have been Matthews around here for ages. We traced them back three or four generations. I'd not given it any thought, not until Martha came, which just goes to show, doesn't it?"

"Goes to show what?"

"That however far you run, there's bound to be some bugger waiting, ready to trip you up."

* * *

The police HQ had moved out to Wymondham in 2002, so John had never actually worked there. That didn't prevent him from having an opinion about the modern, hard-edged

27

design that had cost £216 million to build. It was a measure of his distress that he passed no comment today.

Mike led him inside. There had been talk about mergers with Sussex and Cambridgeshire, and the relocation of one or both police forces to the Wymondham base. Mike wondered where they would put everyone if that were to happen. He presumed that the open-plan space would become less open. He'd had to fight to maintain his own tiny office on several occasions already.

Now, sitting on either side of Mike's desk, John nursing a mug of strong tea, they surveyed the mass of paperwork taken from Martha's room. Glancing through it all, John was sure there were some items missing.

"What did she do for a living?" Mike asked.

"She said she'd been a nurse, but I can't recall if she told me where. More recently she'd been involved in some sort of home care scheme, but she didn't talk about it much. I gather it was rather stressful." He frowned, wishing he'd asked more questions, sought to justify his uncharacteristic lack of curiosity. "When she first arrived, I wanted to keep her at arm's length, so I didn't ask her a lot. Then, as we became friends, it either didn't arise or it felt intrusive to be interrogating her."

"With hindsight, do you think she was being deceitful?"

"Deceitful? No. Just not expansive. She was careful about what she told me. Oh, she'd chat for hours about this distant cousin or that great-great somebody or other, but . . ." He shrugged. "I know she was married and that she divorced years ago. No children. She said he went off with another woman and I didn't like to pry."

Mike took note of the 'no children.' So how did the boy fit in? Had this Martha lied to John, or was the teenager that Mrs Beal had described making things up? He put the question to one side for the moment and asked, "This cousin, Billy. How well did he know her?"

John shook his head. "Not well, I imagine. She was introduced to him at some family gathering or other. A wedding, I think it was. You know what it's like. The clans gather and you suddenly realise you've more relations than you ever wanted."

Mike nodded. "Was there any doubt that she was? A relative, I mean."

John shrugged again. "Not that I know of. Billy was a bit too eager to pass her on to me, but then family history was never his thing. He's into football and vintage cars, anything else goes right over his head. And anyway, Billy didn't know a thing about my mother's side. You think any of this is the reason she was killed? Mike, I know you have to look at every possibility, but this seems terribly unlikely."

"I'd agree," he said, "if it wasn't for the phone call."

"Phone call?"

"And a visitor she had two days ago. Did she mention anyone calling at the B&B?"

John shook his head. "What's going on, Mike?"

"Wish I knew. I talked to the landlady, Mrs Beal. She said that a young man, a kid she called him but from her description he's probably in his late teens or early twenties, had called at the Two Bells looking for Martha Toolin. He claimed to be her son."

"She doesn't . . . didn't have a son."

"Not that she told you about. Anyway, Martha took him up to her room and it seems they got into a big fight. It was noisy and aggressive enough that Mr Beal went up to see if everything was all right."

"She didn't mention anything like that."

"Well, Mr Beal asked the boy to leave but he said he'd be back. That he hadn't finished with her. Mrs Beal says Martha was very upset. They made her a cup of tea and she sat in the lounge bar for a good twenty minutes afterwards while she recovered."

"No police report?" John asked.

"No. The Beals wanted to but she was having none of it, and I don't suppose they pressed her. Not the best of publicity."

"Better than having someone murdered on the premises," John said dryly. "If they'd called it in . . ."

"May all be coincidence, you know that. But he phoned her last night, just before you dropped her off. Mrs Beal took the call and recognised his voice."

"Did he say what he wanted? Do they know what the argument was about? And why not call her mobile?"

"I don't know." He frowned, trying to recall if he'd seen a mobile phone in the room. It might have been in her handbag but no one had mentioned finding one and it was the sort of thing the CSI would have drawn his attention to. "Maybe he didn't have her number. Maybe he's not what he claims. If Mrs Beal heard anything significant, she either didn't realise it or she's still reluctant to be seen to have been listening. Jude — ds Burnett — will hang on at the Two Bells for a while and probably pop back this evening, when the Beals have had a chance to talk about it."

John nodded. People recalled one set of facts immediately after the event and they were often crucial. In the hours that followed and the initial shock wore off, random memories would arise. Or they'd realise that it was better to admit to facts that might be embarrassing than to risk being accused of withholding later. "I don't know Jude," he said.

"Been with us about a year. Transferred up from Ipswich to be closer to her family. She's sharp. If there's anything the Beals don't know they know, she'll ferret it out."

"And the phone call?"

"Last night. As I said, he called about an hour before you dropped Martha home."

"So he may have come to see her?"

"Possibly. It would be fairly easy to get to Martha's room without being seen from the bar. But, John, we're getting ahead of ourselves. You're making the assumption that this young man killed his mother. If she was his mother."

John Tynan shook his head. "Why not tell me she had a son? Why deny it outright? I asked her, as you do, if she had any children. I mean, odds are, a woman that age, unless they're a confirmed spinster, will have acquired at least one."

"You and Grace didn't," Mike said gently.

"No, but it wasn't for lack of wanting. Why would you deny a child?"

"People do," Mike reminded him, "for all kinds of reasons. Broken relationships, estrangements, disapproval . . . who knows?"

Mike allowed the silence to grow between them for a minute or two. He shuffled through the paperwork spread out on the desk. Notes on possible locations, copies of birth and marriage records, photocopies of church registers and sepia photographs of stern women dressed in long skirts and silly hats. "Did she put a family tree together? I thought that was the way you started on this sort of thing."

John Tynan shook himself from his reverie. "I assume so," he said. "In fact, I'm sure . . . well, now I think about it, no, I'm not so sure. Mike, I was quite happy to drive around and look at old churches and pore over gravestones, but to be honest, I don't think I took half of it in. I'm not interested in the Matthews family. I don't see them, don't have anything to do with them and frankly I'd be content to leave it at that."

He frowned. "There was a notebook, though. A blue, hardback thing. Maybe a diary or an address book, and a couple of other photographs. I remember one showing a teenage girl and a baby, I think. Sorry, Mike, I can't tell you any more than that." He drew a rather shaky hand across his eyes. "I think I'd like to go home now, if that's all right."

"Of course. I'll drop you off and take you out later to get your car. John, there's something I want you to do for me."

"Anything. You know that."

"Phone your cousin and get him to tell you everything he knows about Martha Toolin. Talk to anyone else that had dealings with her."

John nodded. "I'll get onto it this evening. Billy's older than me but he still runs his car restoration business and I'm not likely to find him home until then. You're wondering," he said without bitterness, "a woman who hides the fact that she had a son — what else might she be hiding?"

CHAPTER 6

John asked a neighbour to drive him out to collect his car, rather than wait for Mike to take him. He had decided that he would go and see Cousin Billy, rather than trust his questions to a phone call. He'd called Caroline, Billy's wife, managing to catch her at home between coming in from shopping and going out again to an exercise class.

"For the over-fifties," she confided, then giggled. "I think I just about qualify."

"I think we all do," John agreed. She listened with increasing concern as he outlined the reasons for his call and the hope that he could impose upon them both that evening.

"John Tynan, since when have you been an imposition? It will be lovely to see you. You'll come in time for dinner, then, and I'll give Billy a call and tell him all about it."

It won't be just Billy she tells, John thought wryly as he hung up. He couldn't see the over-fifties exercise class getting much exercise done that afternoon, not unless you could class churning the rumour mill as exercise. Some people, he reflected, never really change, they just gain a few wrinkles. Caroline was one of those. She was still running around as busily as ever, still queen bee. Billy let her get on with it, as he'd always done.

The drive to King's Lynn and Billy's home was not a long one in terms of distance but John chose to take the coastal route and meander. He arrived to find Caroline there but Billy not yet home.

"He won't be long," she told him. "Let me get you something. Tea? Coffee? Something stronger?" She tilted her grey bob to one side and regarded him thoughtfully, her light blue eyes concerned and appraising. "You look tired," she said. "And old. John, I do believe you are finally getting old."

"Well, thank you for that."

"You're welcome." Her smile was warm and humorous and she hugged him tightly. "Oh, John. I think we're all getting old. And I don't mind telling you, I don't like it one little bit." She clattered around the kitchen, filled the kettle, then took a bottle of single malt from the cupboard and poured him a large measure. "Do you know, I actually tried dying my hair. Oh," she waved her hands in mock despair, "what a mess, what a palaver. I kid you not, I came out orange. Orange! I had to go down to the salon and get it fixed. The stylist told me I couldn't just use any old thing, not to cover all my grey."

"Silver," John said. "It's much too pretty to be called grey."

She paused, smiled at him. "Well, thank that gentleman over there. In any case, I decided I'd stick to being *au naturel* or whatever."

She poured herself a drink and came over to join him at the breakfast bar. "I don't *feel* old," she said. "I don't feel any different inside. Sometimes I just catch sight of myself in the mirror and I think, oh Lord, who is *that*?" She laughed and looked keenly at him. "But you look as if you're feeling the years right now. That's what I meant."

"I suppose I am," he agreed. He covered his glass as she aimed the bottle in his direction. "No, dear, I've got to drive back later."

"No you don't," she said firmly. "The spare room's made up and Billy can lend you a shirt or whatever. We often have

33

people stay over. Our Vera stops in once a fortnight or so, and her Tracy's got friends near here. When she's had, you know, one too many, she stops here rather than go home."

John laughed. "Better that than face her mum." Vera had always been oddly straight-laced.

"I don't know where she gets it from. She must have caught it from the Matthews, that's all . . ." Suddenly horrified by what she had implied, she covered her mouth with a pink-tipped hand. "Oh, John, I didn't mean . . ."

He chuckled softly. "Billy always reckoned I was the milkman's. No, the Matthews were a mirthless lot on the whole. Mum had a sense of humour, but not when her dad was around."

"Not a happy bone in his body," Caroline said. She refilled John's glass, and then hopped off the stool and went over to check on the dinner. The scent of roasting chicken permeated the kitchen, the aroma intensifying and adding thyme and lemon to the mix when she opened the oven door. "There's new potatoes and garden veggies, but I'll put those on in a minute when Billy gets here. And gravy, of course. I think Billy would have gravy on his salad if he could. Not," she added, "that he ever eats salad."

"Rabbit food," John said. "What time will he be back?"

"Ten minutes or so. You go and get washed up so I can have my kitchen back. I'll let you lay the table if you're good. Guestroom is . . . well, you should know by now."

John slid down from his stool a lot less elegantly than Caroline had done. "You think he'll ever retire?"

"Only when they nail the lid down. He's handed off a lot of the coach work, got himself a young apprentice and still has the same mechanic. Thick as thieves they are, the pair of them, and the young lad's just as daft. But Billy loves his cars. If he comes home one day and tells me he's going to stop, I'll know to make sure his will's in order."

On that note, John did as he'd been told and took his drink off to his designated room. A clean shirt had been laid out on the bed for him and the tiny en suite shower room had clean towels. He had a wash and mentally thanked Caroline for her thoughtfulness, especially as, come to think of it, it must be five years since he'd last visited. He patted his face with a thick burgundy towel and stared at his reflection in the mirror. She was right, he was looking old and tired. Sighing, he hung up the towel and retreated to the bedroom. Hearing Billy's voice drift up from the hall, John pulled on the borrowed shirt and made his way back down.

* * *

Caroline and Billy's house always reminded him of a 1980s show home. It was as though she had decided on her style back then and stuck with it. John could not help but wonder if Caroline had bought a job lot of wallpaper and just kept using it — striped paper below the dado rail, floral above. A coordinating scheme, pink in the hallway, green in the dining room. Heavy floor-length curtains framed a view onto the immaculate garden with its close-clipped lawn and massive tubs of summer bedding on the patio. A screen of trellis separated Caroline's vegetable plot from the wonderfully overblown borders. The interior decoration was reflected in the striped lawn and floral theme.

It was not until after their meal, when Caroline had poured their coffee, that the conversation turned to the purpose of John's visit. He was oddly grateful for the reprieve. For the opportunity to gossip about the children whose growing up he had missed, and the small talk about holidays and plans for the garden and the cars. Having no family of his own to talk about, he borrowed Mike's, talking about Maria and Josie and their extended clan. It struck him that both Caroline and Billy saw this as so normal that he must have been doing it for years — practically as long as he had known Mike and Maria.

"I must get a congratulation card for the new one," Caroline said happily. Though she had met Maria only once and Josie never, in her mind they had become family by association.

The air grew heavy as the conversation took a sudden turn. Billy looked at his cousin with concern. "It's a bad business, this. Do they know who did it yet?"

John shook his head. "No real leads. She was heard arguing with a visitor, and it turns out she had a son I didn't know about. Apart from that, nothing yet."

"A son? And she didn't tell you? Now that is strange. Don't you think it's strange, Bill?" Caroline said.

Her husband nodded. "I suppose it is. Especially if she thought he was likely to turn up."

John realised he hadn't thought about that. Martha had known the boy was close by because he'd visited her at the Two Bells, so surely it would have been natural to mention him . . . or had she intended to do so only if the boy happened to turn up when John was with her? Did she think John might think less of her?

Then he reminded himself that he had asked her if she had any children and she had definitely said no. He was back to the question he had asked Mike: why deny a child's existence?

Caroline was watching him closely. She reached out and patted his hand. "You and Mike will get to the bottom of it. Try not to fret."

"I've retired, remember."

"Have you?" Caroline asked innocently. "I hadn't noticed. More coffee?"

"I've phoned around the family," Billy said. "No one seems to have known anything about the woman till about eighteen months ago, when she turned up at a wedding. Cousin Alfred's granddaughter. Well, you know what Alf's lot are like. The world and his wife have to come."

"I seem to remember getting an invite," John confirmed. "I sent my apologies. I don't think I ever even met the lass."

Billy nodded. "I don't think we've seen her more than twice. Once at her wedding and once when she was christened. Anyway, we went along. It's nice to catch up and Alf can be relied upon to put on a good bash so . . . and it was there we met this Martha. Funny thing is, no one can recall who she came with. She knew enough about us to pull it off, though, and everyone just thought she was related to someone else."

"Presumably she had an invitation," John said.

"Well, I suppose so, but it was held in this big hotel. Wedding, reception, big disco thing in the evening. Frankly, if she looked the part, it would only have taken a bit of cheek to help herself to a glass of champagne and mingle. No one would have been the wiser. Half the family that was there I wouldn't have known from Adam if I'd met them in the street. Remember, this wasn't a Matthews affair. It was a full-blown Tynan shindig. One or two of Grace's people came. You remember Edie and Malc. Well, they were there and asked after you. But from your mam's side, there was only Raymond and his wife, and I'm never quite sure where they fit on the family tree."

"Grandma's relatives," John said. "But no, I can't recall exactly how they fit in either."

"And one or two of your dad's people, though I don't think they stopped long. Alf kept in touch with them, but I'm not sure who or what. We all assumed *she* was a Tynan. It was only a few weeks later, when we found out she'd started visiting old Jerry, that we realised she was from the Matthews camp."

"So, did Jerry remember her?"

"He seemed to, bless him." Though not directly related, Billy had liked John's uncle Jerry a lot when they'd all been growing up, and he and Caroline, living only a mile from Jerry's nursing home, had been regular visitors. "But she seemed to come out of nowhere and when we asked him about her he was a bit vague."

"But we didn't think anything of it," Caroline added. "Jerry could be a bit vague about *us* sometimes. He always seemed to think we were Gloria's children. Even though Gloria was your mum, not Billy's," she added, as though John might need reminding.

"Jerry seemed to think she was related to Eric in some way."

"Uncle Eric? We don't even know where he buggered off to. He left home before I was even born. He's probably long dead by now."

"Probably, but his brother Jerry was ninety when he went and Eric was only, what, four years older."

"Something like that." There had been three siblings — Jerry, Eric and John's mother, Gloria, each born, with a nice sense of symmetry, just two years apart. Gloria had been the middle child and the only one, so far as John could make out, that their father Ernest had truly cared for. "She could have been related to Eric, I suppose. Who knows what he got up to once he'd left?"

"Escaped, more like," Billy supplied the word John had not used. "Your mam reckoned he went into the merchant navy."

"Apparently. He sent her Christmas and birthday cards for a few years, then they stopped, and I think she assumed he was either dead or he'd given up even on her. There was never a return address and I think it hurt her that he lost touch so completely."

"Pity Jerry didn't follow him," Caroline said. "Poor man, I don't think he was ever happy. That father of theirs kept him under his thumb till the day he died. It was as if Jerry never dared cross him, even as an adult, not even in small things. Living in that dark old house. Do you know, Jerry didn't even get central heating in that place until his father passed on. Said Ernest didn't approve. It took us all giving him a good talking to before he got proper heating installed. You remember how cold that place was, I'm sure. Bitter, it was, and dark. He'd never have a light on anywhere if he could help it."

John nodded. He remembered.

"I offered to do some decorating for him, but he wouldn't have it. Said he could manage. Manage! He bought a job lot of magnolia and did the whole house. Said it looked clean."

"Well, compared to the mausoleum it was before, it did at least look brighter," Billy said. "Been me, I'd have moved out, sold it to a developer and found somewhere small and bright and with all mod cons, but he couldn't seem to leave the place. Couldn't let it go."

"Well, he must have sold it in the end," John said. "When he went into the home?"

"Well you'd have thought so," Billy said. "We assumed he must have, but it seems not."

"Really?" It seemed this was also news to Caroline.

"Well, like I said, I've been doing a bit of phoning round the family today, after John's call, and apparently it went like this. He put the place on the market five years ago, when he finally had to give in and go into the home, but he tied the place up with all these conditions and, whatcher callems, covenants. Got the solicitor to make it so the place couldn't be pulled down and redeveloped without them jumping through a load of hoops. Of course, no one wanted to deal with that, so the place never sold."

"So how on earth did he pay for the nursing home?" Caroline asked. "Cedars isn't a local authority home and I don't expect it's cheap."

"Savings," Billy said. "Who'd have thought it?"

"Savings? From what?" Caroline said.

Billy shrugged. "Maybe we should do what Ernest did and get rid of the central heating."

"So who was the house left to?" John asked.

"Well — and this is the other weird bit — it wasn't. Neither was what he left in the bank account. When Jerry died there was a bit of a will he'd written six months before and got someone at the home to witness. When he went in, all the bigger stuff and a lot of his bits and pieces were shared out round the family. You remember, he had some things sent to you. We had that music box and a few other bits. Jerry said who should have what and we all saw to it." Billy shrugged. "We all liked the old boy, you know. Well, when he passed on, the rest of his stuff was in the will. He left something to that Martha Toolin woman. Some silver knick-knack. A box, I think?" He looked to Caroline for confirmation but she just shrugged. "We sent those bits of jewellery on to you?"

John nodded. He'd been away on a much-needed winter holiday when Jerry had died and had missed the funeral. Jerry's bequest had been some small pieces of what he assumed had been his mother Gloria's jewellery that John had not realised even existed until they'd arrived in the post.

"We all thought that was it," Billy went on, "but it seems not. The rest is going through probate and they're trying to sort out who's next of kin."

"Well that would be John, surely," Caroline said.

"You'd have thought so." Billy looked quizzically at him. "You heard from them?"

"No, or I'd have said. I didn't think Jerry had anything to leave. I assumed the house must have been sold. I mean, who'd hang onto that barn of a place?"

"Well, if the covenants came off after he passed, it might be a dump that's worth a good deal of money. Who's to say?" He frowned. "But if they've not contacted *you*, who the devil are they looking for?"

* * *

Mike had just made a brief statement to the assembled press, gathered close to the Two Bells. They had been corralled into the car park on the North Walsham road but better arrangements would have to be made. Mike wondered about shifting them to the cricket club or the community centre on the outskirts of the village, which would at least minimise the local disruption. Jude had suggested this might look too much like he was shoving them out there so he wouldn't have to talk to them.

She had a point. Mike wondered, instead, about moving the incident room from the St Mary's Church rooms to a less central location. Parking would be easier and so would overall control — for one thing, if the team got any bigger, the church rooms would be pushed to house them.

Well, that decision could also wait a while.

He turned down into The Street and past the primary school. The church rooms stood opposite the post office. Martha Toolin had been to the post office at least twice, apparently, to buy postcards and stamps. He wondered who she might have sent them to — thus far they had not managed to trace any next of kin and, more significantly, the address she had given to the Beals turned out not to exist.

So, this woman might or might not have been hiding the fact that she had a son. She was definitely lying about where she had come from.

The evening briefing had been later than Mike would have liked, but it had taken time to get the major incident room set up and longer still to get the troops back from house-to-house enquiries. The Beals had come up with an extensive list of who had been present at the Two Bells the night before — a mix of locals and visitors, some of whom were staying in the caravan parks on the clifftop and behind St Mary's Church or in other local B&Bs. Catching people in had been a challenge, as the holidaymakers tended to be off elsewhere until early evening and the locals included both agricultural workers — early starts and late finishes in summer — or commuters whose homeward drive didn't get them back to the village until six or seven.

Mike had called everyone back for 6 p.m., hoping by that time he'd be able to construct an overview of the situation but aware that there'd be a lot of catching up to do the following morning.

He had appointed DC Firth as the loggist, charged with keeping track of statements and evidence as it came in. The young man was never happier than when he was dealing with minutiae. He had appointed two uniformed officers, one just out of training, to assist. Mike believed that all officers should familiarise themselves with the way an inquiry was run from the ground up — though he was aware that they'd probably rather be off doing something more active than being stuck in the incident room.

Superintendent Flint, Mike's superior and now Chief Officer in the case, had confirmed Jude's position as DSIO and Mike had appointed Terry Gleeson, who had been first officer attending at the Two Bells, as Community Liaison Officer. Terry knew everyone in the community and was also familiar with the last time this twee little church hall had been a major incident room. He'd joined the police at around the same time. He'd always lived in the area, so if anyone was going to be aware of local feelings, be sensitive to peoples' memories but also able to hold the official line, it was going to be Terry Gleeson.

"So," Mike said, conscious of the sudden quiet as he took up position at the front of the hall. All eyes had turned his way. "What do we know?" Behind him the pinboard that usually displayed public notices and finger-paintings done by the twice-weekly playgroup now bore images of the murdered woman, a plan of the Bells and a sketch map showing possible exit and entry points for the killer. Beside this was an OS map of the village and surrounding area.

"Jude, anything useful from the interviews?"

"Not much more than you had this morning. It seems Ms Toolin stopped off and had a drink, chatted for a few minutes to Harry Pickson — that's the head barman you met this morning."

Mike nodded, knowing that she was not only reminding him of the man's name, but also bringing others up to speed on what the boss knew.

"Mr Pickson says she spoke to a couple who were also sitting at the bar. A Mr and Mrs Crick. We've got an interview with them . . ." she broke off and looked for confirmation from one of the constables. "Good, they've got a caravan up behind the church, and are here for two more days."

Mike switched his attention to the constable, struggling for a name and then hauling it up from the depths. Mary Jeffries, that was it. "Constable Jeffries? Anything to add?"

"They talked about the restaurant she had been to with Mr Tynan. The Cricks were looking for somewhere a bit special to have dinner on their last night. They're newly-weds, apparently."

"And she spoke to them for . . . ?"

"Um, about fifteen minutes. Soon as she came in she walked up to the bar, bought a gin and tonic, drank it standing at the bar and chatting, then they saw her go upstairs."

"They *saw* her go upstairs?"

"They were leaving. They walked with her and she went upstairs, they went past and out the main door."

"And the Bells would have been about to close," Mike confirmed. "What else do we have?"

Amit Jacobs was next to speak. A DS, he'd been appointed as PoLSA — police search adviser. It was a role he had landed because Mike knew he'd had experience in complex cases, in particular a domestic dispute that had escalated into a murder enquiry and a suspicious death that had turned out to be a suicide. The young man involved had changed his mind after making multiple slashes to his wrists, forearms and throat and taking a painkiller cocktail. All over-the-counter stuff but enough to have finished him off, even if the blood loss hadn't done the job. He'd wandered about his flat, dripping blood, and finally lost consciousness close beside his own front door. Initially the thought was that the wounds on his arms might have been defensive. Jacobs had worked closely with the crime scene manager, who now stood and cleared her throat.

"Unidentified fingerprints on the doorframe, the bannister rail and the bedroom door," the CSM told him. "But it *is* a B&B and they might be completely unrelated. No blood evidence beyond the bedroom and little enough there. The PM will probably confirm that she bled out internally. Hypostasis indicates the body was not moved and time of death looks likely to be between eleven p.m. and one a.m."

Jacobs took over. "We have witness statements to the effect that she went upstairs at closing time. So eleven p.m. The landlady was passing the stairs at eleven fifteen and thinks she heard the bath running. So, allow maybe a half hour or so after that and she's unlikely to have been killed before eleven forty-five. So whoever killed her must have been *in* the pub, have stayed in after closing time, hidden somewhere, and waited for her to go back to her room."

"The second bedroom was unoccupied," Mike said.

"And so we extended the crime scene to the second room," the CSM confirmed.

"But until we've got a suspect to compare evidence to, any trace you've collected is speculative." Mike nodded. "And the knife?"

"Matches those in the dining room."

"The cutlery is kept on the far side, from what I remember. Next to the till?"

Jacobs nodded, but it was Jude who answered. "I spoke to the serving staff. The procedure is that guests choose a numbered table, the server takes their order, then gives them cutlery from the trays next to the till. There are two copies of their bill, one goes to the kitchen, one is pinned to . . . there's like a board with numbers on over by the till. It gets pinned by the table number, so when they pay, they give the table number, pay their bill, add a tip to the jar. Low tech but it works."

Mike recalled the process from when he had eaten at the Two Bells.

"So, would someone be likely to notice if a customer crossed the room and picked up a knife?" an officer asked.

Jude shrugged. "From what the staff say, it would be possible when the place is busy. But food is only served up to nine thirty, and the diners are usually all paid up by about half past ten, so . . ."

Mike visualised the layout of the dining area. The till was in an alcove, along with a table on which the cutlery trays were laid and a rack on the wall for leaflets advertising local tourist attractions. "Unless the person went over and collected a leaflet," he said.

Jacobs nodded. "It would be possible to grab a handful of flyers and pick up a knife. No one would notice."

"Not premeditated then — they didn't go equipped," someone commented.

"But once they had the knife, they went upstairs, waited for her to come up to her room, run a bath, go back to her bedroom. At any point they could have backed away, dropped the knife and left. No, they meant her harm and in that sense premeditation was there from the moment they picked up that weapon."

"What we don't know," Jude said thoughtfully, "is if they intended to do her harm *before* they went to the Two Bells that evening or if she did or said something once they were there that provoked the attack."

"It could also be," Mike felt compelled to play devil's advocate, "that the intent was to frighten her but it all went wrong once she was confronted."

"No defensive wounds," the CSM reminded him. "I'd be inclined to think that she felt in no danger until the moment she was stabbed."

Mike was disposed to agree. The single blow had been direct, incisive, angry but not frenzied. Whoever had killed this Martha Toolin, the indications were that they definitely wanted her dead.

* * *

John dreamed of voices in the night. The reminders of his grandfather's house had triggered memories long buried. Feelings long ago set aside and deliberately forgotten now refused to remain that way.

"Hush, keep your voice down. The boy will hear."

He creeps from his bed in his striped pyjamas and stockinged feet. Presses an ear against the door, but they have moved on down the hall and he can hear their whispered voices but not the words.

He shivers. It is November and there is no heat in the bedrooms of his grandfather's house. He thinks there will be no more to hear and then . . .

A baby, crying. The sound sudden and unexpected, it wails and squalls and a man's voice is raised.

"Can't you shut that thing up?"

A woman retorts sharply, but not loud enough for him to hear what she says above the child's cries. Then a door, slamming. Then silence, followed by a man's slow tread along the landing floor.

He flies across the room and jumps back into his bed. Lying motionless under the covers, he hears the handle turn and the slight creak as the door is inched open. Light from the hall falls across the thick, satin mounds of quilt and then across his face. He keeps his eyes tight closed — though not so tight that the man will know he's faking it. He won't make that mistake again, not after the last time.

He breathes again as the door is shut with a slow creak and a quiet snick as the latch falls, risks opening his eyes and tries to make sense of what he heard. His grandfather's voice. He has never heard the man when he isn't angry. His mother, tense and anxious, the only one of them that dares cross her father. The other woman and the child. Who they were, John doesn't know.

He wonders if they'll still be there in the morning.

He wonders when his mother will take him home.

He wonders what his grandfather will be angry about tomorrow and, still wondering, he drifts into uneasy sleep.

John Tynan wakes, senses still dominated by the dream. He can taste the musty, frigid air of his grandfather's house, still smell the cigarette smoke that clung to his clothes. Still hear the baby's cry and the implied threat in the man's voice as he shouts at the woman to keep it quiet.

And more than six decades of life later, he is still none the wiser.

CHAPTER 7

The rain arrived in the early evening, continuing through the night and way past breakfast time. Mike drove from the post-mortem along roads that steamed in the mid-morning sun, between hedgerows that glistened with raindrops. He found himself looking out for the black dog. Until John had spoken about it the day before, he'd been inclined to dismiss the stories, consigning them to the same category as UFO sightings and kids with hysterics after playing with homemade spirit boards. John, though, had spoken of the dog as being flesh and blood. Solid. Teeth that could tear and puncture and the kind of danger that, as a police officer, he should take note of. It was easy to get carried away by the liminal quality that characterised this landscape, even on bright, sunlit mornings that gleamed freshly washed after a rainy night.

Preliminary findings from the post-mortem had simply reinforced what they had already surmised. The weapon was a steak knife taken from the dining room of the Two Bells, death the result of a single stab wound, the path of the knife up from below the ribcage and penetrating the left ventricle of the heart.

A lucky strike? Or a knowledgeable one?

Once that had been established, Mike had left. There seemed little point in staying for the weighing and measuring and examination that made up the rest of the post-mortem. He had other things to do.

John was already at the police station when Mike arrived, drinking tea and yarning to old colleagues who'd been fresh-faced constables when he had been a DS. It was hard to believe that close on fifteen years had passed since he retired.

Jude handed Mike a mug. "Quite a character," she said.

"He is that." He exchanged tea for the file containing the preliminary PM findings, so she could hand it on for copying and distribution. Then he beckoned John into his tiny office.

"You got your car back?" Mike asked.

"A neighbour dropped me out there yesterday afternoon. I drove over to see Billy and stayed overnight. It turns out he didn't know her at all, not really. His aunt Margie introduced them, but she only met her through another cousin and this Martha woman turned up at a family wedding. You've heard me talk about the Tynan family gatherings? The world and his wife turn up and when it gets too complicated to work out a relationship, they just get designated as another cousin. Anyway, Margie thinks Martha was connected to my uncle Eric. Maybe you remember, there were three siblings. Eric was the older brother, then my mother, Gloria, and then Jerry. Jerry died in a nursing home and Margie reckons Martha had been visiting him. Eric left home years and years ago, joined the merchant navy and broke off all contact with the family, so anything could be true and we'd not know about it."

"And this Margie met her at the nursing home?" Mike asked.

"No, Margie lives miles away. I doubt she visited Jerry but of course she turned up to the funeral and Martha popped up there too. Arrived with a wreath and a bunch of stories that sounded authentic, though Billy can't recall being introduced at that point. To be fair, he'd probably have been too busy organising the cars. Anyway, after that she seems to have infiltrated the rest of the family and, as I told you, Billy met up with her at a wedding, then passed her on to me. But — and here's the funny thing — she was mentioned in Jerry's will, so she must have some connection somewhere."

"Maybe. What did he leave her? Did Billy say?"

"Oh, nothing to speak of. The old boy had been in a nursing home for a few years and most of his worldly goods had been distributed round his immediate family before he went in. Billy reckons he left her a silver trinket of some sort. The upshot is, Martha Toolin appeared practically out of nowhere, and if Uncle Jerry actually knew who she was he's taken the information with him."

Mike nodded. "Was he in good health? Mentally, I mean?"

John shook his head. "I wouldn't know. Caroline and Billy reckon he was a bit confused toward the end, but he made his final will six months before he died so he must have at least presented as compos mentis enough to do that."

"And this uncle was your mother's brother?" Mike asked.

"A Matthews. Yes. As I say, Jerry was the youngest son. I knew him, of course, and was very fond of him when I was a kid and a young man. But, as you know, I pretty much broke off contact with everyone besides Billy. Billy always kept himself a bit separate from the rest, didn't get involved in the backbiting, didn't take sides. Anyway, he's a Tynan not a Matthews."

"And what sides were there to take? I'm sorry, John, I know this is painful, but your family history seems to be entwined somehow with that of this woman."

John Tynan nodded. "Oh, I know. The truth is, there's not so much to tell. My grandfather, my mother's father, was a brute of a man. I think Gloria, my mother, was the only one he didn't manage to intimidate. His poor wife, though, and the two boys, well . . . Ernest Matthews was violent and unpredictable and no one blamed Eric for taking to his heels as soon as he was old enough. My grandmother, Elizabeth, was a gentle soul and Grace and I kept in touch with her while she was still alive. I think Grace always hoped she'd finally see sense and leave, but she never did, not even when we said we'd take her in, look after her. And we would have done, willingly, poor love. But it was as if he had some hold over her . . ." He shook his head.

"You see it, though, don't you, over and over again, the women — and the men, for that matter — who stay. They suffer years and years of abuse because the will to leave seems to have been beaten out of them, or they still hope, year after year, that things will change. He never did, of course. Grace and I, we didn't contact him much after my grandmother's funeral, didn't even go to his — which, of course, didn't go down well with the family. My father was furious with us, but then he only met Gloria once she'd left the family home and hadn't had to grow up with the bastard.

"My mother was gone by the time Ernest Matthews died, of course. Cancer. My father kept in touch with her family and even seemed to get along with the old man . . . but then, my grandfather never hit my mother and my father never got mixed up in any of the controversy. Funny how there's often a favourite in families like that, one who seems to avoid the flack and almost not see it. My mother was like that, though he beat seven shades out of the rest of them and out of us kids too if he thought we'd stepped out of line. I used to dread going near the man but my mother was always there with her excuses . . ."

"I'm sorry, John," Mike said softly. He studied his old friend thoughtfully, certain that there were other things he wasn't telling him.

"So you see, when Martha started asking about the Matthews, I wasn't sure I wanted to get involved. It was all past history, better dead and buried as far as I was concerned."

Mike nodded. "Apparently, the home address she gave at the B&B was false. It doesn't exist."

"More lies. Do we even know if that's her real name?"

Mike shrugged. "It matches the ATM cards she had in her purse, but we both know that means very little. We've contacted the issuing bank and should get a home address that way, always supposing she's not scammed them as well. I'm sorry, John, but this woman seems to have had her own agenda."

Jude knocked on the door, handed Mike a manila folder and then withdrew. He studied the contents and then laid it down on the table. "An artist's impression," he said, "of Martha Toolin's supposed son. Jude talked to the Beals again last night and drew it then."

"She's good," John commented. "Talented. Do they think it's a good likeness?" He gazed thoughtfully at it. "There's something familiar. I just can't . . . Maybe I saw him."

"Can you think where?"

John shook his head. "No, it's just a feeling. As though . . . Sorry, Mike. I'll try and remember." He got up, looking as though he felt every one of his seventy-odd years. "I'd best be off, let you get on."

Still puzzled, Mike walked him out to his car and watched him drive away.

"Problem?" Jude asked when he was back inside.

"I'm sure there is," Mike told her. "I just don't know what it is yet."

CHAPTER 8

Jude had already gone across to the incident room. Mike followed an hour later, taking a more circuitous route into the village via the back roads. He drove slowly past the cricket ground, scoping out the community centre as a possible venue for operations, then back down Blacksmith Lane to the crossroads. To his right he could see the corner of the Two Bells, the car park that had now become the media compound and the curve of the North Walsham road. St Mary's Church was now behind him and immediately ahead was The Street and the church hall. Mike hesitated, then decided on a short detour before returning to the fray. He headed up Beach Road, towards the Seaside Tea Rooms and parked up outside. Beach Road divided at this point, swinging left along the clifftop and then the steps down onto the beach. Past the tea rooms was a children's play area and the route John had taken in his rush to get back to the Two Bells when he'd heard the police sirens on the day Martha Toolin's body had been found. It was also the route the dog walker, Jason Matthews, must have taken on the day he and his dog had been chased by the big black beast everyone was talking about. Standing facing out to sea, Mike looked down onto the beach and then across to where the lighthouse raised a white and red striped column to the sky. There was another cut-through onto the beach there, he remembered, close by the lifeboat station.

Mike sighed. So what did any of this tell him? That anyone knowing the area could have left the Two Bells on foot and disappeared in any one of a half dozen directions. A car parked close by would most likely have been unnoticed if left beside the tea rooms or the play area or along Beach Road — narrow as it was. Parked in a residential area, it might have stood out but close to the caravan park, or pulled onto a verge along the road, or even parked up by the lifeboat station . . . this was a bit of a walk but from what Mike recalled, there were areas of hardstanding by the lifeboat station on Cart Gap Lane, there for when the crew were called out.

He could have thought all of this through with the help of the map back at the incident room, he knew, but he much preferred to look —undisturbed if possible, so that his thoughts could ramble.

Almost reluctantly, Mike turned and faced inland. He could not see it from where he stood, the school and the hedges got in the way, but he knew it was there. The Greenway. That short stretch of ancient pathway that had brought him to the village a little over a decade before.

He retraced his steps to his car. Back to the world of motive and circumstance, of TIE strategies — Trace, Interview, Eliminate, a process Mike could not help but think would be a bloody sight easier if they knew for certain who the victim actually was, and who might want her dead.

* * *

Jason Matthews no longer had a dog to walk, but the habit of walking was ingrained and not one he felt entirely ready to give up. He was here later in the day than he would normally have been — Jason and his big wolfhound had preferred the early mornings or evenings as the sun went down, the tourists and holidaymakers dispersed or not yet arrived. Today, though, he had come here, both to escape and to . . . well, test himself.

He was supposed to be working from home today. Some hope of that. He had finally admitted defeat and come out here to escape yet another argument with his wife, who had once again accused him of having an affair. She could smell perfume on his shirt, apparently, and she knew it wasn't hers. Well, maybe she could. The accusations had been regular enough over the years but it so happened that this time she was correct. Jason was seeing someone else and it was reaching the point where he knew his wife really would have her suspicions confirmed beyond any doubt, and soon. It was almost a relief, even if it did mean that all manner of shit would likely hit multiple fans.

His second reason for being here this morning was the memory of the last time he had come here with Carson. He was feeling more than a little ashamed of the fact that he'd run away like the devil himself was giving chase when it was only a bloody dog.

He had, however, chosen to take a different route onto the beach, parking up close to the lighthouse and cutting through the old cart gap. Despite the beautiful weather and the relative lateness of the hour, he was pleased to see that the beach was largely deserted. Only a man looking out to sea, and a family of four down at the water's edge, the children shrieking as the cold waves lapped about their knees.

Jason looked back over his shoulder — a reflex, checking that his dog had followed. He would then have watched as Carson did what he always did once he'd sighted the sea, and run off towards the water. But, of course, there was no Carson today.

This caused Jason acute pain.

He caught sight of the man watching him and nodded politely. The man in the dark jacket nodded back. He looked oddly overdressed for the beach.

He frowned and turned his attention back to the familiar walk.

* * *

The man in the dark jacket watched Jason Matthews walk away. Interesting, him coming out here at this time on a weekday. The man wondered briefly why he had. Then he turned back from the beach, made his way up onto the clifftop and wandered slowly back towards the village. The police activity seemed to have settled into a routine. He assumed that many of the comings and goings of yesterday had been to do with the setting up of the incident room, rather than any degree of progress. He had watched constables going from house to house, others searching the area around the Two Bells. He had gone into the post office and asked what was going on. Gossip there had been plentiful — a woman stabbed to death, police everywhere and, so he learned, a local officer had been first on the scene. This seemed to be a sort of claim to fame for those that lived there.

He shook his head. People were odd, always wanting to be a part of whatever was going on. Wanting to share, albeit obliquely and vicariously, even those events which no one in their right senses would want to have anything to do with. Even when death came to their very doorstep — as long as it was their *metaphorical* doorstep. At one small remove it was exciting. He doubted any of them would get as excited should they be the one facing the knife.

CHAPTER 9

It had, Mike considered, been a frustrating day. Witness statements were still being collated, and the pub was still sealed off, though Mike had noticed that the Beals and a couple he didn't know were now operating a mobile food van in the car park, serving snacks to the press corps. He knew how much the loss of income must be hurting them and was glad they had found at least a small substitute.

If the CSI team and his boss were agreeable, he saw no reason why the smaller bar should not be opened to the public in a few days, though the restaurant would probably not be released for a little while longer. The layout of the pub might make this possible.

Mike parked his car beside his house and sat back in his seat. The lack of momentum tired him more than long hours of busyness, and he did not relish coming home to an empty house.

Mike hated it when Maria went away. He would, of course, never have attempted either to prevent her going or to make her feel guilty for doing so. It was just that he missed her so very much

Daytimes were not so bad. They both worked and were used to being apart. Evenings could be filled with more work, with essential chores, with television. What was so hard was waking in the middle of the night and finding himself alone. He missed the feel of her beside him, missed the sound of her soft breathing. The scent of her. Missed being able to turn over and wrap his body around hers and know that life was about as good as it could possibly get.

He made dinner and spent the evening going over notes and half watching a film on the television, deliberately putting off going to bed until midnight.

When he woke around three, he knew that more sleep was going to be elusive. Rising, he drew back the curtains and looked out onto the fields beyond the garden, trying to see the tiniest glimmer of dawn light, but it was too early even for the birds. Giving in to the wakefulness, he found his phone and made his way downstairs, sent Maria a text telling her that he loved her and would ring in the morning. Then he flopped down in his favourite chair and switched the television on again, hoping to catch some tedious late-night film that might send him off to sleep once more.

They had found this ugly little house three years into their marriage. It had been exactly what they had *not* been looking for. Maria had seen the For Sale sign at roughly the same time as they had discovered that their plans for a family might prove problematic. Suddenly, their search for a large family home, with three or four bedrooms at least, seemed like an unnecessary additional torture. Mike had expected a period of anger, of mourning, even of recrimination, but there had been nothing like that. Somehow, and in a very short space of time, they had both shifted their perspective, changed focus. He was still half waiting for the impact to finally happen.

Then Maria had found this place, persuaded Mike to see it, and that had been that. There was a spare room, small but adequate, and a large bedroom up in the eaves with crooked windows and a window seat set into the massively thick walls. Downstairs, the house was divided pretty much across its middle, producing one large living room and one large dining kitchen, both with oversized fireplaces. If he was honest, it had been the fireplaces and the pretty picture-book cottage garden that had sold it to him.

The house itself was squat and square and really rather unattractive. It seemed, over time, to have settled into the ground, but Mike had walked down the steps and into that bright and scented garden and had been half persuaded. Then he saw the stone fireplaces, and they practically signed the contract then and there. It had since proved to be a happy home.

Flicking through the channels and finding nothing on, he got up and wandered around the room. There were a great many photographs, mostly friends and Maria's family, Mike having little of his own. He paused to study one image that had been taken that spring. Maria and Josie, Josie's husband, Tig, and their children standing together, with Mike leaning in somewhat diffidently. In another picture John Tynan had taken Mike's place while, presumably, Mike took the snap. Essie, childhood beads and braids now forgotten, was a poised young woman of fifteen. Mike tried not to think of the time ten years before when they had almost lost her — taken by a killer Mike had been hunting, they had feared her dead. Now Mike rejoiced when he looked at the pretty face, the determined look in her eye, and recalled the inevitable and oh-so-normal teenage tantrums that drove her mother mad, and the charm she could switch on when it suited her. Her brother, Nate, was ten and had a broad smile and a taste for cartoon T-shirts, and her two younger siblings, Evelyn and Kwame, the terrible twins, were six. Josie had sworn that the latest addition would be the last. They had called her May, after Tig's mother. Josie and Maria looked very much alike, Maria just an inch taller and, unlike Josie, whose hair was relaxed and hung just past her shoulders, Maria always kept hers natural but cropped quite short.

Maria had a few more lines around her eyes than when Mike first met her but in his eyes she had grown even more beautiful.

Beside this picture was another, smaller image. A boy of nine in a striped T-shirt and baggy jeans, standing on a beach, a backdrop of grey ocean stretched out behind him. He was half turned, Mike having just called his name and snatched the picture as he spun round, smiling. Steven had been at that age when the novelty of having his picture taken had diminished, and all the pictures Mike had of him seemed slightly blurred, as though the boy could not ever keep still. This, slightly creased and faded though it was, had been among the last he had taken and was his favourite, the signs of wear testament to the years it had lived in Mike's wallet. Maria had had a copy made for him and this precious original now lived safely in a frame.

His phone chimed and broke through his reverie. Mike smiled. Only one person would text him at that time of the morning. He read Maria's message twice, then turned off the lights and retreated reluctantly to bed, the phone on his bedside cabinet just in case.

CHAPTER 10

John had taken a great many photographs while out escorting Martha. A couple of years before, Maria and Mike had bought him a digital camera for his birthday, rather a good one, styled like a small SLR and with features John was still discovering. He had taken to digital photography with the enthusiasm of a child with a new plaything and was even beginning to be pleased with the results.

With the morning light streaming in through his kitchen window, he sat down with a pot of tea and his laptop and began to work his way through the hundreds of thumbnails, looking for that one face.

The sense of familiarity had grown overnight and he had woken certain that he had seen the boy in Jude's drawing somewhere. He could not shake the conviction that he had encountered him more than once.

It wasn't easy, looking at pictures featuring Martha smiling out at the camera. Martha, who was now dead and gone. He was shocked, too, at just how many he had taken. One thing he had noticed since 'going digital' was that he tended to snap everything, knowing he could get rid of anything overexposed or shaky later and leave no evidence of failure behind.

Now, however, that profligacy could well prove to be useful.

He was on his second pot of tea before he found what he was looking for and, once he'd found that one picture, he discovered more. The boy had been following them and John had simply not noticed him.

"Slipping in our old age, aren't we?" he chided himself as he found the third incidence of the boy appearing in the background of one of his pictures. Although, to be fair, it was not a face you'd pay particular attention to, and the boy was keeping well back and out of the way.

"Question is," he muttered, "did Martha know you were there? Was this a game you were playing on your own, or was she in it with you?" Whatever *it* was.

He called Mike on his mobile, telling him to look out for an email he was about to send. Attaching the pictures, John looked more closely, reminding himself of where they had been taken. One in the Cathedral Close in Norwich. One at the Forum, the big, newish centre with its massive arch of glass and steel that John was still not sure about. Martha had been standing on some steps that led down from the main entrance. From what John could recall, they were probably taken on the same day. He made a mental note to check the date codes on the thumbnails. The third, though, was different, one of the many little churches they had visited in the past week, scanning the gravestones for lost ancestors that John didn't really feel the urge to find. There, half hidden in the background, lost against the massing of dark trees, the boy watched.

* * *

Tom was good at watching. Watching and waiting. He had found a good place from which to watch the Two Bells. From the shadow of the churchyard wall, he could see while remaining unseen, unless someone looked directly and looked hard. He had found the spot a few days before. At night, when the porch light was on, he could still see the comings and goings easily enough, and by day he had a clear view. Of course, he hadn't kept up surveillance all the time. He hadn't needed to. He'd a good idea of her routine, and it had only been on that last day that she'd really fooled him, not coming back to the B&B in the late afternoon but instead going off somewhere else. With *him*. Returning late, so late that Tom had almost come to believe she had moved on.

That, he considered, would be just like her.

But she'd come back. *He* had driven away and Tom had gone down to the Two Bells, slipped inside and been waiting in her room when she'd come out from having a bath.

That had been the easy part.

The hard bit had been knowing that she didn't want to see him.

Since yesterday, he had watched the police come, and the ambulance, and the man she had been seeing talk to someone Tom decided must be a detective. He'd watched the ambulance go and the police cars and the detective and then the other police come back in the evening. He'd been careful not to stay too long, to keep away for an hour or so and then come back, parking each time in a different spot. He assumed the locals would recognise a stranger's car, just as he would have done if it had been parked in his street. He hoped they would just assume it belonged to a visitor, though Tom hadn't seen that many tourists. The village was small with not much to do, so it stood to reason no one came. It had never occurred to Tom that these were the precise reasons people might choose to visit.

He had arrived about an hour before. The Two Bells was still closed to visitors, the No Vacancies sign hanging by the door, even though Tom knew they had no one staying there. He hadn't expected much to happen. In fact, he'd decided that this would be the last day. After all, she'd gone now. He had done everything he needed to do, so he might as well pack up and leave. He was annoyed with himself for letting the woman that owned the place get such a good look at him, but he thought the story about him being Martha's son was a good one. Good enough to throw them off for a little while. And it wasn't so far from the truth, was it?

Well, nothing to keep him here now.

He watched as a familiar car pulled up in front of the door to the Two Bells and the man got out. The man Martha said knew what she wanted to know. Tom was sure now that she'd been wrong. After two weeks she'd been no further on than before she came here. He watched as the man knocked on the door and stood on the porch step talking to Mrs Beal. When he got in his car and prepared to drive away, Tom knew he should follow him.

He sprinted back to where he had left his car, tucked on the verge, almost in the hedge, on the edge of the village. The man would have to pass this way, unless he turned round outside the Two Bells, in which case, Tom would soon know.

He made it to his car and ducked down inside just as John Tynan drove past. He counted to twenty before pulling off the verge and preparing to follow. He knew the roads round here by now, so he didn't have to get too close. The coast road had only a few turnoffs, mostly heading back towards villages, and the low hedges gave a good view across the flat plains of the countryside. He could stay well back, observe without being spotted, follow him.

What then?

Tom hadn't thought that far.

* * *

The man in the dark jacket lowered his binoculars.

Interesting. He'd seen the boy several times, of course, assumed he was yet another innocent drawn into the woman's schemes — how many had there been over the years? He had expected the young man to leave, to head for the hills once the police investigation began and had been surprised that he had not. What did he want? What did he hope to gain by remaining? Watching and waiting, much as the man himself was doing?

* * *

John had printouts of the photographs on the seat beside him. He had emailed copies to Mike at work and then driven straight to the Two Bells to talk to the landlady. Mrs Beal had told him she was 'almost certain' it was the young man who had claimed to be Martha's son. She had reached that stage — John recognised it well from his police days — when she was beginning to feel the need to distance herself from what had occurred. He would be willing to bet that the day before, she'd have sworn on her grandmother's grave that the boy in the photograph was definitely the one she had seen. Now she would rather not know. Certainty implied further involvement, and Mrs Beal was running from that. But John had seen the flicker of recognition in her eyes. She knew.

John pulled off the narrow road and onto the verge. The first time he had come here, down this tiny byway, he had thought they were lost. There was no village down here and no church showed on his satnav. "It's one of those lost medieval villages," Martha had told him. "You know, deserted after the Black Death or something." John vaguely understood what she had meant. "Apparently some big house took the church on and kept it going but I don't think it's used much now."

The sign outside the church reminded John that this was the house of St Michael and All Angels. Nothing like hedging your bets. Services, apparently, took place on a bimonthly basis. He wondered who constituted the congregation or if the vicar found himself alone, preaching to St Michael and the rest of the angelic host.

Sunlight slanted through tall trees as John opened the gate and wandered slowly up the path towards the porch. Grass banks flanking the gravel pathway spoke of long years of burials piled one atop another. He wondered if Martha had been right and the church really was a medieval relic. He could see that it was old, but church architecture had never been his thing.

She'd stood just outside the porch that day and he'd taken her picture and then a panorama of shots on either side of her, recording the churchyard and the trees beyond the wall. It was here that the boy had stood leaning against the wall, framed by dark trees that John now identified as yews. He had been in shadow, dressed drably in a long-sleeved T-shirt and John, concentrating on what Martha was saying to him while trying to frame his shots, had simply not noticed him. Not consciously, anyway.

Padding slowly on grass that the last time he was here had just been cut but was now long and soft and dotted with dandelions, John made his way around to the side of the churchyard.

It was here that they had found the graves.

Matthews graves. One a century old and the second, a simple wooden cross, weathered and aged to grey, marked crudely with the name. John knelt, his fingers tracing the ill-formed letters across the crude little crosspiece. It seemed strange to find such an object here, in this once so ordered churchyard. It was such a makeshift marker.

And such a little grave.

He sat back on his heels, hearing his knees crack, and tried to recall what Martha had said that day, just why they had come here. He seemed to remember that it hadn't been anything she had discovered from her research, but some article she'd read in a local paper or magazine.

He shook his head. No, it wouldn't come. But what did seem to float just at the periphery of memory, as it had when he had come here with Martha, was the odd feeling that he had been here before. Years before. And that day had been in winter. It had been raining and bitterly cold and his mother, standing beside him in her old tweed coat and headscarf, not dressed for a funeral or even for Sunday church, she had been crying.

A soft footfall roused him from his reverie and he looked up. The boy, standing just a few yards away, hands clenched tightly at his sides.

Shocked, John stared at him for a moment or two before he gathered his thoughts enough to react. A slurry of random thoughts slid into his mind. What if this boy had killed Martha? What if he meant to harm him, too? Why was he here?

The boy, rising on his toes, poised between — what? Flight? Fight? John couldn't tell. It was as though the boy was changing his mind, second by second.

John struggled to his feet. "Hey!" he called out. The youth half turned, as though he had finally settled upon the flight option. "Hey. I want to talk to you."

The desire for conversation was distinctly one-sided. The boy raced away across the churchyard, weaving between the graves and heading towards the lychgate. Cursing his clumsy feet, half asleep from kneeling and now getting the blood back in a painful rush, John staggered inelegantly after him. He finally picked up his pace for a proper pursuit in time to hear a car engine start and glimpse a small brown vehicle haring away.

"Damn and blast. Damn it all." John hurried to his own car and opening the driver's door, looked down. His curse this time was somewhat more colourful. The front tyre was still going down, but a large slit recorded the stab that the boy must have inflicted as he fled the scene.

John bent to examine the damage. He had been shocked when the boy turned up, but now that shock solidified into anxiety. Martha had been stabbed. One single, swift and competent strike. The use of a knife now, albeit only against his tyre, chilled John to the core.

CHAPTER 11

Tom didn't know what to think. He drove away as fast as conditions on the byway allowed, and swerved out onto the main road without looking for other traffic. He was profoundly grateful, as he came to his senses enough to be grateful, not to have hit anything. He wasn't sure why he had followed John Tynan in the first place. He had formulated some vague notion that he would talk to him whenever he got to where he was going and then, confronted in the churchyard, Tom had simply lost his nerve.

What could he, should he, have said? What did he actually want to ask this man who had become so big a part of Martha's life for that short time? Tom realised that when it came down to it, he had been jealous. He had been close to Martha, had reached the stage of actually trusting her, depending on her and then . . .

Tom could not even put into words what he had felt when she had cast him aside. And to see her fawning on this man, going everywhere with him, telling him . . . though Tom didn't know what Martha had told John Tynan. And he no longer knew if he should trust what she had told him. Was all of it lies?

And then this man was police, or had been, and that was another barrier to Tom mustering the nerve to speak to him. He'd had enough trouble with the law in his short life, and now Martha had brought him more.

Tom blinked. Why was it getting so hard to see? It took a second or two to realise he was crying. He pulled over in a farm gateway and wiped his eyes impatiently with the heels of his hands. It just wasn't fair. Martha had promised him so much and then, just when he had started to think she might really care about him, had snatched it all away. Tom could not forgive her for that. Of all the unfair things in Tom's life, Martha's betrayal seemed the worst.

He reached across to the glove compartment, searching for tissues. Martha had kept all sorts of stuff in his car while he'd still been the taxi driver of choice. Rummaging, he found a packet and then noticed something else that he'd forgotten about and, evidently, Martha had too. After wiping his eyes and blowing his nose, Tom reached back into the glove compartment and withdrew the things she had left there. A photograph of a baby, crumpled and faded and folded across to obscure the other figure in the picture, a woman holding the baby. Now the baby was alone, only the woman's arm remaining visible where it crossed the small body, and a glimpse of her patterned skirt.

Tom had seen the picture many times. It had once been in a silver frame but Martha had taken it out, replacing it with a picture of someone else, a girl of about sixteen. She had never told Tom who it was but he had assumed at first that it must be her daughter. Later and purely by chance, he had spotted the same photograph in another frame. That frame among a display of many, all with the same picture, and he had realised that the image Martha had seemed to treasure had just been one she had taken from a cheap, shop-bought frame.

Another lie. Tom was no longer sure where the lies ended, or if even Martha herself knew any longer.

Folded up and placed with the photograph were some newspaper clippings, photocopied and highlighted. These were new to Tom and seemed to be the Births, Marriages and Deaths columns from an unnamed newspaper. Tom looked at them for a moment and then put everything back. It was probably something to do with this family history obsession she seemed to have caught. What had started out as (she had told him) a search for her daughter and her daughter's child had become something far bigger and led her in directions that Tom couldn't fathom. Was it even her own family she was researching? Tom had come to doubt even those basic details.

Secrets, she'd said. Secrets families keep and want kept. He had the notion that she had found something she could profit from, maybe even by blackmail — he wasn't blind to this side of Martha's past — but she hadn't confided and he hadn't asked.

CHAPTER 12

Staring out of the back window of the car. Funny how you so often see yourself in dreams, only this isn't a dream, it's a half memory. He sees the boy he was then, maybe ten years old, maybe a little older, gazing out of the rear window, kneeling on the back seat — no compulsory seat belts in those days . . .

John shakes himself and tries to remember what he saw. Whose car was he in? He can smell the old, cracked leather of the seats, the beeswax his grandmother applied to try to revitalise the ageing skins, the lavender polish she used on the dashboard. It came in a large, flat tin and she rubbed at it with her duster, applying and then allowing it to half dry before buffing it off.

"You all right, sir?" The question was an unexpected one. The vague concern on his face even more so. The man tapping on the half open window seemed a little put out to find John half dozing in his car.

John stared, uncomprehending, then recognised the uniform of the recovery firm he had called and glimpsed the orange van behind. Glancing at the dashboard clock he realised he'd been waiting three hours for them to arrive. He'd been warned it would take at least two when he had called them. He eased himself out of the passenger seat and the man stepped back to give him room.

"Sorry it's taken so long to get here, it's been one of those days and I'm afraid you weren't top priority."

John laughed. "Yes, they told me. Women and children first. I'd have fixed it myself but realised when I got the spare out that I didn't have a jack. Really stupid of me."

The man smiled sympathetically. "It happens all the time."

Not to me, John thought. He was always so careful about such things, or used to be. Was it old age getting to him? Or just that he'd finally given in and retired? He settled on the latter explanation. His knees might be shot but he certainly didn't feel any older than he had done on the day he had reluctantly left the force. Certainly not as old as he had felt on the day Grace had died. On that day he'd felt old enough to have lain down beside her and given up on life altogether.

The recovery man was examining the damaged tyre. "What happened here, sir?" His voice was now cautious — evidently he recognised the cut for what it was, knew John could not have driven here with such a gaping wound. He was probably wondering what he was dealing with.

John took refuge in something close to the truth. "A young lout with a knife."

"Out here?" The man glanced around, suspicious and ill at ease.

"Yes," John said. "Out here." He fished his jacket from the car and went to sit in the shade of the lychgate, not ready to field more awkward questions or suspicious glances. He saw the recovery man return to his van and speak into a radio or mobile phone, John couldn't tell from the angle. No doubt he was telling control that he had a somewhat dubious customer. No doubt he'd be asking if there was any chance of backup. At least his unease might speed up the wheel change. He called Mike to give him an update, amused him by telling his friend that the recovery driver now thought he was a serial killer, given to luring people out into the middle of nowhere by slashing his own tyres and then asking for help.

"Are you all right?" Mike asked. "You sound a little odd."

"I fell asleep in the car," John confessed. "All that adrenaline, I suppose. I dreamed about myself as a child of about, oh, ten, eleven years old. One of those really vivid dreams that won't be shaken."

"I know them well," Mike said heavily.

"It isn't the first time I've had one lately. Mike, I know I've been here before. I felt it the first time I came here with Martha. Then again today. It's like one of those half memories you're not quite sure is really yours, or if it's based on something you've been told, but I know it's real and I get the feeling it's important."

"You think it has something to do with Martha?"

"I don't know," John confessed, then, "No, this is something else. Martha may have triggered it, but what's going on in my head is tied up with my uncle Jerry and my grandfather, and so, I suppose, maybe with Martha's family too, if she really was related to the Matthews."

In the background, he could hear someone speak to Mike. "Better let you go," he said. "I think he's about finished with the wheel."

The recovery man was placing the damaged wheel in John's boot and, as John walked over to him, he took a cloth from his pocket and began to wipe his hands.

"All sorted," he said. "Remember, sir, the spare is only rated at fifty and it's a bit smaller than the regular wheel so watch yourself on the rough track." He paused. "The kid who slashed your tyre," he said. "What if he's still around? Don't you think you should report this?" Suspicion seemed to have transmuted into concern.

John shook his head. "He's long gone," he said. "I saw him drive away and I'm sure we should have heard his car."

"Well, I'd best be going then. I'm only allowed so long for a wheel change. But you should let the police know. It's vandalism if nothing else, and I'm going to have to put it into my paperwork, you know."

"I'll call in and get a crime number on my way home," John promised. He watched as the man walked away, noting that he glanced anxiously left and right before getting into his van and, with a wave of his hand, drove away with more speed than was really sensible on the rutted track.

John felt the unease settle upon his shoulders. He had not felt it earlier when that odd sense of familiarity had pervaded. It was as though the mood of the day had changed, the story shifted and he no longer wanted to be alone in this isolated place so filled with half-felt memories.

Shaking his head and chiding himself for being all sorts of fools, John started back towards his car.

* * *

Mike studied the images on the screen. John had sent him three pictures, one a close-up of a detail from a picture taken in a churchyard. The second, he recognised as a local street and it took him a few moments to find the familiar face in amongst the holiday crowd.

In the outer office the phone rang again and he could hear someone fielding yet another call from the local press. It was a wonder the national media hadn't homed in by now. Something more exciting must be happening elsewhere – some celebrity having a bad hair day, perhaps – though no doubt they'd be on the scene soon enough.

He examined the churchyard picture again, the original showing the church porch, Martha standing beside a group of Matthews gravestones and the wall in the background with the boy half hidden by the trees. And then another detail caught his eye. Further back in the trees, a large black dog stood as though on guard, staring directly out of the picture at Mike, so it seemed. Could the black dog have something to do with this boy?

Mike frowned, something from the morning briefing jogging at his memory.

He got up and put his head around the main office door. "Jude, the witness who reported our black dog the other morning, what was his name?"

She laughed. "You mean the one who wasn't ex-DI Tynan?"

"That would be the one."

"It was Matthews, I think. Jason Matthews. Any particular reason? The dog man went out, couldn't find a trace."

Matthews. Coincidence? It was not that uncommon a name. Five minutes later, Jude driving, he was on his way.

* * *

Jason Matthews was a tall, solidly built man. Mike noted the dark brown hair that looked in need of cutting and the tired grey-blue eyes. He could do with a shave, Mike thought, but maybe Matthews regarded it as designer stubble.

If he had been surprised that two detectives should turn up, asking about the black dog, he chose not to show it.

"My dog died." Jason Matthews poured himself a drink, waved the bottle in Mike's direction but took no notice of his response. Jude, sitting quietly, photographs in hand, exchanged an amused glance with her boss. "Heart attack, the vet said. Said he was getting on and it could have happened any time, but I'm telling you," he turned from his ice bucket and waved tongs in Mike's direction, "I was shaking like the proverbial all the frigging way home."

He came over and sat down on the brown two-seater leather sofa that was a twin to the one Mike occupied. Jude had taken the only chair. It faced an impressively sized plasma screen TV and Mike guessed that it was Jason Matthews's seat of choice.

"What scared you, especially?" Mike was genuinely curious. John, not easily disturbed, had been truly upset by his own encounter with the beast. He guessed from Jason Matthews's manner that this was a man impatient of the normal weaknesses.

Matthews frowned. "You mean apart from the fact it was a bloody big dog and it thought nothing of chasing my car."

Mike smiled. "*Was* there anything apart from that?"

"I'm not a man given to imagining things, Inspector, but yes, there was something more. It was, I don't know . . . intelligent. I mean, don't get me wrong, I'm a dog man, always had one since I was a boy and I've owned some smart dogs, but this was, I don't know, like it knew what it wanted and it wasn't giving up."

Jude got up and handed him the photographs John had sent, including an enlargement of the black dog at the churchyard. "Is that the dog?"

Matthews peered at it. "Could be. Hard to say." He shuffled through the others. Paused.

"Do you recognise anyone?" Mike asked.

Matthews shook his head, then nodded. "The kid? No. But I know her." He held out the picture and pointed at Martha. He sounded angry.

"Martha Toolin?" Jude asked. "You recognise her? From where?"

"Well I recognise the woman, but that wasn't her name. She called herself Julia. Julia Matthews. Said she was a relative researching the family history. I told her I didn't give a flying whatsit about my family history but she was the persistent sort, didn't know when to give it a rest. In the end I threatened to get the police involved if she didn't clear off."

Mike and Jude exchanged a glance.

"When was this, Mr Matthews?" Mike asked

"Oh, I don't know. A year, no, closer to fifteen months ago."

Fifteen seemed oddly precise.

"She turned up here one day, said she was looking for some long-lost relatives." He laughed. "Fortunately Katie and the girls were out. I told her I didn't have much to do with the ones I knew about, so I certainly didn't want to find any more."

"How did she find you?"

"She said she looked in the phone book. Maybe she harassed all the Matthews in there."

"Did she say exactly who she was looking for?"

Jason Matthews thought about it. "She had a bee in her bonnet about a child that was adopted by some relative of mine. I told her I thought family history was something to do with tracing the bloodline back, not forward, and anyway, so far as I knew, no one in the family had adopted a kid." He laughed uneasily. "I told her there were days when I'd be happy to lose one of mine to the right bidder, you know, joking like. She nearly hit the roof."

"Oh?"

"You know, she started swearing and yelling and telling me I had no idea what I was saying and how kids are the most precious thing anyone can have. I mean, I was joking! People say that sort of thing all the time, don't they?"

"I suppose they do," Mike agreed. "And then?"

"That was when I told her to bugger off. I told her that if she'd tracked me down through the phone book, she could do the same with the rest of them."

Mike rose to leave, Jude following his lead, though her uneasy glance told him that there were a lot more questions she thought he should be asking.

"Here's my card, Mr Matthews, if you remember anything more. Dates, things she asked, anything that might occur to you."

"Right, I'll have a think. What's all this about, anyway? She been harassing other people?"

"Thank you for your time," Mike said. "Oh, by the way, do you happen to have a Jerry or Gerald Matthews amongst your relatives?"

Matthews looked flustered, put out at being deflected. "Some distant cousin or other, I think. I remember my parents mentioning him. Why?"

"Martha Toolin. Julia. Did she ask about him?"

"I'm sorry, Inspector. I really don't recall."

* * *

Back in his car Mike called the pathologist who had performed the post-mortem on the woman they had been calling Martha Toolin.

Yes, he was told, she'd had at least one child. They would get back to him on the other question. They had, in fact, been about to call him. Mike listened, thanked them and said goodbye.

"Dog hairs?" Jude asked. She laughed. "Black hairs, by any chance?"

"I was thinking more German shepherd," Mike said. "But hairs from a mythic black dog might be interesting as well, don't you think?"

Jude laughed. "Right. Any that turn up we'll set in that clear resin stuff and sell them off on eBay."

"It'll all have to go into police funds, you know," Mike warned, "but if we find any, I'll pay for the resin, you sort out the eBay account. What did you make of him?"

"Jason Matthews? I think he's a jerk. Apart from that, well, he likes to get his own way, I think. I'd like to have talked to the wife."

Mike nodded. "We'll have to arrange that. The pathologist was about to give us a call anyway."

"Oh? Something else come up at the PM?"

"Yes. We may have to rethink our time of death."

"Really? By how much?"

"Couple of hours, maybe. Stomach contents," he added. "Rate of digestion. We know she finished her meal just before ten, then had a gin and tonic at about ten forty-five. Well, the level of digestion suggests she may well have died later than we thought, closer to two or a bit after."

"Right." Jude started the engine and they pulled away from Jason Matthews's house. "So how does that impact the case?"

"Maybe it doesn't, but it suggests that whoever killed her waited longer than we thought. It maybe even calls our initial hypothesis into question — that he hid in the second bedroom and waited for her to go to bed."

"But she didn't, did she? Go to bed, I mean. The bed showed no sign of occupancy."

"On the face of it, no."

Jude laughed. "What, you think the killer made the bed? But why didn't she go to bed? Why was she still up at two in the morning?"

She paused at a junction, turned left and then added, "Could she have gone out again?"

"I suppose she might," he said. "But why? She had a bath, presumably got ready for bed, so why the change of plan?"

"Why not get into bed? Even if she didn't want to go straight to sleep, she might have read or something. Much more comfortable to do that in bed," Jude said.

"No book," Mike said. "For that matter, her mobile still hasn't turned up. No television in the room, so she didn't sit up watching — and even if there had been, it would have made sense to sit in bed and watch." The room was, he remembered, clean and comfortable but very functional. No easy chair, no TV. He remembered from the statements that the newer annexe was better equipped but that when Martha Toolin had arrived, those rooms had been occupied. Or maybe the simplicity and functionality hadn't mattered to her. After all, she seemed to have been out most of the time.

"So," Mike said. "Did she go out? Would she have gone out through the main pub door? What about the alarm — presumably there is an alarm?"

Jude laughed. "Rudimentary," she said. "But guests are given a key to the back door. They can get up the stairs without the alarm going off in the main pub."

"So where would she go? Could she have brought her killer back with her?"

"It's possible," Jude said thoughtfully. "It opens up possibilities. But if she brought the killer back with her, would she have then changed into her pyjamas? I mean if they planned on having sex, they might have skipped that stage."

"True," Mike said.

She frowned. "The window latches in the second bedroom aren't that secure, but it wouldn't have been an easy climb."

"But possible, and there's no security light on that side of the building."

A few moments of silence followed, then Jude said, "Why didn't you press him for more details? On the woman he knew as Julia Matthews."

"Because I want to give him time to wonder what we know. And I want to try and speak to the wife when Jason Matthews isn't there. See if she's aware of this connection."

Jude nodded. "Excuse me for asking this next one," she said. "I know you and Mr Tynan are friends, but why didn't he think anything about her was wrong? I mean, he's sharp as a tack, but he doesn't seem to have suspected a thing."

Good question. One Mike wasn't sure even John Tynan could answer.

CHAPTER 13

John *had* been asking himself the same question, and he had no clear answers beyond the fact that he'd been introduced to Martha by a relative he liked and trusted, and had simply accepted that there was a family connection. That, and the simple fact that she'd been good company and, though this was harder to admit, that he had liked the attention, coming as it did from an attractive and intelligent woman.

He had returned, reluctantly, to the Church of St Michael and All Angels, this time with Mike and Jude in tow. "You've never heard of Jason Matthews?" Mike said.

"I told you, no. The name means nothing to me. I can ask Billy if he knows anything about him."

"John, this boy you encountered here — I want you to be careful. He's seen you with Martha. He followed you here today, so that means he's now watching you. It's likely he knows exactly who you are and where to find you."

"That had occurred to me, you know."

"I'm sure it had, but I'm serious, John. If he did kill Martha, and right now he's a definite suspect, then he's already crossed the line. The second death is always a lot easier, so they say."

"Is it?" John said. "You know, I've always wondered about that. Maybe if you're a psychopath or someone who enjoys inflicting pain but . . . Mike, he didn't strike me like that. He was angry, hurt and, I don't know, scared, I suppose."

"John, he slashed your tyre."

"Strictly speaking, he stabbed my tyre. I'm not in denial, Mike. I know what he could have done."

Mike fell silent, then said, "We could arrange for protection."

"No, you can't. I neither want nor need it. Mike, to turn your argument around, he slashed my tyre, not me. He had every opportunity but all he did was make sure I didn't follow him. He may possibly be a murderer, but he's not a hardened killer — not yet."

Mike looked as though he might argue further but refrained. Instead, he joined Jude, who was examining the tiny grave and those that surrounded it. "All Matthews graves," she said. "Do you know who they are, Mr Tynan?"

"John, please. No, not really. I have a vague feeling that one, Thomas Matthews, was a great-uncle, but I don't recall meeting him. My grandfather was Ernest but he's buried at Cromer. I recall he had a brother or two but he was a solitary man. He didn't have much contact with anything or anyone he couldn't control."

Jude looked hard at him, startled by the sudden bitterness in his tone. "I'm lucky," she said simply. "Both my sets of grandparents are soft as tripe. It's going to rain," she added. "That track is going to be a quagmire in half an hour."

They headed back to the car. Mike found himself checking the tyres.

They drove back down the track and onto the byway, the sky darkening by the second, and the rain began just as they reached the road. John found that he was remembering another journey. That old car with its leather seats and smell of beeswax and lavender. He'd been dressed in a gabardine raincoat, his school coat belted at the waist, and flannel shorts that clung itchily to wet legs. He recalled his mother's voice:

"You make sure you take your shoes off before you come in the house. He won't want you trailing mud in."

They were going back to his grandfather's house.

Somewhere between the present moment and that memory of himself at ten, John strained to see who was driving the big car. He had assumed it would be his father, but now he was not so sure. Listening to the murmur of adult voices coming from the front seats and adhering to the adult convention that he couldn't hear what wasn't meant for his ears, John could not recall the conversation, but he was certain he could hear his uncle Jerry's voice.

"John?"

Mike must have asked him something. "Sorry, I was miles away."

"I could see that. Are you all right?"

"I'm fine. Just wool-gathering." He searched around for something neutral to say, unnerved by his odd reaction to the old church. "Anyway, how are Maria and Josie and the new arrival?"

"Oh, all good. I spoke to Maria this morning. She says it's madness, a constant stream of friends and relatives. I think she feels a bit superfluous. She sent some pictures of May to my phone. I'll show you later."

"Once I remind him how to access them," Jude commented.

"Well, there is that."

John smiled at the exchange, then sank back into his reverie. He stared out of the window, watching the sheets of rain slide in across the open fields, scouring the ground and bouncing so hard on the road that the raindrops seemed to be going back up again. Jude had slowed to a crawl — she could barely see the front of the car — but through the curtains of rain, utterly untroubled by the torrent, John was certain he had glimpsed the black dog running.

CHAPTER 14

Just as the evening briefing was about to start, a man sidled in and asked to speak to someone. He said he was certain that he'd seen the dead woman, sitting in the passenger seat of a small brown car, with a young man in the driving seat.

He was shown the photographs they now had of the boy who had claimed to be Martha Toolin's son, and the witness confirmed that he looked like the same one. He passed Mike as he left the hall. Mike noted a tall man in a black jacket before the door was closed and latched, ready for the briefing to begin.

* * *

Evening, and the rain continued to fall. John, familiar with the vagaries of the local weather, guessed the storm would have emptied itself out completely by midnight and the new day would dawn hot and humid. He liked such mornings, loved the scents that rose up from his garden when he took his breakfast outside and stole an hour away from the concerns of the world.

Back in the here and now, though, he was concentrating upon the task of writing down everything he could remember that Martha had told him, every question she had asked, and anything about her background that might provide some clue as to the truth of the matter. John now doubted everything she had told him, including her motives. He felt used and somewhat soiled by the experience, and was now profoundly grateful that she had at least been honourable enough to have given him the brush-off that last night they had been out together.

Though, on the other hand, if she had come home with him, she might well be still alive.

* * *

On the outskirts of Norwich, Jason Matthews sat down with his family for their evening meal, his head still full of the conversation he'd had with Mike Croft and with his memories of the woman he'd known as Julia Matthews. He'd brought his drink to the table, something he rarely did, and now Katie, his wife, was looking askance at him.

Nevertheless, she poured them both a glass of wine — that, apparently, being all right; a tumbler of whisky not — and water into the children's glasses. The girls chattered like birds as usual, telling him about their day at the Discover Centre in town. A school friend had held her eighth birthday party there and, half listening, Jason gained the impression there had been a fire-eating clown doing science experiments. Michelle, the eldest, wanted to have her upcoming party there too and Sadie, six, and a long way from her seventh birthday, was already starting her campaign. Somewhere in his brain a little voice told him it couldn't be right about the fire-eating clown and another that he should ask them to tell him more, but he really couldn't summon the energy.

"Something wrong?" Katie asked him, leaning over to proffer more potatoes, despite the fact he had not touched those on his plate.

"What could be wrong?" He waved the dish away and lifted his fork, prodding at his food.

"You had visitors earlier, I hear. Molly Greaves saw them. Two people in a car, she said."

Silently, Jason cursed nosey neighbour Molly Greaves. "Trying to sell us double glazing."

Katie looked puzzled, disbelieving. "What? Round here? All these houses were built with double glazing. Any fool can see that."

"Well, that's what I told them then, isn't it?" He got on with eating, hoping that might shut her up. He could feel her looking at him, could see that puzzled, hurt, innocent party look on her face, and was not even sure why he had lied, certainly not why he had come up with such an unconvincing story. Even drunk, he was generally better at it than that. He told himself it was the memory of the chaos Julia bloody Matthews, or Martha Toolin or whatever her bloody name was, had caused when she'd turned up before. Well, he was glad she was dead and gone, and that was the truth of it. Now, all he had to do was ride out the inevitable storm that would hit soon enough. He was damned if he was going to open the window and let in the rain before he absolutely had to.

* * *

Tom was curled up in his car. The clifftop café had closed for the night and the rain kept even the hardiest dog walker at home, so he'd parked up here where he could watch the waves and think things through. The windscreen kept misting up as the chilly deluge of his breath hit. He dried it with the end of the blanket he had wrapped around himself, and had the wipers on intermittent so he could catch swift glimpses of the storm-lashed water before the windscreen flooded again.

With the radio on low, it was all oddly soothing.

Listening to the rain, Tom came to a decision. He'd give it a couple more days and then he was off. He'd like to have thought he'd be heading for home, and for a brief time with Martha he thought he was. Now, though, he'd have to stick a pin in the map or something. He still had money in his account and he didn't need much to live on, so he could get by until he found some work somewhere.

One thing was for sure, he'd have to forget all about the last eighteen months. Put it out of his head. Martha was gone now and there was nothing more he could do for her, so he had to look after himself now. With that thought in mind and the rain still falling hard upon the car, Tom switched off the wipers and closed his eyes, seeking sleep and the oblivion it promised, at least for a little while.

* * *

Mike arrived home to find the lights on and Maria's AuDI tucked in the space beside the house. His mood began to lift, and was practically celebratory by the time he had reached the front door. The scent of herbs and what he quickly identified as roasting lamb filled his nostrils as he opened the door and stepped through the tiny hallway into the kitchen. Both he and Maria liked to cook, and the evening meals were prepared by whoever happened to get home first. She turned from the stove, settling into his embrace. Maria was a tall woman, not quite matching Mike's six feet two but not far off, even without heels. Tall and strong, and he felt that strength now as she wrapped her arms around him, pressing close.

"Oh, it's so good to have you home. I thought you were staying at Josie's till I joined you."

"You needed me more than she does. I could hear it in your voice this morning. Anyway, we can go together when this case is over. I've phoned Oaklands and managed to reschedule my holiday. Pat owes me for all the times I've covered for other people."

He laughed. "So how long do I have to solve the case?"

"I've given you a week. Alright?" Her face was still buried against his neck but he could hear the smile in her voice.

"Generous of you."

She drew back from him, peeling his arms free and compensating with a swift kiss. "Let me check the oven. How's John coping?"

"I'm not sure that he is, actually." Mike leaned back against the counter and watched happily as she removed the meat from the range and checked on the pans simmering on top.

She turned to smile at him. "Go and lay the table, Mr Detective, and you can tell me all about it."

* * *

Later, much later, after dinner and wine and a proper welcome home, Mike woke with a sudden sense of unease that was utterly at odds with his earlier mood. Beside him, Maria slept on, her breathing soft and regular. He leaned on one elbow and studied her face, admiring, as he so often did, the smooth dark skin and the shape of her warm mouth, curving gently as she smiled in her sleep. He slipped from their bed and crossed to the window, staring out into the night. The rain had cleared and the clouds parted to reveal an almost full moon. It was bright enough to see across the fields, to glimpse the rise in the land, beyond which he knew was the sea. The house was quiet and calm, as was the sleeping world outside. He could no longer recall the dream which had so disturbed him.

Maria turned over and asked what was wrong and he slipped back into bed beside her, drawing her close and drifting back to sleep and, it seemed, to some vague half-conscious corner of his mind, back into his dream.

He was running along the shoreline, close to the sea's edge and at low tide, the beach with its jutting wood and concrete teeth some way behind him. The day was warm, though he guessed from the colour of the sky that it was still early in the morning. Mike was not given to running unless it was really necessary. Tall and long limbed, he had once enjoyed the feel of his body pushed to its limits, and he'd been a half decent middle-distance athlete in his youth. More recently, however, he'd come to view such exertion as something he'd rather sit back and admire other people doing than indulge in himself, and the odd game of beach football with Josie's kids had confirmed for him that his days of peak fitness would take some effort to get back.

Now, though, in this dream, his feet pounded the sand and his body rejoiced in the burn that grew in his lungs and flushed his muscles with lactic pain. He knew he could run through it, get through the wall and find his second wind. The beach stretched out ahead of him, longer and further than he knew it to be anywhere along that stretch of coast. And, still in his dream, it suddenly occurred to him that he was not alone. Two others ran beside him, keeping pace, equally exultant as they splashed through the shallows and rejoiced in the feel of the early sun upon their bodies. One was a young boy, sandy haired and freckled and with his mother's blue-grey eyes. The other was a great black dog, strong and sleek and muscled, pacing him effortlessly stride for stride.

"Stevie," Mike whispered softly. Even dreaming, he was afraid to break the spell. "Stevie."

The boy reached out and took his hand. They ran together, man and boy and great black dog, though he knew it didn't make sense. He was keeping up with the dog, and a boy of nine could not possibly match that speed. But who said dreams have to make sense?

And then, too soon and too suddenly, the hand was withdrawn from his. Unable to stop running, he looked back as the others fell behind, dwindling and finally fading away.

"It's all about the kids, Dad." Stevie's voice, soft, and then he was gone.

Mike woke, calling the name of his long dead son, his tears falling.

CHAPTER 15

At the morning briefing, Mike advised the team that further attempts to trace Martha Toolin's next of kin had continued to draw a blank. They had searched under that name and under the name of Julia Matthews. They had tracked down several women of the right age but all had been accounted for.

"She also told witnesses that she had been a nurse," he said. "We've tried to trace her through hospital records, but so far no joy." One of the problems was that they didn't know where to focus the search. They knew that Martha had spent time with Jerry Matthews in King's Lynn, but did that mean she lived in the area?

"And the bank cards?" someone asked. "Do we have a genuine address yet?"

Some laughter at that — everyone knew how slow banks were to release information.

"We're anticipating a response later today," Mike said. "I've set Jude onto them, so hopefully . . ."

More laughter. Jude's persistence was legendary.

After the briefing, he and Jude walked up to the Two Bells. Expecting a media release, the resident press corps had moved from the car park back to the pub yard. Mike surveyed those gathered, noting that some of the locals had set up trestle tables on the verge and were giving out pamphlets about their campaign to save their village from the ravages of the North Sea. One of them recognised Mike and waved. He waved back, and headed quickly inside the Two Bells, not wanting to be ambushed either by villagers or media until he had spoken to the Beals.

"What do we do?" Mrs Beal demanded. "That lot out there and no business. We can't go on like this, Inspector. We've got a friend come over with his burger van, but he can't be here all the time."

"It's been agreed you can open the small bar," Jude told them, "and we can allow limited access to the kitchen. You could maybe set up a marquee, do sandwiches and such, so long as you keep on the far side of the cordon. There's that bit of grass between here and the main car park, would that be a good spot? Unless this lot are a different breed, most journos like a drink and a feed."

Looking relieved, Mrs Beal turned to Mike for confirmation.

"We've no problem with that," he said. "CSI have probably finished here but we'll need to keep the cordon in place for a few more days just in case."

Mrs Beal shuddered. "I doubt anyone will want to sleep here ever again."

"People forget. In a few weeks no one will even think about it." The sad truth, he thought, was that the murder at the Two Bells would enter into local folklore. Still, the frisson of a violent death might well increase their custom.

"If you think you can cope, there's no reason why you shouldn't reopen the small bar and set up some outdoor catering."

"Oh, we can cope," Mr Beal said, "and the staff are already here. We called them in just like you said."

"I just want a quick chat. They've had time to think now, and it may be that some fact has come up in conversation, maybe it's trivial-seeming, but it might be something we don't know yet."

"What should we tell that lot?" Mrs Beal jerked her head towards the window and the waiting reporters beyond.

Jude peeled a sheet of paper from the stack she had in her bag. "Give them this," she said. "We'll be making a statement in a minute, but this outlines the main facts."

"We're having trouble locating her next of kin," Mike said. "Mrs Beal, Mr Beal, can you think of anything else she might have said, about her background, or where she'd come from? Any small thing?"

The Beals exchanged a glance and shook their heads in concert. Mike hadn't really expected anything more. After all, Martha had spent hours in John's company and he was still vague as to where she had said her origins were.

A quick chat with the assembled staff told Mike little more. One thought Martha had talked about a trip to Colchester . . . *'or was it Chesterfield . . . ?'* but that was all, apart from the evident general relief that the Two Bells could at least be partially opened again.

They went outside to read the prepared statement. Mike handed over to Jude for the questions while he scanned the crowd for familiar faces.

"Our main problem is tracing her next of kin," Jude said in response to the request for a picture of the dead woman. "Obviously, we don't want to release a photograph until we've spoken with them."

"We do, however, want to speak to the young man mentioned in the statement." Mike pointed to the relevant paragraph. "The drawing of him, courtesy of the skills of Jude here, is a good likeness, and there's also a photo, but it's a bit on the grainy side." Some laughter at that.

"You need to learn to use a camera, Inspector."

"He is," Mike continued, "someone we need to speak with urgently. He may have seen something without realising its significance, and we understand that he knew the dead woman quite well. He may even be related to her."

"Is he a suspect?"

Mike glanced to where the question had come from, recognised the representative of the local TV news station, tried hard to recall his name. "Usual answer to that — we're ruling no one out and no one in. But he *is* a possible witness. As yet, we have no motive. Oh, and for those of you that are new to the area, have a chat with our friends over there before you leave." He pointed to the couple manning the impromptu information desk, and received smiles and grateful waves in return. "And if you feel the need for refreshment, the Two Bells will be partly reopening for lunch."

General murmurs of approval ensued. Behind him, Mike could hear the bolts being drawn back as the Beals took him at his word. He wondered how much the story would have grown by evening, and in what direction, and what new speculation the morning news would bring. He was aware that the carefully worded statement they had given out had so many holes and omissions that there would be plenty of room for an imaginative journalist to generate some theory to fill them in.

Leaving Jude by the door to field any further enquiries, he made his way over to the trestle table, reaching into his memory for the names of the couple in charge of it. He'd met them before on a couple of occasions. He remembered just in time that they were Laura and Mark something or other.

"Morning to you," Mark said. "Thought we might as well make use of the publicity."

"It might not be in the best possible taste," Laura admitted, "but . . ." She shrugged.

"Do you drink at the Bells?" Mike asked. "You may have seen the dead woman, or this kid. We think he's about nineteen, twenty, something like that."

Laura took the picture. "I couldn't tell you much about the woman, but I've seen him around lately. He drives a little brown hatchback thing." She frowned. "Matter of fact, I think I saw it this morning when we were coming up here." She handed the picture to her husband, who squinted thoughtfully at the picture, holding it out at arms' length.

"You forgot your specs again, didn't you?" his wife said.

"I may have done." He shook his head. "Sorry, I couldn't tell you for sure, but if Laura says she's seen him then it's odds on she has."

He could see Laura weighing up whether this was a compliment or a veiled insult. He was saved from having to worry about it by a familiar voice behind him.

"Hello, Mike."

Mike turned with a smile. Phil Andrews was not exactly a friend, but he was certainly a familiar addition to the scenery, and yet another link back to that long-ago case of the missing child. Today, though, the journalist had a younger man in tow. Mid-twenties and dark-haired, he was glancing wistfully towards the pub and clearly wondering when they'd be joining the rest of the pack inside.

Mike turned with them and they headed slowly back together. "My replacement," Phil said with a jerk of his head towards the younger man.

"You're retiring?"

"Jumping ship before I get pushed. Got to make room for young blood, you know."

Mike laughed. "You don't sound terribly upset."

"Oh, I'm not. I'm ready for it. Not that Geoff here will stay for long."

The young man, hearing his name, glanced over but said nothing.

"My job is just a stepping stone to greater things. Geoff here has an MA," Phil added. "Hope you're suitably impressed."

"Oh, I'm sure I will be."

"So, what's the inside track on this one, Mike? I hear she had something to do with John Tynan?"

"Now where did you hear that?" Mike smiled. "From the Beals, I would imagine."

"Oh, people talk, you know they do."

"A distant cousin," Mike said. "She was here looking up the family tree. John was introduced by another distant relative."

"So why the problem contacting next of kin?"

Mike could practically hear the wheels turning.

"Because, like I said, she was a very distant cousin. You know how it is."

"Not really, no." Phil changed tack. "I hear John's also given in to the local hysteria."

"How's that, then?" Mike asked, though he knew what was coming.

"This here Black Dog. I'm told he's among those who saw the thing on the beach."

"He did see a large black dog," Mike conceded. "Though not on the beach. He reported it and we sent a dog man out."

"I'm betting he didn't make an arrest."

"Superstition." Geoff's comment was both unexpected and scathing.

"Geoff doesn't hold with local myth and legend becoming manifest. He goes for the mass hysteria option."

"It's as good as any," Mike conceded. "But," he added, unable to resist the sudden urge to play devil's advocate, "people have been seeing the dog for a very long time. Black Shuck is famous in these parts."

Phil chuckled. "Famous and deadly. You want to watch yourself, Geoff. Turn down those night-time assignments the boss has been giving you."

The younger man grimaced. "I thought we were here to cover a murder. Not some bloody phantom. Not unless the dog's a suspect."

Mike and Phil exchanged a glance. "Well, since you mention it . . ." Mike said. Geoff was, he gathered from the sour face, not amused. He saw the younger man's expression change to one of sudden interest and was unsurprised to see Jude coming to meet them. With her blonde, pixie cut hair, bright blue eyes and slender, curved body, Jude attracted a fair amount of attention everywhere. He didn't much rate Geoff's chances, though.

She glanced his way, dismissed him with a look, and greeted Phil with a quick smile. "We off then, boss?"

"I think we might be." He said goodbye to the journalists and they headed back to the car.

"Who's the new boy?" she asked.

Mike told her.

"Well, he looks like a load of laughs. Can't see him sticking around. The Beals are holding court," she added. "I had a couple of people ask about the John Tynan connection. Told them he was a distant relative but doesn't know much about her side of the family. There's a lot of speculation, but that's to be expected. It's obvious we're not telling everything, and that lot love a bit of a mystery. You think we should warn Mr Tynan?"

"Oh, John knows the score. I'm looking forward to seeing just how they fill in the gaps," he added. "I'm betting both ex-DI Tynan and our Black Dog get a sidebar in at least one of the tabloids."

Jude settled behind the wheel. "Any particular reason? Anything I should avoid saying? Not been here long, remember."

Mike nodded. "John headed up an investigation here more than thirty years ago. A child had disappeared. She was never found and no arrests were made. Just after I arrived, the same thing happened again. A child missing and no leads, except for some striking similarities with John's case. He offered himself as a consultant and I accepted. Anyone wants to do some digging, there's plenty to find, none of it bad, but . . ."

"Retired detective, locally famous case, violent murder and a bit of folklore stirred into the mix. Right. Got it." She grinned at Mike. "I take it Maria's back."

"Oh, and how would you know that?" He looked down at his feet, peering beneath the dashboard to examine his socks.

"No, not the socks! Though they do match today. You're just, well, happier. You look kind of lost when she's away, as if you've got a bit missing and can't remember where you left it."

Mike did his best to look affronted, which only made Jude laugh. He gave up on the attempt. "She came back yesterday afternoon," he said.

"And the new baby?"

"Is thriving. Same as the rest of the brood." He fell silent, his thoughts turning to his own lost child. Jude, aware of the change of mood, let the quiet lie.

He had not dreamed of Steven in a long time. Just after his death, it had been a daily occurrence, then, as time passed, Mike had realised that days had gone by when he had not dreamed of his son. Slowly, the occurrences had diminished, becoming uncommon enough to be noteworthy in themselves, and then they ceased.

Last night, though, was different from the usual sort of nightmare in which he saw his son dead, or lived through his funeral, or, worst of all, heard him crying in the dark, darkness so thick and so chokingly oppressive that he had no chance of finding him.

No, last night had been different. "Do you ever dream, Jude?"

"What? The other day you wanted to know what I wore in the bedroom, now you want to know what I dream about. I am *seriously* going to talk to Maria."

Nevertheless, she thought about it. "Everyone dreams," she said finally. "I don't often remember mine and they're usually downright weird — mostly they depend on what I've been watching on the telly. Why?"

"Oh, I don't know. Maybe all this talk about the black dog. You know, myth, legends, dreams . . . hysteria."

"John Tynan doesn't strike me as the hysterical kind," Jude said quietly.

"No, he's not," Mike agreed.

"And is he prone to seeing ghosts?"

Mike smiled, remembering. "Oh," he said, "I think everyone is prone to that from time to time."

"Haunted place this," Jude said. "You can feel it sometimes."

Mike was intrigued. Jude was usually so utterly down to earth. "What makes you say that?"

"Oh, maybe it's something to do with the fenland. Like, we're not really meant to be here. It's just borrowed land. I read somewhere that in ancient times they used to think that marshland was kind of between the worlds, you know? Like lakes and peat mosses and suchlike, they were kind of like portals to other worlds. That's why you get the burials, some people think — archaeologists and such who are supposed to know about these things. They reckon they were like messengers, sent to the gods through the marshland."

"Borrowed land," Mike said. "I like that."

She laughed, slightly embarrassed. "I didn't grow up round here, but Mum's family, they come from Somerset, down on the levels."

"And is that haunted too?"

"Oh yes," she said softly. "But it's kind of different there. You stand on the levels and there's this *sound* all around you. Like this hissing, this . . ."

"Susurration," Mike said.

"Oh, good word. But yes, and sometimes it's like . . . like a crackling that seems to fill the air. It's not like that here." She giggled. "God, what do I sound like?"

Mike ignored her attempt at self-deprecation. "So, what *does* it sound like here?"

She hesitated for a moment. "Like the sea. Like the sea is all around and beneath and running through every crevice in the landscape. Like it's telling us that we've had it our way long enough and it's payback time. Like our lease won't be extended, and, like, all the memories of the land that's already been taken back are now in the water. Like it's claimed them."

Mike stared at her. She blushed, laughed, truly embarrassed. Then he settled back into his seat, nodding. "I dreamed of my son last night."

"Your son?"

"He died. Hit-and-run. He'd just turned ten. It was a couple of years before I came here, and that was partly why I did. Funny, but it was a good dream. We were running along the beach and the black dog was running with us, and just for a moment it felt . . ." How had it felt? "It was a good feeling," he said, realising suddenly that it was almost as if he'd finally managed to make peace with his memories.

'*It's all about the children,*' Stevie had said. Mike, somewhere in the depths of his consciousness, felt that statement was important. That it was right. He just could not have explained why.

CHAPTER 16

Mike and Jude arrived back at police HQ to find that more information had arrived from forensics along with the write-up from the post-mortem. There were two types of dog hair found on Martha's body. From a German shepherd, and also from an unknown breed of black dog.

Jude rolled her eyes.

"Unknown means it's some kind of mongrel," Mike said. "*Mongrel*, not mythical."

"If you say so, boss. You think this boy and the dog really are connected in some way?"

"I think it's a coincidence that the dog was at the churchyard . . . *a* dog, that is. Jason Matthews didn't seem to recognise it anyway, and surely you would, wouldn't you?"

Jude shrugged. "Lots of common or garden black dogs around. Mr Tynan saw the blown-up photos and he didn't say 'oh, that's the bugger I nearly ran over.'" Mike laughed. She had caught John's intonation perfectly. "Anyway, back to the real stuff. The dental records are now out there on the system. Hopefully someone, somewhere, will pick up on them."

Mike nodded. He scanned the rest of the report, discovering that Martha had been a healthy, unremarkable sixty-something, who had coloured her hair, was inclined to carry a little extra weight on her hips and had borne at least one child.

So could the boy actually be her son?

In an attempt to get a feel for this woman whose death and, for that matter, whose life was still such a mystery, Mike sat down with the box containing Martha's personal effects.

Among them was a well-worn leather handbag shaped like a small briefcase, with an optional shoulder strap. She hadn't been using the strap — it was tucked into a side pocket — though there were signs of wear and, from the length of it, it seemed she sometimes carried the bag across her body. Her purse was red leather with a gilt clasp on the coin compartment and a billfold on the side. ATM cards in two different names — Martha Toolin and Julia Matthews — from two different banks, three ten-pound notes and just under five pounds in loose change.

"Any progress on getting an address?" Mike asked. "Have the banks released that information yet?"

"I'll chase it up," Jude said. "They promised to call me back this morning."

"I wonder which of these identities is the real one," Mike said. "If either of them is."

He examined the rest of the effects. A case containing reading glasses, a pack of tissues, two lipsticks, one quite pale and well-used, the other bolder, in a deep red, and which looked almost new. He looked at the brand and found that, like the cosmetics from the bathroom, it was a common one available in any large chemist and most supermarkets. Wet wipes, a small mirror and a travel size perfume that had been sliding around in the bag so long Mike could not read the name, and what he thought was a powder compact but turned out to be just a small mirror in a shiny, red plastic case.

"What's missing, Jude?"

"You mean apart from the till receipts and bus tickets?"

"Bus tickets?"

"Oh, everyone has bus tickets in their bag, even when they never use the bus. It's a sort of given." She frowned. "Where are her keys? No car keys. No house keys. Mike, how did she get to the B&B? And no mobile phone, even though Mr Tynan says she had one."

"Ah, now, somewhere here . . ." Mike rummaged among the statements and reports that had come in that morning. He'd skimmed through them before going out to the Two Bells. "Right," he said, finally finding what he'd been searching for. "She arrived at the Two Bells in a taxi, apparently."

"A taxi? Where from?"

"Now that is a bit of a mystery. She took the taxi from North Walsham, but there's no record of her staying in any of the pubs, hotels or B&Bs within what you might consider walking distance. The cab picked her up outside the train station, and dropped her off at the Two Bells."

"Did she say where she'd come from?"

Mike shook his head. "The driver recalls her saying something about staying with friends and someone would be picking her up from the B&B, but apart from that all he recalls is that she didn't seem to want to talk."

"So how did she get to North Walsham? She was picked up outside the station but that doesn't mean she got off a train. And what was she doing there anyway? Do you think there actually were any friends?"

Mike shook his head. "I'm guessing that the boy in the picture drove her out here. For some reason he dropped her off before she went into the Two Bells. Maybe he was going to collect her later. Then, of course, everything, whatever everything was, went, well . . ."

"Tits up," Jude provided.

"Quite. So that would explain the lack of car keys, but people usually keep their house keys with them, even when they go on holiday. Don't they?"

Jude shrugged. "I'd say so. Even if you leave a spare with a neighbour, you'll still want to get in when you arrive home.

Maybe she left them with the young bloke who had the car? She presumably left him the car keys, so . . ."

Mike nodded. "You're assuming it's her car? It might not be." It was almost time for the afternoon briefing, and officers had begun to drift in. Mike familiarised himself with the rest of the reports, quickly glancing through the statements and the phone calls and all the random detritus that such an enquiry generates. A slow, nagging worry was beginning to form in his mind that they should have held off releasing the pictures of the young man they wanted to speak to.

"You worried he'll do a runner?" Jude said. She had, he noted, a disturbing knack of reading his thoughts.

"It had crossed my mind," he admitted.

Jude shrugged. "Bit late now. Though, to be honest, if he did kill her, why isn't he long gone already? I would have been."

Mike nodded. Good question. Why not indeed?

CHAPTER 17

Ever since Julia Matthews, or whatever the woman was called, had appeared on the scene, Jason had become very conscious of his surroundings. He'd thought of Julia as his stalker, always turning up unexpectedly, often not approaching him or even acknowledging his presence but there in the background, watching and waiting.

He'd thought about going to the police, but what could he say? *This woman who claims to be a relative keeps turning up in places I go to.* It sounded pathetic, even to him. Jason thought of himself as a macho, rugby-playing type — even though he'd not played rugby for years — and this Julia woman was half his size. What sort of a threat would a woman like her pose?

But she had been. A threat. She'd known just what buttons to press and had gone right ahead and pounded on them and, no, he wasn't sorry she was dead.

Tonight, he and Amanda, a woman who was definitely not his wife, had taken a chance and gone out for dinner at a country pub. Amanda looked sensational — not overdressed or anything, but the shirt she was wearing revealed the occasional glimpse of breast and, as she walked away from him towards the ladies', her well-fitting trousers emphasised those long legs and the perfect little bum.

Of course, Jason thought, trying to be charitable, Amanda hadn't given birth to two kids. He well knew just how much of a toll that had taken on his wife's body. And the truth was, it didn't really bother him. He could have lived with the bit of extra weight and the boobs that had inevitably lost their firmness after breastfeeding two girls. None of that would have mattered if Katie hadn't been so damned angry all the time.

Jason had come to realise that nothing he could do for her would ever be good enough. To put it bluntly, he was a disappointment. In more honest moments, Jason admitted — to himself at least — that he'd not gone to any great lengths to try and change the faults she saw in him. No, he'd dug in his heels and made the 'this is me, take it or leave it' speech so often he'd convinced himself that he was actually justified in this particular view.

And then Amanda had come back and, well, life had improved and got more complicated in about equal measure.

Jason sipped his drink and glanced around at the other customers. Couples mostly, and one group that looked like a family with older teens — a brother and a sister. Jason watched them for a moment or two and noted that they actually seemed to like one another. They chatted and laughed like that was the natural thing for a family to do. He couldn't recall the last time that his had at least appeared to enjoy themselves that way.

A man entered the restaurant area and waited at the bar, and as one of the waiting staff showed him to a table Jason realised that he knew him. The man glanced in his direction but only in a casual, checking out the surroundings way, as Jason himself had done moments before. There was no recognition in his eyes, but this was the man who'd been standing by the lifeboat station when Jason had gone that way onto the beach. The man in a dark jacket, oddly dressed for a beach walk.

Another bloody stalker. Jason was shocked at how unsettled the thought made him. Then Amanda returned and took her seat and his view of the man was partly blocked by long fair hair and bare shoulder and a glimpse of breast and Jason, with surprising difficulty, allowed himself to be distracted.

* * *

Having spent the evening with Mike and Maria, John arrived home just after eleven. A message on the answerphone from Cousin Billy was waiting for him. Late as it was, John called back, knowing that Billy habitually stayed up 'watching the box.'

"It wasn't a snuffbox old Jerry gave that Martha woman," Billy told him. "It was a picture frame. Little silver thing she took a fancy to. And I've got a copy of the will for you. I stuck it in the post this afternoon. And there's a box of old papers not been bothered with since the funeral, but it might have summat in it you need. I'll drop it over tomorrow night. I pack up early, with it being Friday."

John thanked him and after a bit more small talk, put down the phone and stared at the scribbled name and number Billy had given him. Jerry's nursing home and the name of his key worker, apparently. He dialled, wondering if Trisha Walker would be on duty tonight.

"Oh yes," she told him a few minutes later. "The family said you'd be in touch. I'm really sorry to hear about Mrs Toolin, she seemed like a nice lady. The news said she was stabbed?"

John could hear the hopeful note in her voice. A murder. Something to break up the dull routine. "I'm afraid you heard right," he said. "But maybe you could tell me — do you remember the photo frame that Jerry left to her?"

"Does it have to do with the murder? Well, would you credit it? Just goes to show, like my mum used to say, you never can tell, can you?"

Tell what? John coughed. "No, you never can. The photo frame?"

"Silver. Art Deco, only a little thing but really nice. I remember it especially because the little easel stand on the back broke and Jerry was quite upset. We got our handyman, Phil Beresford, to help out. He made a new little wooden back for it and a little strut on a hinge. Very nice job he made of it. Jerry was so pleased."

"And it was sent to Martha afterwards? Do you happen to have an address for her?"

"Oh no. I think one of the family took it for her, or maybe she even collected it herself, I don't know. I wasn't here on the day the family came to collect his things. Don't the family know where she lived? I mean . . ." She trailed off as though suddenly realising that there was an even greater mystery here than she had suspected.

John interrupted her reverie before it led to further questions. "When did she start to visit him?"

"Oh, must have been about a year before he died, maybe closer to a year and a half. I think she came with another relative, but I really don't remember exactly. Then she started coming every week or so, right up until about a month before he died."

"And then she stopped visiting?"

"I think they had an argument about something, I don't know exactly. He was a lovely old man but he could be a bit irascible, you know. I'm sure she would have come back again if he hadn't, you know, hadn't died."

Right, John thought. "Trisha, was Jerry, you know . . . ?"

"All there? Oh yes, sharp as a knife most of the time. He had his moments, of course, when he forgot things. People had to remind him who they were sometimes, especially if it had been a while, but he was on the ball most of the time. He loved to watch the quizzes on the telly and the news, and he used to talk about how it was in the war and all that."

John felt the need to interrupt. "Did he sometimes forget who Martha was?"

"No, not really. Oh, well, when she first came, I suppose he was a bit hazy, but she reminded him about when she'd last seen him and he remembered after that. He liked her. She made him laugh. Sometimes people forget that old people still like to laugh."

John found himself sympathising with that observation. "Do you remember what was in the photo frame?" he asked.

"Oh yes. It was an old black and white picture of a baby, a very young baby. Someone was holding it but that bit had been cut off. When Phil took the back off the picture to fix it, you could see it had been a bigger picture once. A bit of it was folded over to make it fit the frame, but the rest had been cut off, I think. I thought it was a bit odd, but there you go. People argue, I suppose."

A baby? Jerry had never married, so far as he knew. Never even had a serious relationship . . . A merest thread of memory drifted like a strand of fog through his consciousness. The dream, the child crying, the sad little grave. None of it seemed to fit together and yet . . .

He thanked Trisha and replaced the receiver, thinking about the boy and where he might have gone, and if he'd really been responsible for Martha's death.

CHAPTER 18

Mike walked from the incident room to the Two Bells. With him was Amit Jacobs, the PoLSA, or police search adviser. The victim's mobile phone had been found in a patch of undergrowth a few hundred yards from the pub. The SIM card and memory cards were missing and the phone looked as though it had been stamped on and smashed with something heavy, but Mrs Beal had recognised the bright, floral, after-market back. Looking at the photographs of the smashed-up phone, Mike had to admit that it was distinctive enough to have stuck in the memory. He had emailed the image to John, who had seconded Mrs Beal's opinion. It was the bright pink that had led to it being discovered, the colour spotted in the grass by two little girls who had come to ride their ponies. Their father had called the incident room.

They stood once more in the bedroom where Martha had been killed. "So," Mike said, "what do we think?"

From the doorway, Amit studied the room and the crime scene photos he held. "Her bag was on the bedside cabinet, which suggests to me that her phone was probably in it. It's a small table. If she'd taken her phone out of her bag, the logical place for it would be on the bedside cabinet and she'd have moved her bag elsewhere. Whoever attacked her didn't have to look for the bag, it was in plain sight — always supposing it was the victim who placed it there, of course. They took nothing else?"

"Not as far as we know. It's possible that an address book is also missing, but we can't be certain. If it is, then I see that as significant. An address book plus a phone. Both are items that not only link the woman to friends and family and other contacts, but also give a history of those contacts. So it's a fair assumption that whoever killed her was also listed in one or both."

Amit nodded. "So, they either went down the stairs or out the window. My bet is the stairs. If there's an easy exit, why not use it?"

Mike tended to agree. He followed Amit down the stairs and to the back door. "The keys on the hooks are for guests to use." Mike pointed to a row of three, all with identical keys. All the keys were in place. "If guests are likely to be out after closing time, they take a key, let themselves in and are supposed to leave it on the hook once they've locked the door."

Amit grimaced. "Not very safety-conscious, but I suppose you have to be pragmatic in a business like this. No significant prints on the keys?"

"Nothing useful enough for them to be sent to forensics. The surfaces are dimpled, there were smudges and partials, but . . ."

Amit took a key and unlocked the door. "So, the phone was found at the edge of that field?" He pointed to a line of trees and a hedge.

Mike consulted his map and nodded. "The quickest way is across the car park, out onto the road."

"Security light." Amit pointed to one at the main door of the pub. "So if they knew the lie of the land, they'd have kept close to the wall of the pub and then along the boundary. They might still have set the light off when they got to the road but then . . . Mind you, the Beals sleep on the other side of the building, so the only people who'd notice that security light going on would be passing motorists or perhaps whoever lives at that bungalow on the corner. But I remember from the statements that they don't recall anything amiss and besides, they also sleep at the back."

Mike crossed the pub yard, aware that their presence had attracted the attention of the media camped out in the next-door car park. He ignored the shouted questions and stepped out into the road. Blue and white tape marked the place where the mobile phone had been found. "From here across that way. We'd been focussing on roads and paths going in the other direction, assuming the killer had a car parked close by. I suppose that's how we missed the phone in the first search."

Amit was shaking his head. "That area was searched as thoroughly as the rest of the area."

They walked down to a waiting uniformed constable, who directed them to where the phone had been recovered. The field was rough grass, used for grazing. Two horses watched curiously, weighing up whether or not these new strangers might have anything interesting in their pockets.

Mike crouched by two little markers pegged into the grass. "Rabbit holes. This bit of bank is riddled with them."

Amit knelt, picked up a twig and flicked a tiny fragment of plastic from a rabbit hole Mike had not noticed. "More phone debris," he said. "So whoever took the phone came across from the pub, in the dark, into this field, removed the SIM, smashed the phone and pushed the bits into the rabbit hole. Mr Rabbit probably pushed it out again. Lo, one phone, missed in the first search."

"So they had a torch," Mike said, "and they knew the area. But why bother? Why not take the phone away with you, extract the SIM and memory card at your leisure, then dump what's left in a skip or even a domestic bin?"

"Panic? Maybe they were disturbed, or they didn't think they would get away. Maybe they were local and didn't want to take the phone home. Maybe they *weren't* local but didn't want to take the phone home. Maybe they thought if they took it home, someone might see it, recognise it or at least ask some awkward questions."

Mike shrugged. "Then drive away, dump the phone somewhere en route."

"People don't, though, do they? Not if they're in a panic. They act, react, then think about it later," Amit said.

True. "Which suggests the killing wasn't premeditated, perhaps?" Mike said.

"Or maybe they'd psyched themselves up for the actual act but had no idea how it would affect them after."

Just to be sure, they checked the rest of the rabbit holes but there seemed to be nothing more, or if there was, then it had been shoved a long way in. Mike made arrangements for a more thorough examination, just in case, trying to remember the little he knew about rabbit warrens and how many entrances and exits there might be. It was chance, maybe, that one rabbit had taken exception to the bright pink foreign object in that particular place. There might be other objects that the rabbit community had bypassed or ignored.

Overall, Mike was more interested in the fact that someone had felt the need to take the mobile than where it had ended up. And that they had done their best to hide all her contacts. Chances were, then, that their name was in Martha's phone or in her address book.

CHAPTER 19

As arranged, John collected Maria mid-morning and they drove back out to the Church of St Michael and All Angels. Apparently there was a keyholder at the nearby farm. Maria had spoken to him and found he had a plan of the graveyard, "in case anyone comes looking for Great-Uncle Charlie or summat." The keyholder also kept the grass cut and generally tidied the place up, for which he received a small payment from the church authorities.

"*Very* small, apparently," Maria told John. "He was quite insistent that I understand that. Maybe he thinks we've got a direct line to the Inland Revenue. Mike's off to King's Lynn, by the way. He called me after the morning briefing to say they finally have an address, linked to her bank cards, so the local police and CSI are there, carrying out a search. He's gone over to see what's what. They've also had a call from someone claiming to be an ex-neighbour of Martha Toolin's. Mike's going to have a chat while he's there."

"Oh, well that's progress, hopefully." He told her about the phone call with Jerry's care worker.

"And you've no idea who the photo was of?"

"None at all, but there's a lot I don't know about the family. I suppose I walked away and hoped that I could just keep on walking. And so I did for most of my life."

"You're really angry about this, aren't you?" Maria said.

"What do you mean?"

"I mean, you're angry about being drawn back in. You put it to one side for a bit because you rather liked Martha, but now you're mad as hell about it again and you're feeling bad about that because, after all, a woman has died, and that's what you should be most upset about."

"Is that your professional opinion?" John asked, a frosty note in his voice.

Maria just laughed. "I can't just switch it off, you know. I've been a shrink for far too long. Honestly though, John, speaking just as a friend now, it's OK to feel angry, bitter, to be mad as hell about it all. It's a bloody mess and all the worse because you don't know what to believe about her."

John nodded, slightly mollified and recognising that, as usual, Maria was right. He turned down the byway, the tarmac road swiftly narrowing and becoming a rutted track between high hedges.

"Aren't we somewhere near Walsingham?" Maria asked.

"Ten, twelve miles away," John said. "Have you ever been there?"

"Once, when Josie came over. Middle of winter and pouring with rain. It's an odd little place. I remember standing in, oh, what is it called? The Virgin's House? It was, as I said, this solid grey rainy day, know what I mean, when the rains come straight off the sea and it's like it's brought the whole damned tide inland with it?"

John nodded. A sharp bend and the track opened out into a rough grassy circle. Beyond that was the little church, settled into the landscape between the raised mounds of centuries of burials.

"Pretty," Maria commented. "English picturesque at its best."

"And Walsingham?"

"Oh, definitely not. I've not seen it during the summer with all the crowds and the pilgrims, so it might be different then, but the day we went, there was hardly anyone there. We were just alone in this odd little church within a church with this really lovely statue of the Virgin and Child decked out in an embroidered cope and, I don't know, it felt almost like we were trespassing. Josie felt it too. It wasn't *us*, if you see what I mean. It was just people, like the place wanted its quiet time. You ever felt that in a place?"

John thought about it and then nodded. "I think so. The Greenway was like that." He was referring to a short stretch of ancient pathway close to Happisburgh village. "It didn't mind being used as a pathway, I mean, that's what it was, but I recall that when we were investigating, you'd get those moments of sudden quiet, when we all felt . . . unwanted. Intrusive. We all felt it, but of course no one wanted to say anything."

A man stepped through a gate into the open space and Maria nodded in his direction. "I'm guessing that's our keyholder."

"Looks like it." John got out of the car and advanced, hand extended. The man was middle-aged, probably younger than John but weathered and deeply browned. His skin, when he shook Maria's hand, was not much lighter than hers. He handed John the keys and Maria a sheaf of papers.

"Should be all you need right there," he told them. "Come along up to the house when you've done. I got to be getting back. We're harvesting." With that he vanished back through the gate.

"Thanks," John said to the retreating back. He received a vague wave in reply.

Maria chuckled. "Man's got a harvest to get in," she said. "Mind you, I'd bet he's not much less taciturn in the middle of winter when there's nothing to do. Right, so what do we have here?"

She spread the papers out on the bonnet of the car. There were two parts to the plan of the churchyard, which had once been joined into one sheet, the edge frayed as though it had been folded so often the paper fibres had finally separated. The plan had been hand-drawn and the yellowed paper and spidery handwriting spoke of years long gone. John could not help but wonder if the careful creator of this plan was now interred among those graves he had so assiduously marked.

"Reverend Josiah Grimmer," she read, pointing to a brief note on the edge of the paper which designated the author. "There's a good local name. Doesn't say when he made it, though. What's the other paperwork?"

John laid the clean white sheets down over their older cousins. A photocopied layout of plots marked with numbers, a key giving names to go with them, and references beside some of those that, John guessed, referred to an archive or other record. "Look," he said. "Here are the Matthews graves."

He found the corresponding section of the old map and compared them. "Looks like we may have several layers of Matthews," Maria commented. "Family plots, do you reckon?"

John nodded. "Yes, from what I remember."

They gathered the plans and went through the rather shabby lychgate into the churchyard. "I've not been inside," he said. "Hopefully there'll be a guidebook or some such. I'd like to know a bit more about the place."

Maria nodded. "Graves first?"

"Yes, I think so." John led the way. The day had grown hot and he was made aware that his hair was getting thin, almost gone on the top of his head, like a monk's tonsure. Did monks apply sun cream to their pates? "Here," he said. "Those are all Matthews graves, three or four generations in some plots." He compared them to the plans. "Look, these are on both sets of drawings. Those two, from the twenties, they're only on the later one. Do we have a date on the plans, I wonder?"

"Um, yes, I saw something somewhere. Look," she pointed to the caption that told them that the photocopied plans were from a school project carried out in 1945, "'by children of St Michael's school.' Doesn't say why. You'd have thought there'd be an official record somewhere."

"Probably is — somewhere," John said. "County Records Office maybe? Cathedral? I don't know. Jude just happened to notice the name of the keyholder — it's up in the church porch — so this seemed like the quickest way of getting started."

Maria nodded. "Your little grave isn't here, though, so it must have been dug after 1945." She knelt down and examined the tiny plot, barely raised above the level of the surrounding ground, its grassy curve dotted with daisies and tiny yellow flowers that John thought might be celandines. "Look," Maria said. "This cross is a replacement. The older one must have rotted away. You can see the remnants sticking out of the soil."

She was right. The stump of the first, the wood rotten and friable, could be observed just behind the new one. It had either rotted off at the point where it met the earth or it had broken over time. The newer one showed signs of having been in place over a long period of time. The wood was grey, the grain opened up by wind and weather. The name Matthews was still visible, though it took the touch of a finger running across the words to reinforce what the eyes were seeing.

"No dates," Maria said. "What a sad little grave."

John closed his eyes, the memory of that day returning more forcefully than before. He could smell the damp, almost wet dog smell of his mother's woollen coat, beyond that, the scent of the skin lotion she applied night and morning and which left her skin with the scent of rose and lily of the valley. He had reached out and taken her hand, not really understanding what they were doing here, why they were standing in the rain, his mother wearing her oldest coat, the one she'd kept just for '*round the place, doing stuff in the garden. It'll do for that, so don't throw it out yet . . .*'

"Nineteen forty-seven," he said quietly. "Winter."

"John?"

He didn't reply. Instead, he got awkwardly to his feet, annoyed at how fast his legs went to sleep whenever he knelt down these days. "Shall we look at the church?" His hand shook as he tried to insert the key, rattling against the cast iron of the escutcheon before he slotted it home. Inside was dim and dusty, the summer sun filtered through panes of ageing, greenish glass. John was reminded of woodland, of light filtered through leaf canopies, soft and green and cool and, here, reflected gently by limewashed walls.

They stood silently just inside the door, allowing their eyes to adjust after the brightness outside. The floor was tiled. Victorian, John guessed, black and red and cream set in geometric patterns down the aisle. Maria's heels tapped lightly as she walked towards the altar, the sound echoing and returning. She paused. The regularity of the pattern was interrupted at the crossing by a slab of fine black slate, engraved with copperplate. "Another Matthews," she said. "Arnold, died in eighteen fifty-five and the relict of the same." She laughed. "Lovely word, relict. Oh, she was a Martha. John, isn't that strange?"

He wanted to tell her that it would have been a common enough name back then, but Maria was right, it resonated, echoing and returning like the sound of her heels, tapping again as she moved on.

The church was still furnished with box pews. John was glad to see them. So many churches had ripped them out in the seventies. They were, for the most part, plainly made, with simple decoration and recessed panels. Turned wooden spheres, some of them plain, some carved, decorated the pew ends and John looked with interest at the leaf-like patterns that adorned them and that seemed quite at odds with the restrained style of the pews themselves. Looking closer, John realised that they had been grafted onto the earlier structures. It had been skilfully done but there was still a strange sense of mismatch. John wondered when it had been done and why and if some reverent hobbyist had wanted to add his own idea of beauty to the pretty but sober little church.

"John."

Something in her tone hurried him. Maria was standing in front of an alcove too small to really qualify as a side chapel but which was evidently intended to be separated out from the body of the church. A tiny altar, adorned by a rather modest and somewhat tarnished brass candlestick and a small scrap of embroidered linen, was set before an almost too grand memorial tablet carved from pink marble.

John winced — the pink veining on the marble made him think of raw, chopped liver. Marble he didn't mind, provided it was black or white or grey, but *not* pink.

"Another of your lot," Maria said.

"Not mine," John contradicted almost without thinking. "Gerald Matthews," he read. "Seventeen fifty-four to eighteen twelve. We must have had money back then."

"No relict, but look above the stone. It's so mucky you can hardly make it out but I think it's a wall painting."

John looked closely at the area she was pointing to. Like the rest of the church, it had been limewashed but the whitening was crumbling away and behind it, John could glimpse a picture, black and red and with traces of green.

"Aren't they really rare?"

"Yes, they are, though we have more than our fair share round here. And it must be old, too, before the marble thing. Do you think they knew about it when they put that monstrosity over it?"

"Probably," John said. "I know there was a fetish for painting over during the Reformation and then again during the English Civil War. That's how some of them survived. The people hid them from Henry VIII and then again from Cromwell's lot, but the civil war was long over by eighteen twelve." He frowned. "What is it, do you reckon?"

Without really thinking, John reached up to touch it.

"Careful," Maria warned. "It will be incredibly fragile. Wait." She rummaged in her bag and found her car keys. A small flashlight was attached to the key chain. Maria shone it at the painting but John had already figured it out.

"It's a dog, isn't it?" he said.

"It is. How did you know? Look, you can make out the outline where the limewash is flaking and there's a man too and a boy, I think, but he's still mainly under the whitewash."

John took a deep breath. It was all too absurd for words. "We should go and talk to our farmer friend," he said. "If he's the keyholder then he'll know about this." He turned on his heel and walked quickly away, suddenly in a hurry to leave. Maria said nothing until they were almost at the farm.

"Do you think she knew? Martha, I mean, about the black dog. Do you think . . . ?"

"That she brought a bloody great canine with her and let it loose to cause havoc?"

"OK. Well if you put it like that . . ." She fell silent again, but John knew what she'd been trying to say. He felt it himself, that somehow it was all connected — Martha, the boy, the black dog and the Matthews. Did that include the other Matthews, the dog walker on the beach who had seen the black dog before he had?

* * *

"What makes you think the grave is from 1947?" Maria asked as they drove away. "You remember the place, don't you?"

John sighed. "I *think* I remember it. The trouble is, it's like one of those memories you think is yours and then you realise it just feels like that because you've been told about it so often." He glanced at Maria. She nodded.

"I have this memory of being there, with my mother. It was raining and I know I'm about ten years old. It's such a vivid memory I can even smell the earth, the wet wool from Mam's coat. She's crying and I don't know why. Then we get into my grandfather's car and drive away and I can smell the scent of the lavender polish and old leather. I think it's my father driving. I can hear the two of them talking but I can't seem to remember what they said. Just that it was raining hard and—"

"And you saw the black dog," Maria guessed.

"Running in the fields, keeping pace with the car. I kept glimpsing him when the wind blew the rain aside. You know what it's like when it sweeps across the fens. It acts like something almost solid, a curtain that gets blown this way and that, like . . ." He glanced again at Maria and again she nodded. She'd lived here long enough now to have seen the full range of weather that the fenland had to offer.

"The problem is, there's no one to ask who might remember. I've no siblings, my parents are long gone. Billy was around then, but he's from the wrong end of the family. He won't know."

"Why did you break with your family?" Maria asked.

"My grandfather was not a man I wanted in my life, or in Grace's. Neither was my father, for that matter. It was almost as though my mother found a man as much like her own dad as she could, then inflicted him on me." He shook his head, realising belatedly just how bitter that made him sound.

"But what was the final, decisive break, John? Was it after your grandmother's death?"

He thought about it. "No, not immediately. We buried her in October and we saw him at the reading of the will, and then again at the Christmas when we went to collect the little bits she'd left to Grace. She was very fond of Grace."

"Why the gap? October to December?"

John hesitated. "I suppose I kept putting it off. Grace always thought people were redeemable. I think she felt that we had to give him another chance, but I kept finding reasons not to go. I suppose Christmas is one of those make or break sorts of times, isn't it? We felt we ought to make the effort. My father had been difficult about the whole thing too, saying we shouldn't neglect the old man. Mam was already gone by then. Gran outlived her by just over a year. I think it broke her heart, having to bury a child.

"Anyway, we all agreed to meet up over there, to try and persuade him to come and spend Christmas with one of us.

120

Grace had agreed with my father that it wasn't right for the old man to spend Christmas alone, especially not the first Christmas after . . . you know."

"How old were you?"

John laughed. "This the way you talk to your patients, is it? I was a young man then, twenty-six. Grace was twenty-three and we'd been married just over a year. We'd brought our wedding forward so Mam could be there, so it must have been a year that September."

Grace had been pregnant. They had been so happy.

"Grace was pregnant."

Maria darted a sharp look in his direction. She knew John had no children and he had never mentioned one before. "What happened?" she asked gently.

"Lost the baby in January. Lost another the year after. We never struck lucky again. One doctor said the problem was scar tissue. I don't know if anything more could have been done. We sort of just adapted to the idea — not having kids of our own."

Maria looked away from him then and stared out of the window. John noted the sudden stiffness in her shoulders and cursed under his breath. "I'm sorry, love. I didn't mean to, you know . . ."

She nodded, turned with a half-smile. "Mostly I'm fine," she said. "Really fine. I knew my age would be against me, that Mike had had a vasectomy — and a long time ago, so getting a successful reversal would be unlikely, but I'd kind of hoped all the same. I'd see Josie popping them out like it was no effort and . . ." she shook her head. "Anyway, you were telling me about that Christmas."

Trading her pain for his, but John did not begrudge her. "Jerry came over too, and my dad. He came for Mam's sake, I think. Eric was long gone, of course. Joined the merchant navy and lost touch. Deliberately, I would guess.

"We all arrived on the Christmas Eve, brought food and booze and the makings of Christmas just in case he wanted us to stop there. Secretly, I was dreading it. I hated that house.

You know how some places put a chill in you even on a day like this? Well, my grandfather's house was like that.

"Anyway, he finally let us through the door and took us into the kitchen. Grace made us all some tea and he went to get the bits Gran had left to us. He said he'd had them all packed up and waiting, and he brought these carrier bags into the kitchen, one for each of us. She didn't have much to leave, poor love, a few bits of jewellery and some books and little ornaments. Mostly stuff we kids had bought her over the years. I don't recall one birthday or Christmas when he gave her anything. He was mean to the core, not just where money was concerned but with his time, his love, his . . . I could never understand why she married him."

"Maybe he wasn't always like that. Something could have changed him."

"If he changed, it was long before I came along, and long before his own children were born. That, I am sure of."

"So he gave you your things. Your legacies. And then what?"

"Then he told us to leave. Said we were good-for-nothing scroungers who'd only come to see what we could get out of him and he wanted us gone. Grace tried to reason with him, showed him the stuff we'd brought with us, said all we wanted was to give him a good Christmas, but he wouldn't listen."

"And so you all left."

"So we left, and that was pretty much that. I think my father had a bit of contact but as we weren't exactly close, I couldn't really say. Grace and I had enough to think about anyway when she miscarried. But the strange thing was, a few months after all this happened, Jerry went back to live with his father. Back to that house, and never left until he had to go into the nursing home."

"Maybe they reconciled," Maria suggested. "Maybe your grandfather genuinely felt that after the funeral you'd abandoned him. That after his wife died and you'd lost your grandmother, you ceased to care about *him*. He must have known you had trouble relating to him, don't you think?"

"Relating to him?" John laughed. "That's a polite way of putting it. No, but I take your point. I understand what you're saying and what he might have thought about us. We went over this again and again, Grace and I, we even visited, tried to make things work but," he shook his head, "maybe I didn't try hard enough. Truthfully, I probably didn't care enough. I had my own life, and he made it easy for us all to leave him to stew."

"I'm not suggesting you should feel guilty, you know that, don't you?"

John shrugged. "It's a bit late for regrets, Maria, love. I didn't like the man. I thought he treated people badly and made his wife and his children deeply unhappy. He was mean and violent and whatever his reason for being that way, it didn't stop me from being scared witless of him when I was a kid, or resenting the fact that my parents dragged me over there on a regular basis. Kids shouldn't be scared, Maria. There's no excuse for that, none at all."

He fell silent, staring out of the windscreen, very aware of Maria studying him thoughtfully, waiting for him to calm down before she spoke again. His own bitterness, the surging anger that had risen from the very pit of his stomach, had taken him utterly by surprise. He hadn't realised that it was still in there, after all this time, just waiting for a reason to break out.

"Why did Jerry stay?" he said at last. "That's what I can't understand. Why did Jerry stay, and what did Martha want from him?"

"And did she get it?" Maria added.

CHAPTER 20

Mike didn't know King's Lynn well. Having thought he could do without his satnav, he now found himself lost in a maze of little streets that all looked the same — quiet, terraced, anonymous. He finally phoned the woman he was coming to see and she gave him directions. Ironically, he was only a street away.

Mrs Collins was waiting on the doorstep when he arrived. He pulled into a rather tight parking space a little way up the road. A couple of doors down, a scientific support van sat with two wheels up on the kerb, a police car tucked behind. Mike had made the local police aware that he was coming over and had been told that if he popped into Martha Toolin's house after 1 p.m., the crime scene manager and someone from the police team would talk him through anything they might have discovered.

Mike appreciated the courtesy.

"We've already had a chat with Mrs Collins," Mike had been told. "Expect to drink a bucketful of tea."

The front door of Mrs Collins' house opened straight into the front living room. It reminded Mike immediately of relatives' houses when he'd been a kid. The front room was for high days and holidays, kept spick and span and never touched, unless the guest happened to be important enough or the occasion traditional enough to qualify. He could see Mrs Collins hesitating, not sure whether a policeman warranted the use of the front parlour, and eventually led him through to the more comfortable middle room, next to the kitchen.

"Sit down, please do." The chair she directed him to had wooden arms and was upholstered in what his mother called tapestry: flowers, fruit, little country scenes, always in some variation of beige. An Art Deco mirror hung above the fireplace, its triple glasses reflecting the room oddly. He supposed it was intended to make the room look bigger but, being a bit too large for the chimney breast, it had the opposite effect.

Mrs Collins bustled back in with a tray. He rose to take it from her, but she was already setting it down on the drop leaf table, leaves folded down, tucked against the wall. Two dining chairs, placed like sentries, stood on either side.

"Milk? Sugar?"

"No sugar, thank you." He used to drink his tea very hot and very sweet. He still preferred it hot and strong but had given up the sugar some time ago.

"Oh, I don't know how you can drink it without. Me, I like a bit of sweet."

Mike smiled. Mrs Collins settled in the other chair, expectantly, awaiting interrogation.

Cup and saucer balanced in one hand, Mike fumbled in his document case for a picture of Martha Toolin that he had brought with him, along with both Jude's drawing and a photograph of the boy. He handed them to Mrs Collins, who peered closely.

"Oh, yes," she said. "That's Martha all right and that's the boy too. The nose isn't quite right, if you don't mind me saying. It's a little broad for his face, you know?"

Mike nodded, not quite sure if she meant the nose on the drawing or the one on the actual person.

"She was two doors down," Mrs Collins went on. "You must have seen the police and scientific people rummaging about in the place. I don't know what they hope to find, she'd not been there for some time. Owned the place for about five years, until she moved in herself for a while and then she put it up for sale."

"I'm sorry? You say she didn't live there all the time she owned it?"

"Oh no, one of these buy-to-let people she was. Owned several places, I understand. Then the tenants left and she moved in herself. The young man came about eighteen months ago. She said he was a relative."

"Her son?"

"Oh no, I don't think she ever said that. Just a relative. Of course, I wasn't a friend as such, we didn't have more than a dozen conversations all the time she was here. She'd say hello, but she didn't seem the type to 'neighbour.'"

Mike smiled. He hadn't heard the word 'neighbour' used as a verb in years. "But she was friendly."

"In a . . . in a dutiful kind of way, I suppose, yes. Well mannered, but I don't think anyone in the street knew her well, and these days so many of the houses are let out or they've been made into shared houses." She sniffed contemptuously. "More profit in it, I suppose. I remember when these all used to be little family homes. The kids all played together in the street and in the alley at the back." She sighed, shook her head sadly. "People wouldn't settle for it these days. I raised six children here. You'd be done for overcrowding now, unless you were, you know, of a foreign persuasion. But, of course, they're just doing what we all used to do, aren't they?"

Foreign persuasion. Mike shifted the conversation back, not keen on getting into a debate about social change and immigration.

"Did she drive?"

"Yes, but I don't think she liked it very much. She bought a little car for the young man and I didn't see her own car much after that. I don't know if she sold it."

"I don't suppose you know what kind of car?"

"Hers or his?"

"Either."

"No, I'm sorry. Hers was blue and I think it was a Ford. Maybe a Mondeo? My nephew drives a Mondeo. His was a little brown thing. Boxy looking, not that new, I don't think. More tea?"

Mike kept her company for another cup, listened as she described her life as a young married woman in this street and talked about her six children and assorted grandchildren. He was relieved to be interrupted by one of them letting herself in at the front door and calling out to Mrs Collins that she'd come to take her shopping. After which, duty done, she almost hustled him out of the door.

Two doors down, Mike tapped on the front door and peered in. Boxes had been stacked by the door, filled with evidence bags, ready to be taken away, and a young man was busy sorting through and checking numbers against a clipboard.

He looked up and smiled. "Chief Inspector Croft?" He got to his feet and crossed the room, hand extended. "DC Miles. Come along in."

Mike looked curiously at the boxes. "I understood she'd sold up."

"The sale had gone through but she hadn't moved everything out. It looks as though she was still using it as a letter drop. There are bank statements here from just a week ago."

"It was the bank that supplied this address," Mike confirmed. "She'd obviously not informed them of a change of address. So where was she living? Or planning to live?"

"Your guess is as good as mine. We're presuming she was going to come back and fetch the rest of her stuff. She'd left clothes, some paperwork, a few ornaments and some magazines. We're still sifting through it, so if there's anything you think we should be looking out for?"

Mike thought about it. "Another address? Some sense of where she'd been before this, or planned to be next?" He

127

shrugged. "We suspect she'd been using several different identities."

"Ah, now we might have something of interest." DC Miles crouched down beside a box. "There's a letting agreement with a property agency somewhere . . . Right, here it is."

Mike crouched down beside him. "So they were letting property on her behalf?"

"Two properties. Someone's talking to the agents this afternoon, so we'll keep you in the loop, but it looks as though they also have this as the contact address for Mrs Toolin."

"So she owned three properties? I wonder how she got her hands on them?"

They spent a little more time skimming though the rest of the evidence bags. Mike went through what they knew so far from their side, but at this stage it was hard to know how useful any of it might be.

He had a quick word with the crime scene manager and left shortly afterwards, each side promising to keep the other in the loop.

He was, he supposed, a little further on but not much. He turned his car around and, trying to remember the way out of the confusing little streets, made for home.

* * *

"What's this?" Katie Matthews held out the business card that Mike had left. Jason had tossed it in the bin in his home office but she had spotted it.

"It's a business card."

"I can see that, but what is a business card for a DI Croft doing here? Was that who called the other day? Mrs Greaves said they looked official."

Jason shrugged. "They came about the dog," he said. "It's nothing."

"About the dog? Why would two detectives come to see you about a dead dog?"

"Not our dog, the one on the beach. The one that chased us. They're investigating. It's a dangerous animal. Someone has to investigate."

"A Detective Inspector? I don't think so. Besides, he's the one that was on the telly. On the news, investigating that murder."

Jason sighed, knowing he'd have to give her more than that. "Look, we were down on the beach the day before that woman was killed at the pub. They wanted to know if I'd seen anyone, OK? That's all. He left his card in case I remembered something more."

"If that's all it was, why didn't you tell me?"

"Because I knew I'd get the third degree, just like I am now."

"If you were straight with me, I wouldn't have to go rummaging through the bins to find out what you're up to."

He turned his back on her and left the house, smothering the automatic whistle to Carson. Walking the dog had been a perfect excuse for getting out from under. Now he didn't even have that.

Starting his car, he decided that he'd have to get himself another dog. Jason Matthews cursed softly under his breath, not certain whether his anger was directed at his wife, the black dog they had encountered on the beach or the woman he had known as Julia Matthews. Even dead, she was still causing trouble for him.

CHAPTER 21

Trisha from the nursing home called John early that afternoon. She'd been chatting to the handyman who'd fixed the picture frame for Jerry.

"He says he remembers something written on the back of the photograph," she said. "He thinks it said Silvia, but the spelling was unusual. That's what made him notice. He was at school with a Sylvia, spelt with a y, this was S-i-lvia. He thinks there was a second name, but can't remember what it was. A date, too."

"Does he recall what that was?"

"Well, he can't be sure, but he thinks it was just after the end of the war — forty-six or seven."

John felt his body grow tense. 1947. The baby crying, his grandfather's rage. Himself at ten years old, the age he would have been in 1947. What was going on then?

He heard Trisha asking him if he was all right. "Yes, sorry, my dear, I'm just trying to put it all together."

He could feel her waiting, anticipating more, wanting to be included in the mystery.

"Do you know who this Silvia was?" Trish asked.

"No, I'm afraid I don't."

"She must have been important to him, though, don't you think, for him to keep that picture?"

"Except that he, or someone, had cut her from the photograph. Unless Silvia was the baby, of course."

"No. Oh, I'm such a dunce, I knew there was something else. The photo wasn't cut like I thought. It was torn and there were signs of burning, like someone had tried to get rid of the picture and Jerry just salvaged what was left, but there was a young woman, folded over and hidden behind the baby. Now who do you reckon would want to do a thing like that?"

* * *

Mike stopped at a café on the way home and bought himself coffee and a sticky cake. Suddenly, like Mrs Collins, he felt the need for something sweet. He bought three newspapers from the little kiosk on the way in and sat reading them while he ate his cake, interested to discover what the local and national newspapers had done with the press release. He was slightly embarrassed to find his own picture on the front page of one of them. Mike glanced around, hoping no one else had noticed, but the assortment of lorry drivers and holidaying families seemed bent on their own concerns and paid him scant attention. Reports of the black dog mingled with accounts of stab wounds and speculation about the woman who called herself Martha Toolin. Page four of one local newspaper carried the sidebar Mike had foreseen would appear, reprising the background and careers of John Tynan and of Mike himself. The Greenway warranted a mention and someone had made a big play of the myth, legend and spooky atmosphere of that part of the coast. Much to his amusement, Mike found that the story had been composed by Graham Firth, the new boy working with Phil Andrews, who had claimed to be above such speculations.

The articles gave little more of the story than was known on the day the news of the murder had first broken. A few more days and, if there were no new developments, the columns would dwindle, retreat page by page into the body of the newspapers and then be altogether lost, replaced by feel-good stories designed to entice tourists and encourage holidaymakers to make the most of the beautiful location, rather than dwelling on humanity's darker side.

He drank the last of his now cool coffee, gave up on the too sweet, too sticky cake, tucked the papers under his arm and left, catching the quizzical stare of the woman behind the counter who seemed to be wondering where she had seen him before.

He'd just have to hope that more ex-neighbours came out of the woodwork. Or that Martha Toolin, aka Julia Matthews, had drawn attention to herself in other ways. It now seemed likely that she had an income from rental properties. So where had they come from? There would undoubtedly be a paper trail for the forensic accountants to follow, but their meticulous procedures would not show results for some time.

* * *

Tom, concealed in the shadow cast by a large tree opposite John's house, saw him go around to the side and wander, watering can and bucket in hand, to the end of the long garden.

He still hadn't decided what to do, or if this man was going to be trouble.

Glancing up and down the road, though he already knew there was no one around to see him, Tom crossed over and slipped through the front gate and into the house, entering via the kitchen door through which John Tynan had just exited. The man had his back turned to Tom and seemed to be doing something to a plant trained up a wigwam of canes. Tom did not hesitate, he opened the door and slipped inside.

Just what was he looking for? Tom wasn't sure he really knew.

There was nothing posh or modern about John Tynan's kitchen. A scrubbed table, Belfast sink, cupboards that Tom thought looked like they were from the fifties on the walls. A gas cooker. He'd seen the bottled gas outside, the cottage being a long way from the mains. Everything was scrubbed and clean and well-looked-after, but it was all really old, like the Tynan bloke didn't care for change.

He slipped through into the hall, keeping his ears pricked for any sound of John Tynan's return, and checked the front door to ensure he could make a fast exit that way should he need to. The floor of the hall, like that of the kitchen, was tiled in brownish red. A long runner in bright shades of red and blue stretched from the front door mat almost to the kitchen door. Stairs led up on the right and a wood-framed mirror with coat pegs and a telephone table below it sat close to the front door. Only one room led off the hall. The living room was bright and sunny and Tom stood for a moment, savouring the warmth that had nothing really to do with the sunlight streaming in through the small panes of the old-fashioned windows.

The fire grate had logs laid out and kindling, all ready to be lit. Tom found it pleasing. It was unlikely to be needed at this time of the year but an empty grate always looked kind of sad. Dark wood bookshelves, well stocked, stood either side of the fireplace and the wooden floorboards, also dark, were relieved by the addition of bright rugs.

Looking about, Tom concluded that nothing had changed in this house for a long time. Only the flat-screen television and the chrome and black mini hi-fi jarred. Curious, Tom went over to look at the collection of CDs. He was unsurprised to find that it was mostly classical.

Returning to the hall, he hesitated at the foot of the stairs, reluctant to put himself in a position from which escape would be difficult. He had no doubt that he could outrun the older man, but the thought of John Tynan somehow trapping him upstairs made him anxious. He went back into the kitchen and peered out of the back window. John

Tynan was closer to the house now, kneeling beside a border and pulling weeds and tossing them into to the zinc bucket Tom had seen him carrying from the house.

Tom took a deep, steadying breath and let himself back out of the kitchen door.

* * *

A slight sound caused John to glance up, trowel in hand. The boy stood a few yards away at the corner of the house. John tried to get up, aware again that kneeling was no longer something his legs and feet appreciated. Neither did the arthritis in his right knee, a problem he was sure he hadn't had a year ago.

"Are you all right?" The question was an unexpected one, the look of concern on the young man's face even more so, as was the suddenly extended hand.

"I'm too old and stiff to be kneeling on the damp grass," John said.

"You should get one of them stool things you can kneel on."

The hand was taken, the palm warm and the fingers unexpectedly strong for all that the boy looked so fragile, so small and gracile.

John felt the blood returning to his feet with a gripping, tightening pain and hoped this unexpected meeting would remain on something like friendly terms. He couldn't run now to save his life. It crossed his mind again that this young man was a suspect. A woman had died. The words spilled from his mouth before he could stop them.

"Did you kill her?"

A look of pure rage crossed the boy's face. John's feet still hurt, but he figured the ability to run was academic in any case. He knew that he would be too slow. Ironic, though, to die here in his own garden.

CHAPTER 22

Habit and anxiety had taken Jason Matthews back to the coast. He had walked the beach and wandered down into the village, across the playground and past the café. He had assumed that the Two Bells was still closed, and was surprised to find the bar open and a mix of journalists and locals seated at picnic tables or sprawled on the grass between pub and car park. The scent of burgers and fried onions drew him towards a van manned by Mrs Beal, her husband having stationed himself under a gazebo nearby.

"Well, hello there!" Mrs Beal greeted him with something close to her accustomed cheeriness. "I was sorry to hear about your poor doggie. Now, what will you have?"

Jason purchased a burger, spread the onions with tomato sauce and wandered away. 'Doggie.' Honestly. As though Carson had been some kind of handbag pooch.

"At least they're getting a bit of business while the pub's closed." The voice sounded half familiar.

Jason looked round. A man was seated on the grass, a plastic cup of what looked like beer in his fist. Jason frowned, but replied politely, "Yes. It must be very welcome. I'm sorry, but can I help you?"

The man smiled, knowing full well that Jason Matthews recognised him. "Did you enjoy your meal the other night? You and your, er, friend."

His insinuating tone said it all. Jason scowled at the man and walked away. His burger had suddenly lost its appeal and Jason dumped it half-finished in a bin and strode away.

The man watched him for a few moments, finished his beer and sauntered after him.

* * *

John's phone call had interrupted Mike's journey back to Norwich and he had turned instead towards the coast and the tea rooms on the cliff, close to the Two Bells.

Small, sandy-haired, freckle-faced, the boy didn't seem particularly impressive to Mike. Did he look like a killer? Mike had long ago stopped trying to identify criminals by the way they looked. He was obviously scared, though, and somewhat hostile, glaring at Mike as though he might be the murder suspect and not the boy.

Mike sat down. John left to fetch more tea, leaving Mike and the boy to stare at one another.

"What's your name?" Mike asked.

"Tom. Tom Pollard. He says your name is Mike."

"It is. How old are you, Tom?"

"Eighteen. Nearly nineteen."

"And Martha? What was she to you?"

He shrugged. "Turns out she was nothing. At first she thought I might be . . . family."

John rejoined them, setting the tray down carefully on the wooden table.

"Was Martha her real name?"

"I don't know. That's what she told me. But she told me a lot of things that weren't right. Then she told me to clear off, but I'd nowhere to go, not anymore."

"What do you mean, not anymore?"

"I was brought up in care, foster homes and suchlike. When I turned eighteen there weren't no care anymore. I'd got a job and a bedsit when I was seventeen but that were about it. Then she turned up, said she thought I might be family. I believed her. I wanted to."

"She thought you might be related?"

"Yeah." Tom took his tea and dumped sugar into it, stirring it impatiently so the spoon clattered against the sides of the cup. "She had a kid. Her kid had a kid. She thought it might be me. Then she decided it weren't and she dumped me like I were nothing."

"Is that why you killed her?"

Tom dropped the spoon into the saucer and glared at Mike. "I never killed her. I went to see her when he dropped her off, yeah." He jerked his chin in John's direction. "I went in and waited for her while she was having a bath. When she came in and saw me she got mad, told me to clear out, that she didn't need me now, that she'd been wrong. She said she'd given me money and that should be enough. Said I had to go away. So I went. I slept in my car. Next morning I heard the sirens and then I heard that she was dead."

"So, what time did you leave the Two Bells?"

"I heard the church clock strike midnight about the same time. The back door of the pub weren't locked yet. The Beals don't lock that till Mr Beal's switched off the back security light."

Mike raised his eyebrows. "Switches off the security light?"

"Otherwise it shines in their bedroom window every time a fox or a cat or whatever sneaks by."

And no one had thought to mention this before. "And you know this how?" Mike said.

Tom looked uneasy. "This past week or two, I spent a lot of time just watching what was going on. Nothing better to do, not when *he* was hanging around." He nodded towards John. "Martha didn't want me meeting him. She didn't say why, but she didn't have to."

"Didn't have to?"

"Not good enough to meet the likes of him, I wasn't. Not someone who might really be family." He shook his head, his expression bitter. "I should've cleared off, left her to it. She didn't want me. I wasn't no use to her any more. I should have just gone."

"What made you stay?"

The boy shrugged miserably. "She'd been good to me . . . sort of. I wanted to make sure she was all right, you know? She kept saying she could take care of herself but I was worried about her. She didn't think I was family any more, but she was the closest thing I'd got."

"What made her think you might be family?"

Tom shrugged again. He shifted about constantly, Mike noticed, all tics as though he found it hard to be still.

"On me birth certificate, me mam said me dad's name was Alec Matthews. Me mam gave me up for adoption but I never got adopted. When I turned eighteen they gave me a file. I started looking, you know, for family, and Martha, she was looking too and, well, she found me."

He took a swallow of his tea, refilled his cup from one of the pots John had brought. "She let me live at her place, even bought me a car, just a second-hand Fiat, but more than I could have afforded. I thought . . . but I was just stupid, wasn't I?"

"What changed her mind?" John asked gently. "Tom, you started to tell me . . ."

"She never stopped digging, did she? You know, she didn't even know what her kid had had, a girl or a boy, but someone told her it was a girl, so she kept on looking."

"That must have hurt," Mike said. "You must have felt—"

"Like I wanted to kill her? That what you think, is it? No, she made me feel like shit, but she weren't the first nor the worst. She'd at least given me something, and I thought, I don't know, I thought if I hung around long enough she'd realise that even if I wasn't the one she'd been looking for,

138

we could still get along. Be friends, sort of like a family." He took a deep breath and then another long gulp of his tea. "She had a test done. DNA. That confirmed it. I wasn't what she was looking for. A week or two later she said I'd have to leave. She said she'd help me find a place, give me some money, but she was selling the house so she could use the money to go on looking. She said she knew where to look now, she'd found the bastard that got her kid pregnant."

"How long ago was this?" Mike asked. "Houses aren't selling fast just now."

"No, she put it on the market last winter, let me show people round sometimes. She was away a lot and I did try to sell it, even though I didn't want to move out. I wanted to help her, you know? She sold it this May. It went to one of those ads in the paper. You know, cash sale but you only get about ninety percent of what it's worth. Then she gave me some money and in June she took off."

"And this was the house in King's Lynn?"

"One of them, yeah. She had a couple of rentals there and one in Radford. That's Nottingham, I think."

Mike made a mental note, not wanting to interrupt the flow. "And you followed her."

Tom nodded. "Look, she let me down in the end, but she tried, you know, and she was so . . . I don't know, like she was mad at the world and didn't care anymore. I was scared of what she'd do, I thought she'd get herself in trouble."

"Did she find this man? The one who fathered her grandchild?"

For the first time Tom's expression changed. He laughed and pointed at John. "I thought it might be him," he said, "you know, that he was some old perv. But then she told me it was some bloke in Norwich."

"Did you meet this man?" Mike asked.

"Nah, but I followed her one day and I saw her arguing with him. He was mad with her, said he'd told her not to come back and that he was going to call the police. She said fine, why didn't he just do that, then this other woman came up, wanted to know what the hell was going on. I think she was the wife or something. Anyway, he left with her."

"Do you know his name? Would you recognise him again?"

Tom shook his head, but then nodded. "Jason something. I heard her shouting it after him when he stormed off. He had this big dog with him."

"Jason Matthews," Mike said. "Tom, could it have been Jason Matthews?"

"I saw him a couple of times after that," Tom said, "walking this bloody great dog along the beach here."

John couldn't resist saying, "Wasn't black, was it?"

Tom shook his head emphatically. "Nah, not that one. His was a German shepherd. Martha met him here once but she wouldn't tell me why."

"What was her daughter's name?" Mike asked, realising suddenly that he had no idea."

"Emily? Emily Dawson," Tom said. "Martha stopped using her married name after the divorce."

"Did you ever hear Martha use any other name?"

"Yeah. This Jason bloke, he called her Julia. She told me it was her middle name, and sometimes she used it instead of Martha."

"But still with the last name of Toolin?"

"I guess. Look, I want to go now." Tom stood up abruptly. "I've tried to help."

"I want you to come to the station with me, Tom, make a statement. Write all of this up properly."

"No. I want to go now."

"Tom."

"You want me to go with you, you'll have to arrest me."

"Tom!"

He was out of the tea rooms before Mike could react, running back towards the village. Mike gave chase and was just in time to see him dive into a little brown Fiat and hurtle away.

"Damn!"

John ambled over to join him. "He'll be back, Mike. You don't seriously take him for a suspect now, do you?"

"He's still on my list. Dammit, John, what the hell spooked him?"

"Maybe he doesn't like policemen," John said laconically. "Or maybe it was that." He pointed. On a high ridge close by the church was a large black shape staring down at them. The day was bright, cloudless and entirely benign, but Mike felt the hairs on his neck begin to rise and a chill grow in the pit of his belly.

CHAPTER 23

The late afternoon briefing had been protracted. The first list of items found at the King's Lynn house had been sent over — photographs and scans of documents. The follow-up interview with the property agents who looked after Martha Toolin's rental properties had revealed they had met her once when the arrangement had been set up, and were paid their fee by direct debit — but not from an account the investigation currently had a record of — and she checked in with them by phone about once a month.

They had authorisation to deal with any maintenance issues on her behalf via an insurance policy she had taken out, and she always paid promptly for anything not covered.

No, it was not unusual for a landlord to keep such a distance from their properties — after all, that was what a letting agency was for. But yes, it probably was unusual for her to be so accommodating in other ways. "I wish we had more like her," had been the final comment.

He talked his team through the encounter with Tom Pollard. At least they now had an identity for the boy and knew that he'd been in the care system. Jude had already contacted social services and had discovered that Tom had been a local boy — which, as she commented, was useful.

Other sightings of Martha on the night she was killed had filtered in, and now they had more than one name to search by — combinations of Matthews, Toolin, Julia, Martha.

Maria was already home when Mike finally arrived. Dinner was cooking and she was ensconced in the second bedroom, which served as both guest room and home office for those inevitable times when she had to catch up on patient notes.

Mike could hear music drifting down the stairs. He chuckled to himself as he realised what it was: Nick Drake singing about a black-eyed dog.

"Research," she said, gesturing towards a stack of print-outs on the edge of the desk. "At work today, all anyone could talk about was Old Shuck. I had three patients this morning all obsessing about it, and the staff were no better."

"Real patients or neurotic golf widows?" Mike wanted to know.

She shot him a reproving look. "They are *all* real patients, you know that. But no, these were private patients, not referrals, if that's what you mean. Somehow, they'd heard I'd come back from holiday and all booked themselves in. I've told them I'm off again next week and they'll have to see Sybil or James, but I don't think they believe me. Anyway, it all got me thinking. You know how I just *love* mass hysteria?" She smiled wickedly at him. "John excepted, of course."

"If you except John, you're also going to have to excuse me."

She stared at him. "You're joking? You saw it?"

"Well, I saw something. It was large and black and most definitely dog-shaped."

"Where?"

"Up near Happisburgh church, just standing there, staring." He paused thoughtfully. "Do dogs actually stare?"

"Sure they do. You and who else?"

"John. Again. It seems to like him and a young man called Tom Pollard. Supposed son of Martha Toolin. Except, it turns out, he isn't, just thought he might be."

"The boy? You found him? What do you mean he just thought he might be?"

"Exactly that. And no, you might say he found John and John set up the meeting."

"Did you arrest him? I mean, I thought he was a suspect."

Mike shook his head. "I wanted to bring him in but he, as they say, did a runner. John reckons he panicked when he spotted the dog. I thought, just for a moment, that I saw someone up in the churchyard with the dog but by the time we reached it, there was no sign of anyone. Anyway, I'm shifting my opinion of the boy as a suspect."

"Well, let's hope you're right, seeing as how you let him get away, Mr Policeman. You need to get your running shoes out of the cupboard and dusted off. So, if he's out of the frame . . ."

"Do I have a better prospect?" He nodded. "I think I might, a tenuous one anyway. Oddly enough, my new favourite suspect also claims to have seen our canine friend. Or should that be fiend?"

Maria picked up her sheaf of notes and handed it to him. "Don't say I never do anything for you. And, incidentally, you're right, whichever."

"Whichever what?"

"Friend or fiend. Round here and down in Suffolk, meeting the black dog is definitely not a good thing. Cross the Wash and get up into Lincolnshire and it's as likely to be a friendly meeting, good luck not disaster, but they always seem to have been a bit fonder of their supernatural flora and fauna up there. Maybe it's a cultural thing. Anyway. Dinner. Then you can do your homework."

Over dinner he told her about his meeting with Tom and his suspicion that Jason Matthews might be implicated in Martha's death. He had nothing in the way of evidence, apart from a few dog hairs and Jason's admission that he'd had dealings with the dead woman.

"So," he finished, "I need to show his picture to the Beals, see if we can place him at the Two Bells when Martha was staying there. Then I might have enough to bring him in for questioning, at least."

"But it's still a bit slim."

"Anorexic, really. Any lawyer would argue that as he'd already admitted to meeting with her, the dog hairs could be simple transfer and, of course, they would be right. The rider, of course, is that the hairs were found on her pyjamas."

"Which surely places him in the room on the night she died."

Mike shook his head. "Only happens on TV. It suggests that he *may* have been there. It's equally possible that she had dog hairs on her outdoor clothes. She *may* have laid those clothes on the chair and put her nightclothes on top. Lo. Transfer. We have a balance of probability, not enough to get him past the CPS threshold. Not without clear motive. That's what I need next."

"So, what motive might he have had?"

"Well, Tom gave me a couple of leads, though I don't suppose he realised it. He said he'd followed Martha one day, seen her arguing with Jason Matthews and that a woman had come along and broken up the fight. Tom thought it might have been Matthews's wife. We need to speak to her in any case, and we definitely need to press her on what they were arguing about, and what Martha was doing to wind Jason up so tight."

"And the other lead?"

"The missing child. Martha's daughter was believed to have had a child. Martha seemed to think that Jason Matthews knew where it was, or maybe even fathered that child. Tom says Martha had been told the grandchild was female, which is partly why she discounted him, but we have no way of being certain and we don't know where she got that information from. Martha had reason for suspecting Jason Matthews's involvement, I'm sure of it."

Maria shrugged. "Unless she was just working her way through the phone book. She seems to have tried to inveigle herself into the family. John's uncle Jerry, for instance. What did she hope to get from him?"

"Apart from an Art Deco picture frame? I don't know that any more than I can second-guess the attention she paid to John, or why she was researching a family that doesn't seem to have been her own." He frowned. "Though I suppose that was because she had an idea that her daughter *may* be mixed up with a Matthews. How did the visit to the church go? I didn't get a chance to ask John."

"Oh, interesting. I saw the grave, definitely a child, I'd say, but equally definitely not in the burial records we had. You need to get onto the diocese, though I'm betting it isn't in their official records either."

Mike paused, fork lifted halfway to his mouth. "Someone buried a child in a graveyard and no one noticed? Maria, that seems extremely unlikely."

"Why? It's a tiny grave, turfed over, with just a little wooden cross for a headstone. It's over at the side of the churchyard, behind that bit of a shrubbery with the other Matthews graves, and the church is used once a month if that. I talked to the keyholder. He reckons the churchyard was in a terrible state before he started mowing the grass and keeping it tidy, and that the church hadn't been in regular use for decades." She giggled. "He then assured me, again, that he was paid a mere pittance for all his hard work. I'm quite convinced he thought we were spies from the taxman, but other than that he couldn't really tell us much. He's no interest in the place. He didn't even know about the wall paintings."

"Wall paintings?"

"Medieval, I'm guessing. They'd been whitewashed over, but some of the limewash is flaking off and you can just about make out what's behind. You'll never guess what the painting is next to? A Matthews burial site — well, the commemorative plaque for one, anyway. The plaque is much later, of course, but it's funny, it's as though whoever chose to put it there knew about the association." She frowned. "Though I suppose that doesn't make sense. If the painting had been washed over, then whoever had the plaque put there couldn't have known. Spooky though, don't you think? Do you want this?" She speared the last new potato and began to slice it.

"Looks as though it's too late even if I do." He smiled.

"I'll share if you like."

"Anyway, what's spooky, as you put it? What didn't they know that they should have known? What is the wall painting of?" Mike asked.

"Oh, didn't I say? It's a picture of a black dog."

* * *

The bedside clock stated sulkily that it was 2:15. Mike didn't know what had woken him, but he was fully alert and listening for some sound that had penetrated his dream. The dream was already fading from his consciousness and, even as he glanced at the clock, the sound that had woken him was fading too.

He slipped quietly out of bed and went downstairs, checking doors and windows, switching on all the lights and driving whatever demon had woken him back out into the dark. The sense of unease remained, and he flinched at every slight familiar sound as the house, resentful of his interruption, creaked back into wakefulness.

He found nothing wrong and finally went back upstairs, though sleep seemed a distant and unlikely prospect. Maria, unusually, had not even stirred.

He was still listening out for that mysterious and only dimly remembered sound but wasn't sure if he'd even recognise it should he hear it again.

The notes Maria had prepared for him were on the bedside table. He had glanced through them before settling down to sleep and wondered if perhaps that was what had interrupted his sleep. The formal history of Black Shuck seemed to have started in Suffolk on August 4, 1577, when a great black dog had burst into Holy Trinity church at Blythburgh and killed a man and a boy. The church had been so shaken by the appearance that the steeple had collapsed through the roof and Mike was somewhat surprised that more people had not been killed.

The dog had exited via the north door, a sure sign this was the devil's work and, should any have been left in doubt, had left scorch marks on the door itself.

Later that day, the great black dog had made a further appearance when, according to one Abraham Fleming, a *strange and terrible wonder* had taken place. It had run down the length of the nave and, in Abraham's words, *wrung the necks* of two individuals who had been kneeling in prayer.

Flicking through the various accounts, Mike was struck, as Maria had been, by the different attitudes to the black dog. It could be demon or guardian depending on where it was seen and who did the seeing.

He recalled the image he had seen that afternoon, of the dog high up on the cliff. Why had it disturbed him so much? Was it simply that he'd been subconsciously primed by all the talk there had been? Some of the accounts had certainly verged on the hysterical, and the counterpoint of the murder investigation had probably heightened his sense of anxiety and made him more vulnerable to the general paranoia.

Tired at last, and a little more satisfied now he'd applied some cod psychology to the problem, he set the notes aside and lay down again.

"Something the matter?" Maria asked sleepily, rousing now that the emergency was long gone.

"Nothing. It's all fine." He kissed her and pulled her close to his side, relishing the feel of her skin against his own. The clock told him that it was now 3:15, though he could have sworn he'd been awake for a lot longer. He drifted back into sleep. He dreamed again of running along the beach, black dog beside him and his son joyously keeping pace, though this time Mike was aware of another figure waiting on the beach. Standing at the water's edge, the low tide lapping gently at his trainers, Tom stood, looking out to sea.

He began to turn and then a sound woke him again, but this time it was real, persisting even after he had opened his eyes and stared accusingly at the clock. It was 7:15. He had overslept. Outside, the day had dawned and was sneaking in through a gap in the heavy curtains and the tang of sea salt permeated the air. Mike answered the phone, and when Jude gave him the news he was painfully unsurprised.

"Give me half an hour," he said.

CHAPTER 24

The body had been dumped just below the high tide mark, as if whoever had left him there wanted him to be washed out to sea but didn't quite have the local knowledge to make that happen.

Mike noted the reddish hair, matted with wet sand, and the freckles standing out against the now white skin. He was wearing the same grey long-sleeved T-shirt he'd had on when Mike and John had spoken to him the day before. His sodden jeans seemed to weigh down the too thin legs.

"His name is Tom Pollard," Mike said sadly. "So far as I know, he has no family."

The police surgeon regarded Mike with a speculative look over the top of his glasses. "You knew him?"

"I met him. Yesterday. I should have just arrested him, kept him safe. God, what a bloody mess."

"Cause of death would seem to be a single blow to the right temple, but the pathologist will have to confirm that later. How old was he?"

"Eighteen."

"Poor little sod. He looks younger. Looks like he needed a good meal."

Awkwardly, Mike got to his feet and handed over to the CSI, who were waiting for him to finish his examination.

150

He'd have to tell John. Somehow that felt as bad as if he had to go and tell Tom's family.

* * *

John shook his head. "Who killed him, Mike?"

"I don't know, but Jason Matthews is now at the top of my list. Martha had dog hairs on her pyjamas. They can't confirm it was Matthews's dog until they get a reference sample, but the best comparison they have is with hair from a German shepherd."

"Matthews said his dog died. Are you going to bring him in?"

"Not yet. All we've got are a few strands of dog hair and an allegation based on hearsay evidence from a witness who is now dead."

"Isn't that enough?"

"John, I want more. I don't want him wriggling out of it because I've made my move too soon."

"If you'd moved faster yesterday, Tom might still be here!" He stopped. "Sorry, Mike, that was—"

"What I've been telling myself since I heard. Jude is doing a background check on him. She's got something on Martha, by the way."

"She's got a record?"

"As Julia Toolin. Tom was right, Julia was her middle name, but she had a string of aliases. Blackmail, obtaining money through deception and a slew of petty thefts. Nothing for the past ten years or so, unless she just got better at it. John, did she—?"

"Ever ask me for money? No, always paid her way even when I tried to insist, and she didn't get anything but the picture frame from Jerry."

"The question is, did she try it on with Jason Matthews?"

* * *

Jason Matthews was certainly not happy to have DI Croft turn up on his doorstep. The DI had brought a new person with him, Terry Gleeson, working as community liaison, who, it turned out, Jason Matthews knew "just to say hello to." They'd been co-opted to form a team together at a pub quiz night a few months back.

Jason Matthews frowned at the two police officers. "I've spoken to you already. I've nothing more to say." He peered at Terry Gleeson, obviously registering that he was familiar but being thrown by the uniform.

"We won't take up much of your time," Mike said.

"Now's not convenient." He began to close the door.

"Who is it, Jase?" A woman's voice, curious and a little impatient.

"No one. They were just going."

Mike pushed the door. Jason's hold on it had not been tight and the door swung wide. A small, fair-haired woman stood in the hall. "Mrs Matthews?" Mike asked. He extended a hand, giving Katie Matthews little option but to cross the hall to shake it, Jason little choice but to shift out of her way. "I'm DI Mike Croft. This is Constable Gleeson. We just wanted a few minutes of your husband's time."

Katie Matthews shook Mike's hand in a puzzled, automatic kind of way and turned questioningly to her husband. "Jason?"

"I said this is a not a good time," Jason said.

"Is this about the dog? Jason said you called before. You left a card. But I mean, waste of resources, isn't it? I thought you lot had better things to do with your time and with public money than send a Detective Inspector about a dog."

"That would be a waste, yes," Terry Gleeson agreed cheerfully.

"So what, then?" Katie's eyes narrowed and she peered at Mike. He wondered if she normally wore glasses. "I saw you on the telly," she said. "Investigating that woman who was murdered out on the coast."

"I expect you did," Mike said.

"Jason said you were just talking to everyone who'd been out there the day before."

"Come in for a bit, can we?" Terry at his most cheerful again. He leaned confidentially towards Katie. "Only I can't help but notice you've a fair few curtain twitchers among the neighbours."

Katie Matthews blushed red. "You'd best come through," she said, and stalked off towards what turned out to be the kitchen. Mike could hear the television in another room and children playing. "The girls are in there," she said by way of explanation.

They sat around the kitchen table, all but Jason, who leaned against the sink, looking mutinous.

"So what's this about?" Katie Matthews said. "What do you want to talk to my husband about, because whatever it is, I want to hear."

"Katie, I told you. I just happened—"

"To know the murder victim," Mike put in quietly.

Katie Matthews gasped. "What do you mean he knew her?" she demanded, looking from her husband to Mike. "Who is she?"

"You might have known her as Julia Matthews," Terry said. "Any chance of a cuppa, by the way?"

Katie stared at him. "What? Oh, yes, I suppose." She glared at her husband. "Julia somebody was that woman, wasn't it? The one that caused a scene that day. When we were out shopping. You said she was just some nutcase."

"Which she was! She reckoned one of our lot had adopted her grandkid. I told her, there's no adopted kids in this family. Then she started on about her own kid, her daughter, reckoned one of our lot had been involved with her or summat. Look, I told you about it at the time. She went away when I threatened to set the police on her."

"And now the police are here," Katie said coldly. "So, how many times did you see her? What was she to you? What did she want from you?"

"I told you. That was it."

153

"So she came up to you in the street, just out of the blue and wanted to know about a kid? I don't think so," Katie said.

"Last time I was here, you mentioned that she had come to the house," Mike said.

"You what? She came here? Are you crazy? Bringing a stranger to our house?"

"I didn't *bring* her here. She was just some nutter working her way through the phone book. I told you that." He gestured at Mike, angry and accusing.

"We're ex-directory!" Katie said.

The silence that followed sat thickly.

"So how did she find you, Mr Matthews?" Mike asked quietly.

"How the hell should I know?"

"And how many times did you have contact with her?"

"*Have contact with her*. That's a good one," Katie Matthews was scathing. "So how many times did you *have contact* with her, Jason?"

"Christ's sake, Katie, she was old enough to be my bloody mother."

"And that makes a difference to you?"

Mike was suddenly aware that the sound of the television was louder. He glanced out into the hall to see the living room door was open and two young girls stood in the doorway. Their parents seemed not to be aware of just how loud their voices had become.

Terry had spotted the girls as well. "Hello there," he said. "I'm Terry and this is Mike. What are your names, then?"

"Go back in and close the door," Katie Matthews snapped. Then she softened her tone. "Look, I'll be in in just a minute. You find something nice for us all to watch, OK?"

"Mr Matthews, Mrs Matthews, we need to know everything about your association with this woman. What she wanted, how often you spoke to her, anything she mentioned that might explain how she found you and why she decided you were worth speaking to as opposed to any other

Matthews she might have discovered. If, in fact, she did approach anyone else. Did she mention anyone else?"

Jason Matthews shook his head. "I know nothing about her, Inspector," he said stubbornly. "She came to the house once. She approached me in the street that time Katie was with me. I spotted her in the Two Bells one night, so I decided I'd better stop away for a while."

"But you didn't, did you? You still drove out to the coast and walked your dog."

"But I kept away from the pub. No way did I want that mad woman latching onto me again. But that was it. I don't know what she wanted. She was soft in the head, if you ask me. A sandwich short of a picnic. I don't know anything more than that."

He folded his arms across his chest and looked away, staring out of the kitchen window and seemingly doing his best to ignore the police officers, his wife, the sound of the television coming from the other room.

Mike took a card from his pocket and handed it to Katie. "My number, should either of you remember anything more."

She waved it away. "I've already got one, thanks. I took it out of the bin in his study."

Abruptly, she got to her feet and crossed the hall to the front door, flinging it open. Mike took his time. Terry, following on behind, nudged open the living room door. "Bye, girls," he said.

Katie Matthews flushed and then went pale with rage. "I want you to go," she said. "I want you to leave. Now."

"So," Constable Gleeson asked as they drove away. "Do we bring him in?"

"On what charge? No, we wait and allow Mrs Matthews to soften him up a bit first."

Terry Gleeson laughed. "Maybe just as well I didn't mention him being in the pub for quiz night."

"Oh? I take it the woman he was with—"

"Sure as hell wasn't his missus," Terry confirmed.

155

CHAPTER 25

Late afternoon saw an immaculate Jaguar XJ6 creep cautiously up the lane to John's cottage. Its pristine condition told him that this must be Cousin Billy. John went out and directed his cousin to the rather awkward parking space at the side of the house.

"Can't you move somewhere more accessible?"

"Why, so you can visit in comfort once a decade? More, for that matter. You've not been over here since Grace died."

"I surely have."

"And I'm sure you have not. Come along in."

John led the way. Billy, carrying an old wooden box, followed him into the tiny kitchen and plonked himself down at the table. "Get the kettle on, then. You got the copy of the will?"

"I did, thank you." It hadn't told him anything new, unfortunately. Jerry had made a dozen such small bequests as he had made to Martha, mostly to those who had looked after him at the home. "What have you got in the box, then?"

Billy shrugged and gave John what he thought of as his trademark grin. "Lots of junk, if you ask me, but you might find something of use." The smile faded and he forced his face into unaccustomed seriousness. "Look, John, I have to be frank here. Everyone's a mite upset by all these goings-on. No one seems to have really known this Martha woman. Everyone seems to have assumed someone else knew her better than they did, and they all feel like she was taking the piss. John, what the hell was she up to?"

"I don't know. Not yet. She was looking for her grandchild, that's all we're sure of." Not the exact truth, but it would have to do.

"And she hoped to find it in amongst our lot? John, if we'd found ourselves with an extra child, someone would have noticed, don't you think?"

John shrugged. His boyhood dream echoed in his memory. The child crying, his mother's voice arguing.

"Did Jerry have any children?" The question was out before he was aware he was going to ask it.

"Jerry? Jerry never married, you know that."

"Which doesn't preclude children."

Billy shook his head. "Jerry was old school. That wasn't his style." He looked narrowly at John as though trying to see where he'd come upon such a crazy notion. Gave up. "Now, what about that tea?"

* * *

Billy had left, and John was sorting through the contents of the box when Mike arrived. The blue book and the pictures John had said were missing still hadn't turned up.

"Found anything?" Mike asked.

"Nothing relevant to your case, as far as I can see. Has Tom's car been found?"

"Not as yet. It's possible Matthews, if that is who killed him, picked him up somewhere or maybe he hid it. We'll find it," he added, his tone harsh. "So, what do you have there?"

John smoothed the creases from a birth certificate he had found stuffed among letters and photographs and news clippings. The detritus of a long life. He pushed it across the

157

table. "Silvia Jones, born February 4, 1947. Jerry was her father. His name is on her birth certificate but he never married the mother and the child just disappeared. The mother's name was Isobel. There is no Silvia in the Matthews family, or the Tynans' for that matter. Jerry had a child."

"The baby in the photo frame?"

"I believe so, yes. And I have this awful feeling that I know why she disappeared."

CHAPTER 26

Jude had been busy. By the time the briefing began the following morning she had a stack of files and printouts ready, going back to when Julia Toolin, alias Martha Toolin, alias Julia Matthews, had been eighteen. Her name back then had been Anne Hargreaves.

"A bit of a stretch, isn't it?" Mike commented. "Anne Hargreaves to Martha slash Julia and whatever else she tried on for size."

Jude picked up the few pages that represented what was known of the woman's earliest life. "Anne Hargreaves, born Nottingham, 1957, seems to have had an unremarkable childhood. First came to notice when she was fourteen and ran away from home. Social services finally got involved after she accused her father of beating her, but so far as I can tell nothing ever came to court. The only reason we have any of this is that she was caught stealing a woman's purse, and that did make it to court. Her social worker used the alleged ill treatment as mitigation.

"Anyway, she continued to run away until she turned eighteen. Then, it seems she hooked up with a man called Harry Taylor, in Norwich, and told him she was twenty-one. Her family decided to leave her to it after that. Social services logged it, but nothing seems to have been done. We only know this much because of what I've pieced together from court records."

"So she hooked up with this Taylor. What happened then?"

"Well, a year later, he's gone, she's had a baby and she's calling herself Julia, though she hung on to the Taylor for a while. She was caught shoplifting. Baby clothes, according to the arrest report. But here's the interesting bit. A lady by the name of — get this — Martha Toolin speaks up for her in court, says what a rough time she's had, gets the ear of the magistrate and Julia, Anne, whatever her name is, gets a slap on the wrist and is released into the care of said Martha Toolin."

"So who was this woman?"

"That I don't know yet, still digging. Got a last known address though, so I'll start there. Anyway, everything goes quiet for a bit and then we get a report of an arrest when Julia was twenty-five or so, but for some reason the charges are dropped. Theft again, but it doesn't say what. This is back in '77. The name on the report is a ds Cross and I happen to know he's still living locally, so it's just possible he'd remember . . . Anyway, he runs across Julia/Martha/Anne a couple of years after that and again three years later. You know, this woman must have had the angels on her side. Arrests, cautions, cases dropped from lack of evidence or because the victim wouldn't testify. Twice, families reported she'd encouraged a loved one to change their will and they made complaints, but nothing came of it. She did finally do six months but that was for aggravated assault and she only served three."

"Something of a change in the pattern?"

"Yes and no. A man called Arthur Coates died. This Julia woman had been working at the nursing home and befriended him. The family thought nothing of it at the time, then he died and . . . let's say their expectations were not met. He'd left everything to Julia, along with a very snotty letter telling the family just what he thought of them all. As far as I can gather, the family confronted her and she lost it, big time, got into a fight with one of the Coates children and hit her with a lamp base. Fortunately for all concerned, her aim was off and she didn't do serious damage, but looking at the picture of said lamp base, she could very well have killed someone."

She handed Mike the newspaper clipping she'd been holding, and he passed it around the room. The base in question was what looked like a bronze shepherdess, seriously ugly and heavy looking. "Killed by a kitsch shepherdess," Terry Gleeson commented. "Not something you want on the death certificate. Where is this clipping from?"

"It's on the back. From the *Echo*, I think. Someone had slipped it into the records. There are allegations in the article from previous families that felt they'd been ripped off. We should chase up the details to find out who might still have a serious grudge against this woman."

"Do that," Mike said. "We want the fullest narrative we can get. Who looked after the child while Julia was in prison?"

"That I don't know," Jude said. "It's probably buried in the social service records somewhere."

Mike nodded slowly. "So, from what Tom told John Tynan, the child, Emily Dawson — Lord knows where the Dawson part came from — got pregnant very young and lost touch with her mother. Now, getting on for two decades later, this Martha woman comes looking for the lost child and runs across Jason Matthews. Now, was her contact with Jason Matthews because of her association with the Matthews side of John Tynan's family, or was it the other way around? Did she believe the father of her grandchild was a Matthews, and just searched out various branches of the family, hoping to find the right one?"

"We need to work out a timeline," Jude said. "But my bet is she met Jason Matthews first and, for reasons we don't yet have a handle on, she got involved with John's family after that."

"But why?"

"Because Jason Matthews is sort of the right age to have been an older boyfriend for a teenager like Emily Dawson probably was. John's relative would already have been, well, getting on a bit . . . eighteen, nineteen years ago, and while I'm sure he was a nice bloke . . ."

"Point taken. So, we work up a timeline. Get yourself some help on that, Jude, fill in what you can, and then we pester the life out of Jason Matthews until we get the missing pieces."

A murmur of assent rose from the assembled team.

"Now," Mike said, "we need to consider the death of Tom Pollard." He pointed at the new board that had been set up. Tom's body on the beach looked small and pathetic. "He was eighteen years old, had spent time in the care system, so Looked After Children should have details. He does seem to have been local. He seems to have known this Julia/ Martha woman for about eighteen months and he lived for a time at her house in King's Lynn."

Briefly, he filled them in on what more was known about Tom Pollard and his relationship with the phoney Martha Toolin. Little enough when it boiled down to it.

"As you all probably realise, this second death, if the PM does indeed show it to be suspicious, complicates matters. It also raises the incident category from B to A so we'll be getting extra bodies in, and I'm looking at the possibility of shifting our incident room from the church hall to the leisure centre out near the cricket ground. That will not only give us more space and better parking—"

A small cheer from the assembled officers.

"—which I'm sure will be welcome. It will also move us further away from our friends in the media and make our area easier to control, all of which is a plus. Over the next day or so I should be able to enlighten you all on the additions to the team and what kind of impact they are likely to have."

The meeting broke up to the accompaniment of mild grumbling about the logistics of the move, and of integrating new officers into a team that had grown close over the past few days.

Mike stretched.

"You off, then?" Jude asked.

"Thought I may as well. Someone has to inform Mr Matthews that we might need to exhume his dog."

"I thought the vet said it had been cremated."

"Did they?" Mike raised an eyebrow. "Pity no one told *me* that. I wouldn't want to upset anyone. Have fun with the timelines."

* * *

John Tynan had been on the phone for the best part of an hour, trying to get to grips with the unexpected complications associated with Jerry's estate. It was, he thought ruefully, an apt demonstration of the old cliché that you never really know anyone, even a close blood relation. To make it even more complicated, the solicitor seemed intent on assuming that John was calling about his own inheritance.

"We are very aware of you, Mr Tynan," the solicitor assured him, "but you understand, we have to be thorough. Your uncle's estate is substantial, as I'm sure you know."

"No," John replied. "That's just it. I was not aware of anything until a few days ago when I was told that Jerry's estate had not been broken up when he went into the nursing home."

"I see," the solicitor said, somehow drawing those two words into an extended expression of suspicion and distaste. "Well, you may be assured, Mr Tynan, if no other heir is found then you do have a major claim upon your uncle's assets."

"In other words," John said, trying to make sense of all this legal fencing. "There is a will for the remainder of the estate and I figure in it. Is that correct?"

"There is indeed a will, and yes, you have provision within it, Mr Tynan — under certain particular circumstances which I really am not at liberty to discuss."

"And those circumstances concern a more direct heir." John wasn't asking the question and the solicitor seemed to understand that. He did not reply immediately.

"A daughter." John pressed the point home. "Her name was Silvia, spelt with an i not a y, and her last name is given as Jones."

A palpable recalculation seemed to be taking place in the head of the man at the other end of the line. John could almost hear the cogs begin to turn. "Mr Tynan, what exactly do you want?"

"Just to know the truth," John said. "Jerry had a child. I saw her once when she was still a tiny baby. Mr, er," what was the man's name? "Pettigrew."

"Yes."

"The family don't know about Silvia, do they? I've asked the odd discreet question. No one knows that Jerry had so much as a serious relationship, never mind that he fathered a daughter. But, Mr Pettigrew, I have reason to believe you won't be finding Silvia. If I'm right, she died not long after I saw her."

Silence. That same impression of creaking gears and cranking cogs. "And you think this why, Mr Tynan? Mr Matthews, your uncle, never gave any such indication."

"I don't think he knew," John said sadly. "Mr Pettigrew, I think we should meet, discuss this. As you may know, I was once a police officer. Well, it seems that an investigation currently underway here may be relevant to Jerry and his child. I think it might be good for both of us to pool what we know. Mr Pettigrew, please believe me when I say that my reason for contacting you is not that I want to get my hands on Jerry's estate. I believe a very great wrong has been done. A child is dead, I'm pretty sure of that, and I need to know why and how."

The appointment having been made, John put down the phone and closed his eyes, feeling the tears pricking and not wanting to give way. He could see his mother's face as clearly as he had on that day, standing in that churchyard, rain falling down upon them and the little turfed grave. Even the heavy rain streaming down his mother's face failing to hide the fact that she was crying.

Unable to settle after that, John called Maria and just before lunchtime, drove over, taking with him Jerry's box. He still hadn't worked through all of its contents, the will to do so somehow having fled when he found the birth certificate. What else was he going to find? Uppermost in his mind and the most potent of his fears was the possibility that his mother had been implicated in some way in Silvia's death, or at the very least in covering it up.

* * *

This time Mike did not go to the house. He guessed that Jason Matthews would be at work, and so he called on him there. Jason Matthews worked somewhere called Mason Holdings. Mike picked up a brochure in the reception area and, while waiting for Jason to come out of a meeting, learned that Mason Holdings was essentially a construction company — but rather than building anything themselves, they were responsible for the logistics, bringing together architects, contractors, even scouts whose job it was to look for possible locations for new builds. They specialised, it seemed, in opening up what they termed 'difficult and complex sites,' which Mike gathered were mostly brownfield, together with ex-military and unused agricultural land.

His perusal of the brochure was interrupted when a lift door opened and a group of suited men emerged, Jason among them. He spotted Mike but did not react and Mike, likewise, made no move. He waited until hands had been shaken and the visitors had left.

The receptionist spoke briefly to Jason, nodding towards Mike. He had deliberately only given his name and not his rank, and he could see the relief on Jason Matthews's face as he realised this. This time it was Jason who crossed with hand outstretched for Mike to shake.

"Mr Croft. Good of you to drop by. Come on through."
Mike followed him into the lift.

"Thank you," Jason said, "for not making this difficult.
We can do without the police coming in mob-handed."

"I'm hardly mob-handed," Mike said mildly.

"Yeah, well, you know what I mean."

This, Mike thought, was a different Jason Matthews
from the one he'd observed in the company of his wife and
children. He was assured, confident, at home in his surroundings. The house was not Jason Matthews's domain. It
definitely belonged to his wife.

"What do you do here?" Mike asked.

Jason smiled. "I've got the very fancy title of Head of
Logistics," he said. "Mostly I just make sure everyone plays
nice."

He led Mike past a secretary and into a corner office.
The windows were big enough, Mike thought, but the view
wasn't much to write home about, being mostly car park
and main road. He took a seat on a square and uncomfortable leather sofa beside one of the windows. Jason settled in
an equally unprepossessing chair. Only now did he begin to
look nervous.

"So, what can I do for you? I've already told you—"

"How about filling in all the details you didn't want
your wife to know?" Mike said.

He could see that Jason Matthews was doing his best to
contain his anger. Mike pressed on. "Did she blackmail you,
Mr Matthews? Maybe she threatened to tell your wife that
you were having an affair — oh, I don't mean with her, I'm
not sure she's quite your type."

"What's that supposed to mean?"

The explosion Mike had anticipated happened a little
sooner than he'd expected. Jason launched himself from his
chair and strode about the room.

"Do you have a type?" he asked innocently. "This Julia
Matthews seemed to think you did. Younger than you, I'm

guessing, and probably blonde, like your wife and the lady you took to the Bells on at least one occasion."

"You what?"

Mike could see the wheels turning, the memory of when and where he knew Terry Gleeson from suddenly clicking into place.

"She was a friend, that's all."

"But one your wife might not have been happy to hear about, I imagine. Did Julia Matthews threaten to tell her? About this woman, or others, perhaps?"

Jason Matthews glared at Mike but returned to his chair — though it was clear he felt confined, his anger giving rise to a restlessness that the room, never mind the chair, could not contain.

"It must be difficult," Mike said, abruptly changing tack, "not to have a dog to walk. I imagine it was a way of getting away from it all. The job, the wife, the kids, all the stress that comes with working for your father-in-law."

"You been checking up on me?"

"Of course. You had history with our murder victim. That automatically makes you a person of interest."

"History? Don't make me laugh. The bastard woman was nothing but a frigging stalker. And always the same questions, always on about did I know her daughter was underage when she got pregnant. Like I knew the girl from Adam."

Eve, Mike couldn't help thinking. "She believed you were her grandchild's father?"

"So she said. I kept telling her I never knew her kid. And the only daughters I had were with Katie. But she wouldn't hear it. Said the girl was only fifteen when someone knocked her up. It was nothing to do with me. Not a bloody thing."

"She must have had a reason for thinking it."

"Why? The woman was a fruitcake. And I mean, for real. Mental, she was."

"She had mental health problems?"

"Yeah. Yes she did. On medication for it, wasn't she?"

Interesting, Mike thought. John had not been aware of that, so how come Jason had been? "And how do you know this? Did she tell you?"

Jason Matthews looked suddenly very uncomfortable.

"You went to her room, Mr Matthews?" Though, as Mike recalled, no meds had been found there.

"Why would I do something like that?" Jason asked.

"How do you now she was on medication? Did she tell you? Did you see them?"

Jason was backtracking. "I don't *know*. I'm just saying. No one fucking normal acts like she did."

"Like she did? What did she do?"

"I told you, she was a frigging stalker. Every time I turned round, there she was. I went out with the kids, she was there. I parked my car, she pulled up next to me. I was home alone, she was ringing the doorbell and shouting to be let in."

"Did the neighbours mention this to your wife?"

Matthews shrugged. "I don't bloody know. I told them she was a nutcase," he added. "Told them she was off her rocker and on day release."

"And they believed you?"

"How should I know? Yes, they believed me. The woman was clearly sick in the head."

"And your wife never knew about this? I'd see that as unlikely." Mike remembered the twitching curtains when he had visited.

"She never said — and believe me, she would have." Jason paused for a moment. "The two times she showed up, Katie and the girls had gone away with her mum and dad, so maybe it had been forgotten by the time she came back."

"You didn't go with them?"

Jason laughed. "Like they wanted *me* along. Katie married me because she was pregnant. She lost that one, and didn't fall pregnant again for a few years, but her dad insisted I do the decent thing, and so I did. He gave me a job and you know what, he might have intended just to keep an eye on me, but I'm good at what I do. I've more than earned my keep. But spend my free time with them? Go on holiday? No way."

Mike nodded thoughtfully. "Dog hairs were found in the victim's room at the Two Bells."

"So?"

"Hairs from a German shepherd."

"There's lots of them about. Popular breed, you know."

"And you happen to have owned one. Tell me, Mr Matthews, would you be willing to supply some hairs from your dog for elimination purposes?"

Jason Matthews stared at him. "My dog's dead," he said, "and if you think Katie would have left any of his bloody hairs around, you don't know my wife. And the vet disposed of him for me. I couldn't exactly bury him in the garden."

"Dog hairs are difficult to get rid of, Mr Matthews. It might be a lot less embarrassing all round if you cooperated voluntarily."

"And what's that supposed to mean?"

"That otherwise I will apply for a warrant to search your house and car."

Jason Matthews gave a short laugh. "Well, you just bloody do that then." He stood up. "I think we're done here. You want to look for dog hairs in my house, you get yourself a warrant."

* * *

Maria met John at the door, took the box from him and stashed it on top of the kitchen dresser. "Lunch first," she prescribed. "Life always looks less complicated on a full stomach."

John laughed. "Yes, Doctor. Have you heard anything more from Mike?"

She shook her head. "He said he'd try to give me a call around lunchtime, but it always depends on where he is and what he's doing and—"

"If he remembers what time it is."

"Quite. At some point he'll realise that he's hungry, but that might well be mid-afternoon. Were you expecting news?"

"Not really. I just keep thinking about that boy."

"Tom? Is that his name? Mike says he had no family."

"None that he knew about."

"Sit," she ordered. "Eat. No more talking about any of this until you've got food inside of you and have had at least half an hour talking about something else."

John did not argue. He sat, ate his way through the stack of sandwiches Maria set before him, talked about the new baby and admired the pictures Maria had brought back with her.

"Josie swears this is the last, and I think she means it this time, though I think if they'd got room and money she'd keep on having kids till her body gave out."

"She seems to thrive on it."

"Oh, I think they both do. Some people just seem created to be parents. Others, well, they shouldn't be let anywhere near a kid. You know, John, sometimes I think about all the damaged kids who are damaged adults by the time I get to deal with them and I get very close to being vindictively conservative about parenthood. At the very least, you should be made to apply for a licence to breed."

John chuckled at her vehemence. "You, my dear, are one of the most liberal people I know. I know what you mean, though." He poked at the crumbs on his plate, rolling the fragments of bread into a little ball, belatedly noting what he was doing and looking up guiltily.

Maria smiled. "Bet you got told off for playing with your food."

"Oh yes. Frequently."

"My mother had a thing about ice cream," she said. "I loved to wait until it got all sloppy and half melted and then I'd whisk it all up with my spoon. She hated that. I never understood why, but it somehow offended her sense of what ice cream was meant to be. If she caught me doing it, she'd take it away."

"You do that now," John said accusingly. "I've seen you."

"I surely do. Josie's kids and I, we have contests, seeing just how fast we can mix it up before it all spills over the sides of the bowl. I guess I've never really agreed with St Paul."

John nodded, recognising the reference. "I don't think any of us ever really puts aside childish things. I think we just make a big pretence of it but our childhoods, for good or ill, lie in wait, ready to trip us up, even in old age."

"Go get the box," Maria said. "I'll clear away and we'll see what else your Jerry has to tell us."

CHAPTER 27

Late afternoon and Mike was called in to see his boss — never a good sign in his experience. He remembered when he had first come to join the Norwich force and the shabby little office the previous superintendent had occupied, with its old, frayed carpet trampled to a camouflage of green and khaki. Scuffed desk, cork boards so over-used that it was a challenge to find a place to push the pin into the notices.

Rather a lot had changed since them. Superintendent Reece occupied what could only be described as a suite of rooms on the top floor of the new HQ. His secretary had a little chamber of her own, through which all supplicants had to pass and be vetted, and there was even a little waiting area, complete with obligatory low, uncomfortable seating upon which she could stow those deemed deserving of the punishment of a long wait.

Mike went straight through into the large glass office beyond, wondering why modern architects seemed so enamoured with human aquaria, and if Reece minded being ensconced in such a fishbowl. Reece, behind an imposing blond wood desk, was on the phone, listening, looking bored. He held up three fingers to Mike, which he interpreted as meaning the number of minutes before boredom won and the phone went down. He sat where Reece indicated, a chair set just that little bit too far from the desk to make for easy conversation. Mike got up again and moved the chair closer. Reece's mouth twitched in a smile from which Mike judged he was in trouble but not yet drowning in it.

Reece dropped the phone back on the cradle. "Who'd have kids?" he said. "You'd think by now there'd be an automatic, constitutional right to ship teenage girls off to boarding school the moment they start attracting boys."

"Sadie?" Mike asked, familiar with the trials and tribulations of Reece's fifteen-year-old daughter. "She still a Goth?"

"Oh, I do so wish she was. Life was simple when all she wanted to do was dye her hair and wear henna tattoos and fishnets. That, I could live with."

Reece, Mike remembered, had not been nearly as sanguine at the time.

"Jason Matthews," Reece said.

"Yes?"

"You're harassing him."

"Possibly."

Reece narrowed his eyes, tried to look imposing, gave up and slumped back in his chair. "OK, we're both wanting to get home, so you tell me what you've got on the man, I'll tell you to go easy and then we can both consider job done and get on with doing what we're supposed to be doing."

Which is? Mike wondered. "Martha Toolin and Tom Pollard," he said. "I think Matthews is involved in both deaths."

"So you want a warrant so you can get CSI collecting dog hairs from his home and car."

"Among other things, yes. He's had the dog cremated so we can't get a match there. I want a warrant for the cars as well. I suspect his car might be a better option, seeing as he looks to have a wife that cleans the carpets until they're bald. The house was spotless, despite their two kids. I can't see him being as thorough. And we can also get a look at his satnav, computer, all the usual.

"We need a match for the hairs found on Martha Toolin's body. He admits to knowing her, was seen arguing with her. He claims she was stalking him and making accusations about getting her underage daughter pregnant way back when. So we have plenty of reasons to believe she was making trouble for him, threatening to tell his wife at the very least. And since his father-in-law is also his employer, he has a fair bit to lose."

"But was she threatening enough that he'd want to kill her?" Reece asked.

"Murders have been committed with far less motivation."

"True. We had a complaint from the wife, Katie Matthews, and from her father. They claim you've been heavy-handed."

"Persistent, maybe. Considering the fact that we have two dead people, I think I needed to be," Mike said.

Reece steepled his fingers, a sure sign in Mike's experience that the interview was almost over. He peered at Mike over the tips. "Are you interested in who Katie Matthews's father might be?"

"Not really."

"Well, just for the record, she used to be Katie Edwards, Councillor Edwards's kid. He regularly gives big donations to police charities. He's a respected businessman and highly regarded member of the local community."

"Nice for him. And is he generous with his son-in-law as well? Apart from giving him a cushy job."

"I believe so, yes."

"Well, maybe you should tell them that I've noted their concerns, but I'm still going to make as much of a nuisance of myself as I need to."

Mike stood and so did Reece, picking up his briefcase and collecting his umbrella. Mike had never seen Reece venture out without an umbrella. Never seen him actually use it either, come to think of it.

"I'll walk out with you," Reece said. "I don't know if I should hope you're right about Matthews's involvement, or if I should look forward to you falling flat on your face." He shrugged. "Won't be a good outcome either way, I suspect."

"No, sir. I don't suppose it will."

"So I'd best be practising my damage limitation skills, then."

"Maybe you had, sir. Maybe you had."

* * *

Maria called just as Mike reached his car, requesting him to bring a takeaway for three. She didn't mind what and neither did John. An hour later, foil cartons and blue-rimmed plates had joined the scattered papers strewn across the kitchen table as they helped themselves to a somewhat random assortment of Chinese food.

"What's all this?" Mike asked, nodding towards the papers strewn across the table.

"What's left of Jerry's life, I suppose," John said. "Sorry. That sounds very grumpy and I'm not, not really. I'm just . . . puzzled, I suppose. You assume you know someone just because you might have had some vague contact with them years before and, frankly, now I think about it, that's all I'd had with Jerry. He might have been my uncle, but once he'd moved back in with my grandfather, I don't think I could have seen him more than once or twice a year. Not much to found a relationship on."

"Not your fault, John. Families break apart, nothing you can do."

"Not as a child, maybe, Maria, but as an adult, I could have made the effort. It just never occurred to me that there was any need. Jerry was there, a constant. I liked him but I hated my grandfather and I suppose I saw them as a package deal."

Mike speared a battered chicken ball and doused it in too sweet, orange-coloured sauce. He looked from one to the other. Clearly this was a conversation that he'd landed in partway through and he wasn't sure if he should interrupt

175

and ask for an explanation. He too was getting that 'I don't really know as much about you as I thought' feeling, and it certainly wasn't because he only saw John twice a year. John was certainly a constant in his life, Maria's too. A dear and trusted friend, but, he realised with a slight shock, he knew very little about the older man in real terms. Their friendship had begun some ten years before and gathered momentum from that point on. Only rarely had either of them ventured into the earlier, largely unknown territory of the other's life. Mike knew about Grace and John about Stevie. Mutual grief had been one of the first things both recognised they had in common. Beyond that . . .

"And what does all of this tell you?" he asked at last, scooping noodles this time and adding spoonfuls of king prawn curry and egg-fried rice. "I don't suppose it mentions this Martha woman."

He knew at once that he could have phrased that better. John had been genuinely involved with Martha, and his cavalier attitude was bound to hurt. The truth was that, to Mike, Martha Toolin or whatever her name had been had now become more puzzle than real person. An issue to be solved. Sure, later on he would remind himself that she was a woman whose life had been taken from her unfairly and prematurely, but he had learned long ago that he was a better investigator if he put a little distance between himself and the victim. He hoped that John would appreciate that, remember what it was like.

Maria was glaring at him.

"Martha Toolin isn't mentioned," John said, and Mike was relieved to note that there was no frost in his voice.

"Incidentally," Mike said, "there really was a Martha Toolin. It seems she befriended our dead woman when she was young and pregnant and very much in need of a friend."

"Oh?"

"And that's about all I know as yet. Jude is looking into it. But the woman we knew as Martha Toolin was originally called Anne — Anne Hargreaves. She was born in Nottingham in 1957."

"Anne Hargreaves?" John rolled the name around in his mouth, seeing if the taste fitted the woman he had known. He took a deep breath. "Then she was born ten years after Jerry's child. Mike, I'm sure Silvia's body is in that little grave."

Mike looked closely at his friend, who met his gaze. John's grey eyes seemed to have lost some of their lustre these past few days. They were no longer the colour of rain-filled skies — instead, the intensity seemed to have been washed away from them. They seemed drained. "I contacted the cathedral," he said. "They put me on to diocesan records and they are looking into it. If the grave is marked, we'll soon know who is buried there."

"And if it's not?"

Mike hesitated. "They're talking about the possibility of exhumation. John, if you're right, we'll need a DNA sample, from you, or anyone else who was a close relative."

"What will happen to the body after that?" Maria wanted to know. "It seems so cruel, somehow, just to dig up the grave."

"Whoever is there will be reburied," Mike assured her, "with a proper funeral." He was watching John's face, trying to work out what was going on in his friend's head. "You said you remembered something. About a baby?"

"Oh, half memory, half dream, I'm afraid. I can't be certain any of it happened, not really."

He remembers all too well, Mike thought. Just doesn't want to talk about it. Leaving John alone with his thoughts, he turned his attention back to his food and for a few moments there was quiet, broken only by the chink of cutlery on earthenware and Maria pouring more wine into everyone's glasses, from which Mike gathered that John would not be heading home that night. Whatever he and Maria had discussed that afternoon, whatever mysteries were contained inside of Jerry's box, she evidently felt that it had left John in need of company. He glanced curiously at the scatter of photographs and notebooks, old theatre programmes and cinema tickets that Jerry had seen fit to treasure, and his gaze fell upon something familiar. Puzzled, he tugged the newspaper clipping from beneath a heap of cheap notepaper. The headline he saw could have appeared in any of the local papers at any time over this summer but, when he looked at the date, he saw that the clipping was more than three decades old.

"Black Dog?"

"Old Shuck, yes. Jerry seems to have collected the stuff. I never thought he had an interest in folklore."

John put down the glass he had just picked up and rustled around under the same stack of notes Mike had just disturbed. More news clippings emerged, some cut from newspapers, others photocopied from earlier editions. "The earliest one we found goes back to the nineteenth century," he said, "the most recent just three years ago. And there's so much more, look. He must have made notes on every story he ever heard about the beast. He recorded legends, hearsay, gossip, anything he could lay his hands on. There's even a photograph of the wall painting we found in the church. The keyholder may not have noticed it was there, but Jerry knew."

Mike took the picture from him and examined it closely. It was, at first, difficult to make out what was going on, to pick out the image from the overlay of flaking paint and the dirt of ages. "A dog?" he said. "A man and what looks like a child?"

"That's what we think," Maria confirmed.

"But why the interest? I mean, everyone and his dog, if you'll pardon the analogy, has a passing interest in Old Shuck. It's part of the landscape, the spirit of place, I suppose, but you seem to think it was more specific than that?"

"More like a lifelong obsession," John said. "Beyond that, Mike, I don't have a clue."

CHAPTER 28

Above the beach where Tom Pollard's body had been found, the man in the dark jacket stood up on the cliff, looking out to sea.

In truth, he was sorry about the boy, the little scrap of humanity who'd survived eighteen difficult years for it all to end here, on this lonely beach.

But that was the way of things sometimes, you didn't get to choose your mode of passing or, on occasion, who would be responsible for that passing — or how.

* * *

A few miles away, Jason and Katie Matthews were fighting. Not that this was anything new, nor was the fact that their row was carried out in fierce whispers so that, in theory at least, the children wouldn't hear. The children, of course, lay in the semi-darkness of their room, trying both not to hear and straining to catch each muffled word. Their parents argued, nothing new there. But, lying in their single beds, each catching the eye of their sibling across the dimly lit room, they sensed that this argument was different from the usual ones about their mother's spending and their father's

179

lack of attention and the fact that they spent no 'family time' together — something neither of the little girls particularly wanted to change. Those times when their father did manage to go out with them usually ended in frustration and full-scale arguments as their father grew bored and their mother angry. Far better, they thought, just to go out with Mum or with Gran and Grampa.

"It's about that woman again," Chantel whispered.

"That *old* woman?" Vicky wasn't so sure. "Daddy said she'd gone away."

"He said that before and she hadn't, had she? We saw her in town."

Vicky nodded solemnly and turned over, pulling the covers over her head.

Chantel sighed. She slipped out of bed and put the radio on low, placing it on the floor between their beds. "Listen to the music," she said, then dived back into her bed as footsteps sounded on the stairs.

"Where are you going?" Her mother had given up on the stage whispers now. "Don't you walk away from me!"

"What the fuck do you want me to do? I've said all there is to say."

"Have you? Have you really?" She lowered her voice again and Vicky heard her mutter something about waking the children.

Vicky rolled her eyes and, following her sister's example, pulled the duvet over her head and tried to focus on the music coming from their little radio.

Their father's footsteps receded and, as Vicky had come to expect, a moment or two later she heard the front door slam.

Time was, Vicky would have padded downstairs after their father left, gone to find her weeping mother and to offer what comfort she could, listening as Katie raged and stormed on about the no-good man that had fathered the girls.

Frankly, the novelty of that had long since worn off. Nowadays, all she wanted to do was get off to sleep and forget about it all. She closed her eyes and listened to the soft music that she recognised vaguely from her piano lessons.

Downstairs, Katie had indeed given way to tears, but the storm soon passed, replaced by a raging anger at having been thwarted once again. She made her way into Jason's office. Silent, furious, she emptied his bin onto the carpeted floor, scrabbled through the mess, looking for . . . for what? Last time she had gone through his bin she had found that policeman's business card.

This time, nothing. She subjected the desk drawers to the same treatment. Post-it notes, stapler, diary, drawing pins all strewn across the floor. Filing cabinet. Empty but for a handful of customer files. She sat down in his chair and switched on the laptop, knowing full well that it was password protected and she didn't know what he might have changed it to this week — not, she suspected, that he kept anything much on it anyway. What did that idiot really know about computers? What did he really know about his job? Her father only kept him on the books because they were married, not because Jason was good for anything.

Exhausted now, she stared furiously at the prompt asking her to input the password. Then swept that too onto the office floor, the laptop landing half open and still blinking atop the stack of files.

He had promised her, hadn't he, that the woman, Julia, or whatever she was called, had gone away. But he'd lied, hadn't he, and Katie was not really sure if he had encouraged this Julia's return or if, as he said, she had just reappeared and it was nothing to do with him. In reality, Katie didn't really care. Jason had let her down yet again. Her and the girls.

A noisy flood of angry, disappointed tears relieved a little of the tension but not the sense of betrayal. And on top of all this, Jason's ex was back on the scene. Katie had known all along that Jason had started going out with her while on the rebound from the other girl, and she knew he'd only married her because her dad had practically bribed him to do so when

Katie had fallen pregnant. The sad part was that Katie had lost that first baby only a month after the wedding.

He'd been sympathetic, loving, but still the doubt remained. The feeling that he'd rather be with that other woman. With his ex. It was why she'd waited until they'd been married for what her family saw as an overly long time before pushing for children. Vicky had been born after eight years of marriage, mainly because, in her heart of hearts, she'd been afraid that Jason didn't really want kids.

But she'd thought that in time, he'd put all of that behind him. Katie wiped her eyes on the backs of her hands and stared blankly across the small office space. She was unable to fend off the thought that even before this Julia woman had arrived with all the accusations Katie had chosen not to tell the policeman about, and before his ex Amanda had come back on the scene, she had known that for Jason she would only ever be second best.

CHAPTER 29

The offices of Pettigrew and Pettigrew were a five minute walk from the cathedral, tucked away on the third floor of a building that looked as though it was trying to be Tudor but not quite making it. John always found it hard to judge the age of Norwich buildings — the lower levels so often given over to plate glass and window displays, so you had to look up to guess the actual age of what might well be a medieval house. He loved the city, just wished that the seventies planners had been a little less active in their efforts to modernise and, in their eyes, improve.

Pettigrew and Pettigrew's offices were reached by several flights of steep stairs and through glass doors bearing their twin names in rather tarnished gold. A secretary, also looking somewhat worn, knocked on the inner door and announced his arrival, then ushered him straight through. John wondered which of the paired solicitors he was meeting or if it really mattered, or even if, seeing as only one office led off the waiting area, there really were two of them. Perhaps it was a job-share.

"Sit yourself down," the solicitor said, waving John into a leather upholstered captain's chair. "Would you like some coffee? Tea?"

"No, I'm fine, thank you. It's good of you to see me at such short notice."

"Oh, I was intrigued," the solicitor told him. "Besides, between you and me, we aren't so busy these days that a little diversion comes amiss. Oh, and when we get all this sorted out, I'll be billing the estate for my time, so you needn't feel guilty."

"Fine," John said, not really sure what to make of these rather contradictory statements.

"So," Pettigrew sat back in his chair, a match for the one in which John was seated. He folded his hands across a very ample belly and beamed encouragingly. "You have a theory about Silvia Jones."

John took a deep breath, not certain where to begin. He toyed with the notion of sharing his childhood memories, voicing his anxiety about those childhood incidents that had returned so unexpectedly to his consciousness, but that seemed an odd and far too personal place to begin. Instead, he said, "Martha Toolin. She befriended Jerry while he was in the nursing home. He left her a silver picture frame."

"Your uncle left a number of small bequests."

"Well, about a month ago she turned up here, asking about my relatives. She said that she was a member of the family, a distant relative but a relative nonetheless. My cousin vouched for her, said that Jerry had seemed to know her and so I felt, well, not entirely easy about talking to her, but justified. She said she was tracing the family tree — the Matthews, that is — and asked about my family."

"From which, I believe, you had largely been estranged."

John's surprise must have shown on his face.

"I was your uncle's adviser for a number of years, Mr Tynan. I won't claim to have been his bosom friend or anything like that, but in the course of our business dealings he told me certain things, and that was one of them. I don't believe he held any grudge regarding your estrangement, he understood your reasons, but I do believe it saddened him all the same."

Pettigrew leaned forward abruptly and picked up a sheet of paper from the oak desk. "Have you seen this?"

It was a copy of the will that Billy had sent to him. John nodded. "Yes."

"Your uncle had this drawn up a few months before he died. He'd had a similar document created a few years before — small considerations for those who might want a souvenir of his life. I believe that in between the making of those two provisions, some beneficiaries may have died; others, perhaps, had fallen from favour. Others, such as this Martha Toolin, appeared and assumed importance."

"And so you drew this will up for him." John nodded.

"I did indeed, but it isn't actually a will in the usual sense of the word. It is, in the original conception, a record of your uncle's *will*, if you see what I mean, though it is by no means the main document but simply an addendum."

"I hadn't realised that," John said. He doubted Billy had either. "And the main document?"

"Was created thirty years ago and, with minor revisions, remains as he wished it then. His estate should go to Silvia Jones, being his natural daughter, recognised as such in law and in Jerry's conscience. Upon his death, we were to find her, or find any children she may have had should she have predeceased him. Failing that, all the remainder of his estate should come to you to dispose of as you saw fit."

John stared at him, stunned. "Why me?"

"Because he liked you, I suppose. If he had a particular reason, he didn't share it with me. When the will was drawn up I did urge him to set the search for Silvia Jones in motion. I told him that time had already passed and the more that went by, the more difficult it would be to track her down. He refused. He allowed the search to begin only when he was certain that he had very little time left on this earth. Three weeks before he finally passed on, he called me in, had me bring both sections of his will for him to check over, and had me promise that I'd begin the investigation into Silvia's whereabouts, but with one small proviso."

"And that was?"

"That if we happened to be lucky in our quest and find Silvia before he died, we should wait until after his passing to make his wishes known. It seems that he had every wish to provide for his daughter but absolutely no wish for her to be part of his life or he hers."

"Didn't that strike you as very odd?" John asked.

"It seemed all of a piece with the fact that Jerry went back to live with a man he, if you'll pardon the presumption, so obviously hated."

"You mean my grandfather."

"Ernest Matthews. Yes. A man as cold as the house he lived in. You know, I went there once at the height of summer and it was still like walking into an industrial freezer. But I'm sure I don't need to tell you that?"

John shook his head. No, he didn't need telling. The chill of that dreary place still ate into his bones, causing him to crave the comfort of a fire even at this time of year, when the sun blazed in through the windows of this dusty little office and he could glimpse the bright blue sky through the little diamonds of ancient glass.

"And have you found her?" he asked.

"Not a trace. Jerry gave us a time limit and a budget. A generous one, but both budget and time are now running short and there has been no sign. Silvia Jones was born and then seems to have dropped off the planet." He gestured, palm out, as if to say, 'over to you.'

John nodded thoughtfully. "I think she died. I think she's buried with other Matthews in the Church of St Michael and All Angels and I'm forced to think that Jerry either didn't know or chose *not* to know, but that my mother did and possibly my grandfather too."

"Can you prove any of this?"

"Not yet, no. But I'm wondering if Martha Toolin found out somehow. I can't ask her because she's dead too, now, and so is the boy she thought might be her grandson."

Pettigrew was looking narrowly at him and John realised that he must seem to be rambling. "Could I see the records of the investigation?" he asked. "It might be that I can bring other resources to bear."

Pettigrew considered this for a moment and then nodded. "I'll get everything copied and sent over to your address. Don't worry, the estate can cover the costs."

John thanked him, wondering if, by the time anyone eventually did inherit anything, there would be anything left.

CHAPTER 30

Mrs Green was now a supervisory social worker, running, as she told Mike, a very busy office. She agreed to give him twenty minutes if he arrived at eleven o'clock sharp — something of a tall order as it was half past ten when she delivered her injunction.

He managed to be only five minutes late. As punishment — or so it felt — she kept him waiting for another fifteen, emerging eventually from an emergency case conference accompanied by a half dozen other intense-looking men and women and glaring at Mike as though wondering what a stranger was doing lurking in the corridor.

"Mrs Green?"

"Yes?"

"We had an appointment at eleven? DI Mike Croft?" Uncomfortably, he found he had made that sound like a question too, as though he was no longer certain of his own name. She glanced irritably at her watch as though the delay was Mike's fault. She sighed. "Oh yes, you'd better come in."

There was no apology for having kept him waiting.

"Find somewhere to sit," she instructed, rummaging through the paperwork on her desk and cramming a stack of folders into an already overfilled bag. Mike moved another stack of files off a chair and sat down. He could not help but wonder how the six that had just left had fitted into the cubbyhole of a room and where they'd sat. Maybe there was a special training course that taught social workers to hover or to shrink into the available space. Belatedly, he noticed a second door, leading out into what he assumed must be a larger room. He felt almost disappointed.

"Now," she said. "What was this all about? Oh yes, Tom Pollard. I have his file here somewhere, though you understand there are issues of confidentiality."

"I don't think confidentiality will concern him anymore," Mike said quietly. "This is a murder investigation."

"Others will have been mentioned in his file. It won't just be about Thomas."

Mike frowned at the reprimand, but bit his tongue. She searched her desk, finally tracking down the folder that she wanted from among those she had stuffed into her bag. Mike brought out his notebook and prepared to write. He did not for one minute expect her to hand over the file.

She read, silently, frowning at the pages. Mike coughed to remind her that he was still there.

"Thomas Richard Pollard," she said at last. "Found abandoned on the steps of a pub, apparently, just before opening time. His teenage mother came forward after an appeal and she seems to have given a father's name on the birth certificate but according to the records I have here, never even wanted to see the baby. As far as she was concerned she had left him where he could be found, and she could, or would, do nothing more. No word from the alleged father. The paediatrician's name was Thomas, the landlord was Richard, so in the great tradition of naming abandoned children, that's what he became."

"And the Pollard?"

"Name of his long-term foster carers. He went to them when he was a few days old. They would have adopted him, I believe, but sadly, Mr Pollard died when Tom was eight, and Mrs Pollard felt she couldn't carry on alone, so Tom went to a children's home and stayed in the care system until he was eighteen. His support worker is away on holiday at the moment but apparently she lost touch with him a few months after that anyway. He said he'd found a relative but declined to tell her more."

"And she didn't push him?"

Mrs Green pursed her lips. "He was an adult, Inspector Croft. He was free to make his own decisions. The role of a support worker is to support. If a client does not want to be supported, there is very little any of us can do. The best option then is to focus on the long list of those who are, inevitably, clamouring for help."

She closed the file, evidently expecting Mike to disappear. He wished he had Jude with him. Jude, like Maria, had the knack of getting on the right side of people like Mrs Green, Maria because she worked closely with them and understood the ways and means and Jude just because she always seemed to know exactly what to say.

"Please, Mrs Green, can you tell me about Tom? Was he happy in the foster home? What friends did he have? Did he do well at school? Did he maintain friendships after he left care?"

"I can tell you only what it says here." She tapped the file. "His support worker may be able to tell you more, but as I told you, she's away." She sighed, reopened the manila folder. "He was doing well at school until his foster father died. You've got to understand, he'd been with them since infancy, never known anything else. After that, well, he never really settled anywhere. By ten he was shoplifting, by thirteen stealing cars. No doubt your colleagues in King's Lynn can fill you in on that. He seemed to have had a settled period from age fourteen until he left school, even managed to get himself some GCSEs." She sounded surprised.

"Oh?"

"Yes, five good grades and a couple of mediocre ones. That's more than most manage. Then a series of dead-end jobs until we found him a bedsit and yet another job at seventeen."

"Seventeen." Mike knew the score. The halfway houses, the 'preparation' for the outside world, but it was still so terribly young to be fending for yourself. "Mrs Green, I need a list of jobs, of schools attended, of his past addresses. Of friends."

"Some of that information may be—"

"Mrs Green, Tom Pollard is dead. Someone killed him. We just need to know if anything in his past led up to this, or if it was his current associations, or even if it was just someone who mistook him for someone else. Unless we can piece together a picture of Tom's life, such as it was, we don't have a hope in hell of finding out why he's dead." He took a deep breath, wondering where that surge of anger had come from. Across the desk, she was staring at him.

"I'll see what I can do," she said frostily and then rose, signalling that his time was at an end.

Mike filed the experience under the 'could have handled that better' category; subheading, 'get Jude to deal with her next time.' He thanked the woman and took his leave.

* * *

It had taken a bit of persuasion to get the solicitor to loan him the keys to Jerry's house, but John suspected that most of the fuss had been for show, and that Mr Pettigrew was as curious as he was to get to the bottom of what was going on. He had the feeling that the solicitor would have liked to have come with him and get his impressions, but that he didn't think it quite proper. John certainly didn't think that it was a glut of client appointments that had prevented him.

It was years since John had come to the house. The Willows, it had been called in his grandfather's day and there had, indeed, been willows in the garden, down at the far end of the lawn where the land was still marshy. He almost missed the entrance and had to reverse several yards back up the narrow road in order to make the turn down what had once been the little track down to the house. The track was a leftover from when the Willows had been a farmhouse, long before John's time.

There was little evidence that anyone had been down there in years and after about twenty feet or so of pushing through nettles and fighting the brambles that reached across what had once been a cart track, John gave up and abandoned the car. He had forgotten just how far back from the road the Willows had been set and now wished he had come better equipped for jungle warfare or at least bramble wrestling. At last, his arms stung and slashed by his battle with shoulder-high nettles and blackberry suckers trying their best to behave like trees, he saw the gate. It was as if even nature had learned to give his grandfather's house a wide berth. Just before the gate, the vegetation thinned out and he could see that the wooden bars and stone gateposts were relatively clear of the overenthusiastic growth that now dominated the track.

As the solicitor had told him, the gate was padlocked and John dug in his trouser pocket for the keys he had been given before realising that padlocked it might be, but in need of unlocking it was not. The padlock, being a mere five years old, was intact and even still slightly shiny. The wood to which it had been attached had largely rotted away and when John reached out to touch the padlock, the gatepost broke with a crack, followed by a rather pathetic creak.

John pushed what was left of the gate aside and stepped through into his former life.

In his grandmother's time, roses had bloomed here, tall foxgloves and then, later in the season, hollyhocks had sent spires of pink to reach way above his head. Lavender had edged the cobbled path that led to the door and bees filled the place with sound all summer long.

The house may have been bleak and cold and uninviting but his grandmother had ruled over her garden and brought the magic in, despite the disapproval of her dark king of a husband. John stood just inside the gate, blinking back unexpected tears, and looked for traces of the paradise that she had created and found, much to his astonishment, that there were still signs of what had been. Roses, tangled now with wild honeysuckle and columbine, sprawled across the cobbles. Wild thyme, self-seeded herbs and the children of the lavender she had planted thrust their heads up boldly in the pavement cracks.

John breathed deep, felt the sense of calm she had always instilled fill his lungs and his limbs and his heart until he thought he might burst, and the tears no longer pricked at his eyes, they poured down his cheeks. They fell for the woman who had made the garden, for his beloved Grace, for Martha, whatever name she might have chosen to go by, and for the boy, Tom, who John could not help but see as a lost innocent in all of this mess of grief and pain.

Treading on the fragrant herbs, the scent of lavender and thyme rising up around him, John made his way slowly and reluctantly to the old front door and went inside.

* * *

Jude was staring at a stack of paperwork on her desk when Mike got back to the office. Unusually for Jude, she looked daunted.

"Is that all about Martha Toolin?" Mike was duly shocked.

"Mostly. I put out a general call and this is what came back. She only actually ended up in court three times and was sent down twice. Six months for kiting. She did three, and you know about the assault charge, but as you are also aware, she'd been in the system since her teens, once you start to take account of her real name and her assortment of aliases. Not much in the last eight years, though."

"Oh? Do we know why?"

"Well, it seems she had no need. Old man by the name of Thomas Ellis left her some money and three properties he'd been renting out, including the one you visited in King's Lynn and presumably the other two. She seems to have lived off the rent and the legacy since then. Either that or she just hit her stride and didn't get caught."

"And we know what about this Thomas Ellis?"

"Well, he seems to have been a genuine, if distant, relative. Nottingham way, somewhere called Carlton. She seems to have started going to see the old boy just after he went into a nursing home. His family didn't live locally so she had pretty much established herself by the time they realised he'd got a new friend. According to statements the staff made, she visited a couple of times a week for nearly three years. Played chess with him while he was still able, carried on visiting even when he'd had a serious stroke and couldn't remember her which, it seems, was more than his family did. They said they found it too upsetting. Anyway, he died, she was sole beneficiary, family contested and lost. The will was made only six months after he went into the home and everyone agreed he was fine in the mind department, totally on the ball at that point."

"Three years, you said? She played the long con, then."

"Well, you could see it like that, yes. But it's not like she knocked on his door and tried to sell him double glazing he didn't need and then told him his house would fall apart if he didn't hand over all his cash so she could fix it. No, this is different. I'm not saying it's right, but it's different."

Mike nodded, taking her point. "Obviously the family didn't agree. How long ago was this?"

"Ten years, give or take. It took a while for probate to complete, what with the family contesting the will and everything, but she was left with three rental properties and something close to a quarter of a million in the bank."

Mike whistled softly. "And while she was charming this old man out of his money, what else was she doing? She must have been living on something while she waited."

"She was. There's another complaint about a woman in Norwich, similar set-up. Mike, it seems like such an odd way to make money. It takes time, commitment, there's no violence or pressure applied. She seems to have just gone in and been nice to people."

"Put like that, it does sound weird," Mike admitted. "Anything more on Tom? Jude, I didn't do so well with his social worker. I wondered if . . . ?"

She rolled her eyes at him. "Who cleaned up after you before I came?" she asked. "How you ever ended up with Maria, I'll never know."

Mike grinned. "Oh," he said, "she just told me what to do and picked me up when I fell on my face." He handed Jude the number and searched his pockets for his car keys.

"You off out again? Before you go, I've made contact with the grandson of the real Martha Toolin. She's very elderly but apparently still possessed of all her marbles. I've spoken to him on the phone and said we'd like to set up a meeting. I thought you might want to call him back?"

"Can I let you deal with him?"

"Sure, and if anyone asks, you are where?"

"Going to see the Beals, see if they can pick Jason Matthews out of our picture gallery. We know he drank there but I want to see if they ever saw him in the company of *our* Martha Toolin. You know, we've got to figure out what to call her. This is just getting too confusing."

* * *

Inside, his grandfather's house was as bleak as John remembered. How, he wondered, could Jerry have borne to go back there, to stay there even after the old man died and Jerry had the opportunity to sell up and move on? He stood for a long time in the hall, holding the door half open, reluctant to completely shut out the sunshine and the scented garden and surrender to the dust and chill of air smelling of long years of damp and cold that even high summer sun could not mitigate. John doubted that even after Jerry had taken Billy's advice and installed central heating, it would have won the battle against the chill. It permeated the wood and stone and the very fabric of the house, as though the spirit of his grandfather, mean-minded and cruel and utterly cold, still held sway here.

Unwillingly, John let go of the door, winced as he heard it close behind him, reminded himself that he was not just a grown man but almost as old as his grandfather had been when he passed on. There was nothing here to scare him now as it had when he'd been a boy of ten — he was stronger than that. Even so, he found that he trod softly across the dusty floor down the short stretch of corridor that led to the kitchen, with as much trepidation as he had way back then.

Only his mother had ever stepped boldly here, only she had ever raised her voice to the old man. Only she had stood defiant, even with the blood pouring from the cut above her eye and the split lip and the force of her father's rage. John closed his eyes, knowing that particular memory was not his own, but one inherited from whispered family stories. Ernest Matthews had beaten his two sons black and blue, but he had struck his daughter only on that one occasion, which had been the day she had left home, she had vowed, for good.

"You came back, though, didn't you?" John whispered softly. Ironically, it had been his father who had persuaded Gloria to come home and make peace. *She* had done it for her own mother's sake. John's father, he had come to realise, had persuaded her because in some very real sense, Robert Tynan had recognised in Ernest Matthews something of himself.

"I don't suppose I never really forgave you, did I?" he whispered, though he had no real faith that the ghost of his mother, Gloria, would be listening. She rarely had in life, why should death make a difference? "You forgave him and you married one just like him. Why would any woman do that? Believe me, if Grace and I had been lucky enough to be blessed with a child, we'd have moved heaven and hell to keep them away from men like him." John shook his head, knowing that he loved her in spite of that. That he had loved his grandmother even while he despaired of what seemed like her almost wilful stupidity in remaining with Ernest, even when they offered her an escape route.

He still didn't really understand why both of these otherwise strong, wise women should have made such basic, tragic misjudgements, but it was a pattern he had seen over and over again in his career, both men and women succumbing to the same trap. It had never ceased to baffle him or to cause him deep and very personal pain.

He opened the door to the kitchen, and was amazed to find it practically unchanged. The cooker was still in place, so was the dresser, plates still in the racks, dust-smothered and heavily cobwebbed. The heavy blue glass bowl that had always been used for fruit sat in the centre of the wooden table. John reached out and drew a finger through the dust.

Why exactly had he come here? Just what did he hope to find?

He retreated from the kitchen, went up the stairs and into the spare bedroom where he had slept during their visits. The room was smaller than he remembered. The sun slanted through grimed glass and illuminated the tiny grate that John was sure had never seen a fire. The bed had been stripped and the mattress looked as though mice had taken possession of the ancient padding. John found himself wondering what had become of the thick, red quilt, the only comfort in an otherwise cheerless room. With some difficulty, he opened the transom window and let the fresh air into the dank room, recognising, as he did so, the underlying scent of mice. He wondered, vaguely, as to the size of the mouse population. He looked out across the garden, then further, to where, across the fields, a hawk was hunting. "You want to come in here, my friend," John said. Laughter rose unexpectedly, escaped, echoed strangely around this room that had never heard it before, frightened the shadows away.

What did you keep this place for, Jerry? What was so important that you had to carry on living in this mausoleum?

Impatient now, with himself, with the memory of his oh-so-dysfunctional family and its closely guarded secrets, John closed the window with a crash that rattled the loose glass in its frame. There was nothing to be found here, not in this tiny room, only mouse droppings and a stinking mattress. Not even the faint shade of the boy he had once been. John left it all behind and strode off down the hallway to his grandfather's once forbidden room.

* * *

Mrs Beal had no particular recollection of Jason Matthews having anything to do with the woman calling herself Martha Toolin, but she knew who he was.

"The man with the big dog," she said. "Funny thing, but I think he must be missing being able to walk his dog. He was out here yesterday — no, the day before. Bought a burger from the van and had a chat with one of the journalists, I think."

"Oh? Who?" And why? Mike wondered.

"Oh, I don't know. Not one of our locals." She looked concerned. "Sorry, my love, is it important?"

Mike reassured her that it was not and she turned back to serve the next customer.

Harry Pickson, head barman at the Two Bells, proved to be more helpful. Yes, Jason had been in the night the woman had been killed, but earlier, long before the victim had returned. "He wasn't there for long," he told Mike. "I did see him talking to her a few days before that. But at the bar, as part of a group, you know. Casual. I didn't get the impression they were friends or anything."

"Mrs Beal mentioned he was back here a couple of days ago."

Harry was curious now. This was obviously more than casual questioning. "I don't remember that," he said. "But I was over serving in the marquee, so I probably wouldn't have seen."

Marquee, Mike thought, glancing at the large gazebo that had been set up as a cooking area and the second one that offered a shaded place to sit and eat.

"Boss tells me you lot might be moving up to the community centre," Harry said.

"Probably, yes."

"Well, you'll be wanting food and such. Want me to see about opening the kitchen? We do for events and that, so . . ."

Mike smiled and said he'd let Harry know. It would, he thought, probably be a good idea, but they'd not progressed that far yet. The post-mortem examination of Tom Pollard was scheduled for later that day. After that he'd know if suspicious death number two would become a fully-fledged murder enquiry.

CHAPTER 31

A search of domestic premises is never invisible or subtle. There is nothing unobtrusive about a scientific support vehicle parked in a cul-de-sac, or the accompanying police cars, and Katie Matthews could not remember a time when she had felt angrier or more embarrassed. She was furious with her husband for having brought this down on her head and even more furious because she didn't fully understand the cause of it.

"Dog hairs? You're looking for dog hairs?"

The police officer shrugged. "Among other things," he said. "Please, Mrs Matthews, if you just let us get on with it . . ."

"I don't understand what the fuck you're doing here!" She was incandescent now. She'd have to go fetch the kids and they'd see the police car. The neighbours were already rubbernecking. What had he done to her, to their family? Abruptly Katie Matthews made a decision. She slammed the keys down on her kitchen table. "There you go," she told the officer. "You bloody lock up after yourselves. I'm picking my kids up from school and I'm going to my father's, if anybody is interested. I take it I'm allowed to do that?"

The officer looked discomfited. He had been given no specific instructions about Katie Matthews. The husband had not been there when they'd arrived and she claimed to have no idea where he was.

"I need your father's address," he said, "and I'm afraid you can't take your car."

"I can't do what? What's my car got to do with it?"

"I'm sorry, Mrs Matthews, but the warrants are for both cars and for the house, and in particular your husband's office." He frowned. "By the way, what happened in his office?"

Katie Matthews just glared at him. It was still in a state from when she'd ransacked the place looking for evidence of an affair, but she wasn't about to tell this snot-nosed young constable that. "I take it I can call a taxi?"

"We would rather you remained here while we were searching. It *is* your right to remain."

"Well fuck that, and fuck you," she told him.

The officer blinked, a look of grave annoyance crossing his face, but he decided to let it go. He'd heard worse. "I'm afraid I have to ask for your mobile phone," he said as she removed it from her bag, ready to call the taxi.

"You what?" Angrily she slammed the mobile down on the table and emptied the contents of her bag on top of it. "So you'd better call the taxi for me then, or better still call my father."

The officer eyed the mess on the table, the mix of purse, cosmetics and receipts and all the debris that women, in his experience, always seemed to carry around with them. "I can do that for you," he said calmly. "Now if you could just give me the number?"

Katie glared at him. In many ways it would have been easier if he hadn't been so damn polite. She wanted him to shout, to be rude, to treat her like a criminal, because that was the way she felt just now. But he and the female officer with him had been very calm and very polite and somehow that made it worse. Angrily she wiped away the tears that she found were streaming down her face and she managed to choke out the number. Her dad would come and rescue them. Her dad had never approved of her marriage anyway. So what if she had to walk out with nothing? He would sort it for her and besides, Katie just didn't care anymore.

CHAPTER 32

A message arrived from the diocesan office. The little grave in the yard of St Michael and All Angels should not have been there. No record of it existed and the bishop announced himself to be concerned.

Putting aside the reverend's concern, Mike went to talk to his boss. Phone calls were made, discussions held, and an hour later an agreement had been reached and a time set. The child's grave, for that was what everyone now assumed it must be, would be exhumed. No one had said it out loud but the word that hung in the air was murder. Why else would a child be buried illegally in a remote churchyard?

"It shows remorse, I'd say," his superintendent asserted.

Mike nodded. "John Tynan is certain that his mother knew about it," he said quietly.

"Maybe she did; that doesn't mean she was directly involved. Do you think he'll object to giving a DNA sample? We'll need something for comparison, always assuming we can recover anything from the body."

"We don't *have* a body, yet," Mike pointed out, but it seemed like a fallacious comment. What else could be buried there?

* * *

Mike was late back that evening. John's car was outside and for a moment, Mike felt resentful. He had a lot on his mind, and wanted time to relax and leave the business of the day behind. Not that it ever turned out that way. He tried not to bring his work home with him, but . . .

He thrust the irritation aside almost as soon as it arose. John was always ready to listen to him and, truthfully, he was always happy to see his friend. The real problem was that it meant telling him about the call from the bishop's office, that the grave was going to be exhumed and whatever was buried there, whatever the story behind it, would now be exposed.

Maria met him at the door. "John's here."

"I saw the car."

"He went to the house. Jerry's house. He's brought some things over. He seems a bit . . . upset."

Mike sighed. "I don't think I'm going to improve his mood."

He went through into the living room. John sat in one of the fireside chairs, a full mug cradled in his hands. Mike could see that the tea had gone cold — a shadowy skin had formed on the top. John was not usually one to let his tea go cold, not since he had retired at any rate.

He looked up, and Mike was suddenly struck by how old he was looking. John was a man with more than his fair share of lines on his face, but they had deepened these past days, crumpling his features. There was nothing for it. He sat down and told John about the grave, the exhumation, the mystery. John merely nodded. He had expected as much. Yes, he would give the sample for the DNA. No, he would not be staying for supper, he needed to be getting home.

"Stay," Mike said. "John, you look all in."

"I am," John admitted. "The trouble with walking down memory lane is that it's so bloody far." He managed a small, unconvincing smile. "I need to get to my bed. Have a good night's sleep. The world will look better in the morning."

"You think he'll be all right?" Maria asked as they watched him drive away."

"No," Mike said. "I think it will be some time before John is all right again."

* * *

Miles away at the Willows, one-time home of Ernest Matthews, a soft sigh seem to echo through the house as outside, a large black dog padded through the garden.

CHAPTER 33

John finally slid the key into his lock. It had seemed to take a long time to drive home. The twenty minutes or so from Mike's place seemed to have stretched for an eternity, as though he was driving through treacle. He had dreams like that occasionally, in which he ran as fast as he could with as much effort as possible and yet his legs felt impossibly heavy and his destination further away with every step.

All he really wanted to do now was sleep. Maria had insisted he have a late lunch when he had first turned up that afternoon, and had plied him with strong coffee and then less strong tea, but he knew he should eat something now and not just give in and take to his bed.

He paused in the kitchen doorway and glanced at the clock. Twenty past eight, that was all, the sun still bright in the evening sky. Sighing, John filled the kettle for tea he didn't want and rummaged in the fridge for food he wasn't hungry for, eventually settling on cheese and crackers because everything else was too complicated. The box of possessions Billy had brought over sat on the shelf below the kitchen window, nestling beside Grace's well-thumbed collection of recipe books. John glared at it and was suddenly doubly thankful that he had left the assortment of objects he had taken from his grandfather's house with Mike and Maria.

Jerry's little bundle of assorted memories he had just about managed to stomach, but to bring anything of his grandfather's into his own home was something he could not face. Ernest Matthews, John felt, had contaminated everything he touched with his coldness and cruelty, and he was damned if he'd bring that contamination here.

With a wry smile, John realised that he'd had no such qualms about contaminating the home of his dearest friends — but then, Ernest Matthews, dead or alive, would be no match for Maria.

* * *

A few miles away, Mike poked at the objects Maria had laid out on the table. The papers smelt of damp and mould and felt cold to the touch, even though they'd now spent several hours in a warm house. The photographs were foxed and creased — not creased in the way Mike's precious picture of his son had been, from much carrying and handling. These had never been treasured in an album or protected in a frame. Rather, they'd simply been shoved at the back of a drawer and forgotten, years of other junk shoved in on top, crushing and mangling them.

Why keep them if they were so unwanted and unconsidered? Mike presumed they had simply been forgotten.

"Do we know what all of this is?" he asked Maria.

"Um, no, not really. John asked me for a bin bag, went back out to his car, dumped the contents of his boot in it and then stood staring at it like it might bite."

"So . . ."

"So I took it away, fed and watered him, as you do when someone is upset, and told him maybe we'd take a look first."

"But we don't even know what we're looking for," Mike said.

"No, but then neither does he, I suspect. Mike, I think he dared himself to go to the house, dared himself again to go into his grandfather's room, grabbed what he could and then lost his nerve."

Mike looked sceptical. "I've never known John to run away from anything."

"You saw how he was today."

"True." Today, John had looked old and defeated and yes, now Mike thought about it, scared. Scared in the way that a child might be scared, not thinking about why or from where the fear emanated, not reasoning, just responding. It disturbed Mike a great deal that his friend should feel this way. What had this man done, this Ernest Matthews, that even now he created this pall of terror and dread?

"OK," he said, "let's at least sort them out. Photographs in one pile, papers in another and then we'll subdivide the papers according to what we find."

Maria nodded. As plans went it was pretty simple, but it was a start. She made more coffee and for the next fifteen minutes or so they simply sifted the contents of the black plastic bag first into two piles and then, as it became obvious that the paperwork was a mix of bills, letters and other documents, further subdividing and then finally sorting them into some kind of date order.

"So, what do we have?" Maria sniffed delicately. "My nose is full of the smell of mice and damp. If it was anyone else I'd have chucked the whole lot outside."

"I'll find a box in a minute," Mike said, "and some manila envelopes so we can separate things out. Then we'll put it in the shed. Anything John wants to keep, we can disinfect."

They had laid out dustbin bags on the table to protect the surface and donned pairs of thin rubber gloves but the smell of mice and damp was pervasive. "Well, there's a stack of utility bills and bank statements, but they are all for Ernest Matthews, so we can probably put those aside for now." But curiosity winning, he flicked through the bank statements and found regular credits for a pension and direct debits for bills. In addition, there seemed to be a savings account which contained just under £8000. He presumed that Jerry must've inherited that after his father's death. He pushed the stack to one side and picked up another. "From what I can see, these are letters, mostly from one sibling to another, and a few birthday cards for John's mother, Gloria." Mike skimmed them briefly and assessed them as things which might be of interest. "Some of these letters seem to be from Eric when he first joined the merchant navy," he said. "I think John said that he kept in touch for a time before he completely dropped off the planet."

"And the rest of this miscellaneous bunch?" Maria frowned at the papers she was holding. "OK, I have shopping lists, there's a little accounts book and there are some solicitor's letters. It looks as though Jerry thought about selling some of the land at one point."

"I think John said that the house was put up for sale after Jerry went into the home but that there had been no takers. John thought that he might have put restrictions on use or something. So those letters might be of interest."

"Though not tonight," Maria said. "Frankly, I'm finding this all very depressing." She flicked in a desultory fashion through the photographs and then stacked them together again with a sigh. "Find that box and those envelopes and let's just put this lot away for the night. It will be fine in the shed."

Mike nodded. It was almost as though John's distress had transferred to them, that they too felt something of Ernest Matthews's presence come into their home, and now they wanted rid of it.

CHAPTER 34

It was the following morning before Katie Matthews finally got hold of her husband. Truth was, she hadn't tried too hard. She had been so angry with him the night before that she didn't much care what happened to him or where he was. The girls had asked, of course, but he had been so grumpy lately that they seemed relatively unconcerned, and anyway a few nights at Grandpa's house was always a treat. Katie knew that her mum and dad spoiled the girls rotten, but right now she was just grateful for a refuge and willing to put up with them having too much chocolate before bed.

The following morning, while her parents were getting the girls breakfast, she found a quiet corner in the summer-house and called Jason on an old phone that her father had given her to replace the one the police had taken. Jason hadn't called the house last night, though he would probably have guessed where she'd bolted to, and of course he couldn't call her mobile.

Katie felt utterly humiliated, and Jason was not going to get away with that.

He answered after about seven rings, sounding sleepy.

"Where are you?" Katie demanded.

"Slept over at Cam's. Why?" Cam was Jason's sister.

"The police were at our house. Your fault, Jason. I have never been so—"

"Nothing I did," he said. "Katie, I swear it's all that bloody woman's fault. I've done nothing wrong."

"So why were the police there? Looking for dog hairs, they said. What does that mean, Jason? What does that even mean?"

"I suppose," he said heavily, "that it means they were looking for dog hairs."

Katie blinked rapidly. He couldn't see that she was crying but he would know. She didn't want to give him the satisfaction. "Were you having an affair?"

"What, that again? God's sake, Katie, I told you. That woman turned up from nowhere looking for some kid. She reckoned she was a distant relative or something. I told you that."

"And your ex-girlfriend?"

"What ex-girlfriend?"

"I know it. You're seeing her again. You were on the rebound from her when we got together."

"Oh, for Chrissake. How long have we been together?"

Actually, Katie thought, she doubted he even knew. Jason always had to be reminded about anniversaries. "Have you been seeing her again?"

Jason sighed. "What does my old girlfriend have to do with the police coming to our house?"

Reluctantly, Katie had to admit he had a point. "So why were the police at our place? What were they looking for? And don't say dog hairs."

"In case you hadn't noticed, a woman was murdered. A woman that was stalking me not so long ago."

"Stalking you? Don't make me laugh. Why would anyone be stalking *you*? You said she was making a nuisance of herself, that's all. You said she'd got something to do with your family."

"So she told me, and I told her I didn't know anything."

"Do they think you killed her?" The thought occurred to her very suddenly.

Jason laughed harshly. "Fuck's sake, Katie, you do come out with some bollocks, you really do."

Katie took a very deep breath and then she said, "I'm leaving you. You know that, don't you?"

If she'd expected protests she was disappointed. "Yeah," Jason said, "I'd sort of figured that one out."

Katie stared at the phone. He had hung up on her. It occurred to her that he hadn't even asked about the girls. Her first instinct was to call him back. Instead, she chucked the phone onto a nearby chair and stared at it. Tears of grief, but mostly rage and anger and humiliation, poured down her cheeks. She was aware of footsteps, someone crossing the lawn and stepping onto the deck in front of the summerhouse.

"Oh, Katie." Her mother sat down on the bench at Katie's side and put her arms around her. "It's time for the school run. Your dad can take them, and when he gets back we'll sit down and work out what to do next."

"I'm going to take that bastard for everything he's got," Katie said, forgetting for a moment that most of what Jason had her father had paid for, or her father still owned.

CHAPTER 35

What to do next? Jason Matthews sat with the phone in his hand, wondering. He'd told the truth about staying at his sister's that night, not wanting to go home and face yet another row, but his sister had not actually been there. He knew she'd be away working but he had a spare key for emergencies, so he had let himself in and made up the bed in the spare room. He knew Cam wouldn't mind — it helped that she couldn't stand Katie — but it was hardly a long-term solution. He had, briefly, thought of going to stay with Amanda but common sense told him that if Katie found that out it would only make matters worse. It would also send a message to Amanda that he was thinking of committing to her, and at the moment that really wasn't on the cards.

This renewal of their relationship had been fun, but it was clear that Amanda was thinking in the long term and, frankly, Jason wasn't. He wasn't planning on leaving one long-term relationship just to plunge straight into another. Marrying Katie had been a big mistake, and there was more than an element of truth in what she said about him being on the rebound.

Whichever way you looked at it, he was well and truly screwed — unless he took action now and tried to sort things out. Two phone calls later, he had made up his mind. He got into his car and drove out to the police incident room.

* * *

Terry Gleeson plonked himself down opposite Mike and dumped a sheaf of papers on the desk. "Two witnesses," he said, "reckon they saw Tom Pollard on the beach last night. Both agree he was walking along and chucking stones in the water. Well, one said he was skimming them not very successfully, but same thing."

"At what time?"

"Between nine and ten. Nearest we can get is probably about nine thirty when the second witness saw him. Mrs Prichard. She was up on the cliff walking her dog. But there is a third witness, and this one is a bit more interesting. Reckons she saw the boy about half an hour later, by which time it was starting to get dark. But she is certain she saw him on the beach, and he was talking to someone."

"Any idea who?"

Terry shook his head. "That's about as helpful as it gets. The witness estimates that they were both about the same height. It was getting chilly by then, so whoever it was had a hoodie on and the hood was up."

"Convenient," Mike said bitterly. "And this was right down on the beach, you say. Anywhere near where he was found?"

"Between the same two breakwaters, the witness thinks, but admits she can't be certain. Again, she was up on the cliff and the only thing that makes her certain it was Tom was that she'd seen the boy before. She'd even spoken to him, just to say good evening, but she remembered him. She said he looked like a lost soul and she remembers wondering where he'd come from."

Mike nodded, wondering if this witness's reflection was really contemporaneous with that meeting or was simply the result of twenty-twenty hindsight, but whatever, he would

214

agree with the assessment. Tom Pollard had indeed looked like the lost soul that he was.

The main door swung open with a crash. Mike looked up and was very surprised to see Jason Matthews standing there, another man beside him.

Mike rose and crossed to greet him. "Mr Matthews, we've been hoping to talk to you."

"Katie says you searched our house. I've not been home."

"Your house was searched, yes. We invited your wife to be present but she preferred to go to her father's and take the girls with her. She said she didn't know where you were."

"As I said, I didn't go home, and I still haven't been there. We had another row and I went to my sister's. This is Mr Collins, my solicitor."

"Actually," Collins said, extending his hand for Mike to shake, "I'm one of the company solicitors but Jason and I are also friends, so when he phoned me . . ."

"Of course. We can appoint legal representation for you, should you need it," Mike said, turning to Jason. "Someone more familiar with criminal proceedings."

"I'm not going to need that," Jason said, "but I wanted an independent witness, and in any case, Rob here knows perfectly well what he's doing."

Mike considered the situation. "You could make a statement here if you wish, but I would prefer you to go back to police headquarters for a formal interview, under caution."

Jason glanced at Rob Collins, who nodded. "Do it by the book, Jase. Let's get this done with."

Jason shrugged. "Whatever. Let's do that, then, so you can go back to work and let me sort out the rest of the mess my life is in."

Collins and Jason Matthews left. Mike phoned headquarters to arrange for an interview room, spent a few minutes handing over to Jude and then followed them back to Wymondham. Jason Matthews seemed very confident. It made him uneasy.

* * *

The man in the dark coat had watched Jason Matthews arrive at the incident room. He had followed Jason from his sister's house that morning and was somewhat taken aback when the other man had joined him and the two had gone into the incident room together. He sat on the wall outside the school, enjoying the sunshine and waiting to see what would happen next until, unexpectedly, Jason Matthews and his friend left after only a few minutes. They got in their respective cars and drove off, so he took a leisurely stroll back to his own car and activated the tracker that he had fixed onto Jason's some three or four weeks before. He hadn't anticipated that they'd head towards Wymondham, and was even more surprised to see Mike Croft emerge from the incident room a few minutes later, fetch his own car and drive away.

"Curiouser and curiouser. So what is going on now in the life of Mr Jason Matthews?" He wondered if the beautiful Amanda had anything to do with this. She certainly seemed to have been the prime motivator behind many of Jason's actions this past month.

* * *

Mike arrived at Wymondham to find that the post-mortem results on Tom Pollard had already been sent over. The report had been rushed through the evening before, Superintendent Reece informed him. It had been prioritised on the grounds that if it was certain that Tom had been murdered, they would need to increase the size of their team, and Reece wanted to get that set in motion as quickly as possible.

"It's a little more complicated than that," Reece told him. "There were large quantities of alcohol in the boy's stomach, and not much in the way of food. Blood-alcohol levels were twice the legal level for driving. There are scrapes and bruises on his legs as though he'd fallen over something, no defensive wounds and the blow to the head could just as easily have been caused by a fall. He was found close to one of the breakwaters, I believe?"

"Not close enough that I'd have said he had fallen, but the tide could have moved him, so . . ." Mike shrugged.

"So we hold fire and see what this Jason Matthews has to say. With luck, it'll be a confession to both murders, we can tie everything up with a nice neat ribbon and that will be that."

Mike laughed. "Now wouldn't that be nice. Though something tells me it's not going to be that simple."

"I can dream, can't I?" Reece said. He handed the post-mortem report over to Mike and wandered off.

Mike took a few minutes to look at the report in more detail. It made for sad reading. The boy had consumed a lot of cheap cider, he'd eaten chips, but these were mostly digested, so his final meal had been much earlier in the day. Mike didn't need telling that he was skinny and underweight but it saddened him all the same. What chance did this poor little scrap have? It was no wonder that, when this Martha woman held out the possibility of something better, Tom had practically snatched her hand off. He had probably been willing to do just about anything if it meant a change in his fortunes.

Had her motives been purely cynical? Mike wondered. The things he was learning about her did not square with the woman John Tynan had become fond of. She was obviously multifaceted, complex, capable of fooling someone as experienced as Mike's old friend, a man as astute as any Mike had ever met. And she had inveigled her way into the lives of others, who had left her property and money and regarded her as a valued friend, valued enough that they had been willing to cut their own families out of their wills. On the one hand it indicated manipulation. On the other? Mike really wasn't sure.

Jason Matthews and his solicitor friend had been put in one of the interview rooms, given coffee and left to stew. Mike decided he'd probably kept them waiting long enough, and went in.

* * *

217

Mike settled himself in a chair opposite Jason and the solicitor, having introduced himself and the sergeant he had brought with him, for the recording.

Jason Matthews seemed restless and ill at ease, but then so are most people in interview rooms, Mike thought. But there was a pent-up energy about Jason that didn't seem the same as the usual nervousness he observed in those accused of crimes.

Mike was about to tell him this would be an interview under caution and as such might be admissible as evidence, but he never got that far.

Jason Matthews exchanged a swift glance with his solicitor and then announced, "I have an alibi for the night she died. I was with someone and she's going to come into the station and tell you so. I've been seeing someone. Having an affair. I was with her that night. Her name is Amanda Levinson and she is going to vouch for me."

Mike was a little taken aback but he gathered his wits quickly and said, "And yet you were seen at the Two Bells, alone, earlier that evening."

Jason nodded vigorously. "I called in for a drink. I was hoping *she'd* be there because I was going to tell her that she could tell my wife anything she bloody liked. I was going to tell Katie myself, tell her it was all over between us and I was moving out. So I went to the Bells and asked if she was there, but she was out for the evening, or so the barman said. He reckoned he'd seen her leaving with someone around seven o'clock, and she had told the Beals she was having dinner somewhere."

No one had mentioned this, even though Harry Pickson remembered Jason Matthews being at the pub. "Which one of the bar staff did you ask?"

"I don't know his name — that young kid that helps out a couple of nights a week, not Harry and not the Beals."

Mike made a note to follow this up. "And this woman you are having the affair with? We need all her details, obviously. What time did you meet her?"

"Eight thirty. We met at the Lifeboat, a pub just ten minutes down the road. They do food. We had a drink, something to eat, went back to her place and I spent the night. I've been seeing her for a while now. I was with her before I was with Katie. Amanda came back about eighteen months or so ago, we met up and, well, things developed, you might say."

"And the woman you knew as Julia Matthews, she knew about this?"

Jason nodded. "She found out. She threatened to tell my wife, and my wife's father. She wanted money."

Mike raised an eyebrow. "Are you saying she was black-mailing you?"

"She was trying," Jason Matthews said. "OK, I'll admit I paid up a couple of times. I wasn't . . . I wasn't ready for the flak right then, it would have made things difficult. But then as time went on and things changed, I decided, what the hell, she could do what she liked. It was over between Katie and me anyway, bar the shouting, and there's been plenty of that lately. So I decided I was going to tell her that I was sick of the whole thing and she could tell who she liked, because I was going to come clean anyway."

"You have to admit that the timing was convenient," Mike said. "You decide to confront this woman on the very night she died. Perhaps you came back later. Can anyone else vouch for you?"

Jason Matthews sighed impatiently, opened his mouth, barely biting back some facetious comment or other. He shook his head. "Look, I'm telling you, Amanda will. We left the Lifeboat at closing time and drove back to her place. We got back there eleven thirty-ish. Her next-door neighbour saw us arriving and Amanda stopped to have a few words with him. Apparently she had taken in a parcel a couple of days before, and this was the first chance she'd had to give it to him. He came up to her flat, she gave him the parcel, we stood chatting in the hall for a few minutes, and he must have left us about midnight or just after. Amanda will probably remember better than I do and Giorgio, the neighbour, will no doubt know. Amanda and I had a drink, watched a bit of telly and then went to bed. She'll vouch for the fact that I was definitely there, if you get my meaning."

"You say you paid this Julia Matthews a couple of times. How much was she asking for?"

Jason Matthews looked abashed. "I paid her five grand in total. Look, I know it was stupid. Then I realised that I'd be paying for the rest of my natural if I didn't do something about it — and I don't mean kill her. Like I said, Katie and I were done but I needed a bit of time before I chucked everything in. Now, it doesn't matter."

"And why is that, Mr Matthews?"

Again Jason Matthews glanced at his solicitor, who had so far been silent, merely adding the odd note to the jotter in front of him. "I've got another job," Jason said. "I'm sick to death of working for the family — Katie's family. I've more than earned my pay, but all I get is constant reminders about how much I owe them, and a man can only put up with that for so long. I needed time to negotiate the new contract, get it signed off. Dig my escape tunnel, if you like. That woman turned up just at the wrong moment, so I paid her. I'm not proud of it, but I needed a way out, and if that meant paying her to keep out of my hair, then that's what I did."

"Must be one hell of a job if it was worth paying some woman you claim hardly to know to keep quiet, just in case it made a few waves."

"Oh, believe me, it is. Twice what I'm on at the moment and a bit of recognition for the work I've done. They know my wife is not willing to move with me, that our marriage is all but over, and they're fine with it. I saw a solicitor yesterday afternoon and everything's been set in motion. We'll be getting a divorce and, as far as I'm concerned, she's welcome to the bloody lot."

"And does this Amanda feature in your future plans?" Mike asked.

Jason fidgeted, looked awkward. "Probably not," he admitted.

"Something she is probably not aware of?" Mike suggested. "Maybe you want to keep her onside while you still need her for your alibi."

"She *is* my alibi. Look, I'm not proud of any of this. You can judge me how the hell you like, but I did not kill that woman. I wanted her out of my way, and the best way I could think of doing that was to pay her off."

There was a pause. All of them seemed to be reflecting.

Mike said, "When I spoke to you before, you said she thought you might have fathered her grandchild."

"And I told you I never knew her daughter." Jason brightened slightly. "But I do remember the name she gave. I got to thinking about it after you'd gone. She said her daughter's name was Emma or Emily Dawson. She said she'd been adopted, but I know nothing about any of that. Like I told you, she was a flaming nutcase."

There was a gentle knock on the door and a constable handed Mike a note. Amanda Levinson was in reception and asking to see him.

Mike folded the note and tucked it into his pocket. "I spoke to the Beals yesterday," he said. "Mrs Beal said that you had been walking on the beach and went to buy a burger from their stand. She said you were speaking to one of the journalists. What was that about, Mr Matthews?"

Jason Matthews looked blank, and then his expression cleared. "Oh, right. Yes, I stopped off at the burger van and we had a bit of a chat. There was some bloke in the car park. I spoke to him too, but I don't think he was a journalist." He frowned and then said awkwardly, "Actually, I've seen that bloke around quite a bit lately. I don't know what his game is. He was on the beach one day, and Amanda and I went out for a meal a few nights ago and there he was again, table opposite us."

"And you don't think he's a journalist? Why is that?"

"He doesn't act like one, and besides, I think I've spotted him around before all this happened. He looks kind of familiar."

"Can you give us a description of this man?"

"I don't know. Just a man. Medium height, greying hair, middle-aged, not heavily built or anything. I really only noticed him because he was wearing a dark suit jacket on the beach, which seemed like, a bit odd. I'm not a big fan of the jeans and a suit jacket school of dressing. It looks like you can't commit one way or the other." He gave a slight nervous chuckle.

Mike nodded, aware that the description was familiar in some way. He said, "Miss Levinson is in the reception area. I will go and have a word with her, and then we'll decide how to proceed."

Jason Matthews sat back in his chair and crossed his arms over his chest. He looked pleased with himself.

Mike looked away. Self-satisfied bastard.

* * *

"And did his alibi check out?" Maria asked. Mike was cooking this evening, and she was perched on a stool, glass of wine in hand, watching him with interest as he chopped peppers and mushrooms.

"Unfortunately, yes, and unless both this Amanda Levinson and her neighbour are lying on Jason Matthews's behalf, he was nowhere near the Two Bells at the time of the murder. Which puts him on the back burner but doesn't completely rule him out, as far as I'm concerned."

"And so what now?"

"Well, tomorrow, Jude and I are going to see the real Martha Toolin and her grandson, and see what they can tell us in terms of background. Plus what else this woman who called herself Julia Matthews, along with every other bloody thing, might have done to upset other people along the way. There are a number of families who consider themselves to have been done out of their inheritance and who won't be well-wishers. And if she was given to blackmail, who knows who else she might have tried it on with."

"Any way you look at it, it's back to square one," Maria observed.

"True, and there's nothing definitive on Tom Pollard either. Did he fall? Was he pushed? Was he facing someone and they hit him on the temple with a rock?"

"Which is going to imply that he knew them, I suppose."

"Apart from the fact that he was so blind drunk he wouldn't have recognised his own grandmother if she'd taken a swing at him." Not that the boy had actually known his grandmother, Mike remembered. Tom had been an abandoned baby and then an abandoned child.

"Has John called today?" he asked.

"No. He sent me a text giving me the time of the exhumation, just in case I could make it. I feel a bit bad, but I can't take any more time off, not if both of us are going to go over to see Josie after this is done and dusted. I told him I'd try, but I think his cousin Billy is going with him, so he's not going to be on his own."

Nodding, Mike added chopped onion to the mix of peppers and mushrooms, remembering belatedly that he really should have cooked the onion first. "I still have the feeling Jason Matthews is hiding something," he said. "No, it's more that he's so crooked he has to screw his hat on, but that might not have anything at all to do with this Julia Matthews or Anne Hargreaves or whatever her name is. I suppose we have to make up our minds what to call her," he added. He realised suddenly that he was pinning a lot on his meeting with the real Martha Toolin, hoping she could fill in some of the gaps. "You know what surprises me — I mean surprises me most of all?"

"That John was taken in by her?" Maria said. "John might be getting older, but he's no fool. He liked her but then from what you tell me, so did a lot of other people. She seems to have been a real Jekyll and Hyde."

Mike crushed garlic and then chopped the chillies. She was right. John was no fool, so what did that make this Julia Matthews woman? An expert con artist or someone who got lucky? Her attempts to blackmail Jason Matthews seemed crude and opportunistic, whereas everything else they knew about her appeared to have been planned and careful. He stirred the vegetables in the pan and then added tomatoes and red kidney beans. He paused. "Er, did we have some leftover lamb from that joint the other day?"

"This is meant to be vegetarian chilli. It's veggie day, remember?"

"It's a veggie base," he argued.

Maria sighed. "Go on, then. I'll check the rice."

That night, Mike dreamed about the dog again. This time it was walking beside him along the beach, and his son and the shadowy figure of Tom Pollard sat on a breakwater, watching as he advanced towards them. Again the dream was peaceful and on waking, the alarm sounding in his ears, Mike remembered that his son was smiling.

CHAPTER 36

There was a slightly muted atmosphere at the morning briefing. Disappointment that a suspect had an alibi was inevitable. Jason Matthews had seemed such a logical and easy possibility.

Mike knew that somewhere in the back of his mind he knew or remembered the man Jason had been talking to and that both he and Mrs Beal had described, so he put it to the team in the hope that somebody's memory would be jogged. He was rewarded when Terry reminded Mike of the man who had come in to report having seen the dead woman as a passenger in the little brown car they now knew belonged to Tom Pollard. The description matched that of the man in the dark jacket. Mike remembered now.

"Follow it up," he instructed. "We've got his address — hopefully it's genuine. And keep your eyes open for him. He seems to be hanging around, taking a little too much interest in our comings and goings." They were all well aware of the theory that offenders like to observe and perhaps even insert themselves into the investigation in some way. Mike had never had it happen to him personally, but there was always a first time.

There were two other developments. The hairs found at Jason Matthews's home and in his car were a forensic match for those found on the dead woman's clothing in her room.

A check on Jason Matthews's banking activity showed sums to the value of £5000 being transferred into another account, but the name on that account was neither Martha Toolin nor Julia Matthews, or any variation they were so far aware of. The recipient was someone called Mary Tealby — probably another alias to chase down. Jason Matthews had been asked about the bank transfer but had informed the police that all he had been given was an account number and sort code.

Tom Pollard's little car had now been found. It turned up parked in a side road a couple of miles from the village, and it was perfectly conceivable that Tom had left it there and then walked back towards the village along the beach. He had probably intended to return to his car later, but sadly that had not happened. CSI were currently on scene.

By ten o'clock, Mike and Jude were on their way to meet the real Martha Toolin and her grandson.

"You think Jason Matthews's alibi is for real?" Jude asked. "I don't know . . . there's just something not right about it."

"I agree," Mike said. "His alibi seems solid but there are things he's not telling us, I'm certain. Whether or not they have anything to do with the case is a moot point right now. Amanda Levinson is quite convinced that she is the next Mrs Matthews, and I think Jason is equally convinced that she is not. I did suggest to her that perhaps he was stringing her along, but she is adamant that he loves her and has left his wife to be with her. And while she believes that, there will be no shaking the alibi."

"Perhaps now you've planted the seed?"

"I think that depends on how Mr Matthews handles things," Mike said. "She's an intelligent and successful woman, so far as I can tell, but even intelligent and successful women believe what they want to believe when it comes to romance. And, yes, I do know men are no better."

"You're thinking about Mr Tynan."

"I'm thinking about Mr Tynan. John is a shrewd operator but he liked this woman. She was funny and friendly and intelligent and good company."

"And basically, that's all anyone is looking for in a long-term relationship," Jude observed. "I mean, the romance and the sex is also important — you've got to be attracted to somebody, after all, but when that's worn off a bit and the gloss is gone, you want a friend, don't you?"

Mike laughed, but nodded. "I guess you also hope the romance will continue. And the sex, of course."

Jude chortled. "Well, well, Inspector Croft. Who would have imagined? I've got a preliminary list of items found in Tom Pollard's car," she added, pulling a sheet of paper from her bag. "Mr Tynan mentioned a couple of things that were missing. The blue book and a photograph and a couple of other things, I think."

Mike nodded. "He said there was an address book?"

"No address book on the list, but there is a blue book with notes in it and a photograph of a young woman and child, and a couple of other similar bits."

"We'll get him in to take a look," Mike said. "Was there anything written on the back of the photograph?" he asked, suddenly remembering something John had said, and wondering if the picture was the same one.

"Um, yes. It said Silvia, spelt with an i, not a y and a date. 1947. And it also had another name, written in pencil and a bit faded, like somebody had tried to rub it out. It looks like it might have been Isobel."

Mike nodded. Isobel Jones. The woman named on the birth certificate. Jerry had been the father and this Isobel Jones had been the mother.

* * *

The real Martha Toolin's house was on the edge of the village, set back from the road and approached through an attractive front garden surrounded by a low picket fence. The abundance of summer flowers reminded Mike of his own house, and he found himself disposed to like this woman he had not yet met.

The door was opened by a man who introduced himself as Toby Merrifield, Martha Toolin's grandson. He led them through to a terrace at the back of the house, where an elderly woman sat in a garden chair, a cup of tea between her hands. She looked frail but the intensity and intelligence in her eyes told Mike that this was only physical.

Introductions were made and refreshments brought out and set on a low table at Martha Toolin's side.

"It's nice to finally meet the original version," Jude said.

Martha Toolin nodded sagely. "It isn't the only time she has pretended to be me. The first time, she ran up a number of debts. That was years ago, of course, but it caused a lot of problems at the time. Fortunately I am well-off and well-connected enough that I could bring the correct forces to bear on the situation and get it all sorted out, but I've often wondered how many other people she did it to. That, of course, was almost the last straw, after which we all refused to have anything more to do with her. But perhaps I'd better start at the beginning, rather than at the end of our relationship. I have to say that for a long time I was very fond of that young woman. I wanted to help her and I thought that I really had made a difference, but sadly she proved that she really was capable of biting the hand that fed her. Not just *my* hand. There comes a time when you have to cut your losses and let go, however painful that is, and believe me, it was painful."

"There was nothing more you could have done, Grandma. She had caused enough chaos in our lives by then." Toby turned to Jude and Mike. "I was very young then, but I do remember that that woman almost caused our family to break up, and I doubt we are the only family she affected."

Mike sipped his lemonade, savouring the sharp flavour. It was a long time since he'd last had it homemade. "I believe you first became involved when she was in court?"

Martha Toolin nodded. "Anne Hargreaves was only a teenager then, eighteen or nineteen, I believe. She had been caught shoplifting baby clothes. My husband was a magistrate and I belonged to a voluntary organisation for the rehabilitation of prisoners. We arranged what you'd now call work placements, I suppose, and I heard about this young woman. The police officer who arrested her contacted social services, learned something of her background and I suppose knew that I was always on the lookout for another good cause." She laughed self-deprecatingly. "Anyway, I became involved. The social workers stated that there were mitigating circumstances, these were accepted by the court and I arranged for her to be released to a mother and baby home that I was involved in running. It was a charity and I was on the board. I seemed to be on the board of every damn thing back then. Anyway, a place was found for her, and the long and the short of it was, the baby was born and adopted."

"So she didn't keep her daughter?" Jude asked. "We'd been assuming that the child was still with her."

"Oh no, a private adoption was arranged, the parents collected the baby and that was that."

"Did she want to give the child up for adoption?" Jude asked.

"My dear, what else was she supposed to do? The wastrel of a man that she had been living with had disappeared at the first sign of pregnancy, her parents were a dead loss, she had no one. How was she supposed to raise a child? She knew her baby would be going to a good family."

"And there was no contact afterwards?" Jude persisted.

"Well, not in those days. Of course, the law changed not long after that, allowing children to access their records when they reached eighteen, but the mothers didn't have the right to make first contact, and as far as I'm concerned that was a good thing. Girls made mistakes, and the best thing that could happen was that they had that mistake sorted out and could get on with their lives."

Toby shifted uncomfortably in his chair and Mike guessed that he probably wasn't in total agreement with his rather forceful grandmother. He cast a glance in Jude's direction. Enough was enough for now. "You kept in touch with this Anne Hargreaves afterwards?

"I did, yes. And I wish I could say that I kept her out of trouble. We found her a job and a place to live and all seemed to be well for a while, and then one day she didn't turn up for work. She'd disappeared. I heard nothing from her until about three years later. By that time she was calling herself Julia Matthews, Lord knows why. She told me at the time that she simply wanted a change, to make a fresh start, but from what I gathered afterwards it seems that perhaps she had, shall we say, purloined somebody else's identity. Of course, at the time I had no idea."

"And how did you make contact?" Mike said.

"Well, she ended up in trouble, shoplifting again I think, but it's a very long time ago. Anyway, when she was arrested she gave my name as next of kin. Of course I explained that that wasn't the case, but I did what I could for the girl. With hindsight, it might have been better if she'd gone through the process and ended up inside for a while — short sharp shock and all that. But once again I stepped in and did what I could. I found her a place in a hostel, paid for what she had stolen and persuaded the shop not to press charges and hoped that would be the end of it. It wasn't, of course. Oh, she tried, I think. She would hold down a job for a while and would seem to be settled, and then off she'd go again, and then, of course, turn up once more like the proverbial bad penny."

"What was she like?" Mike asked. "According to people who have got to know her recently, she was intelligent and amiable and good company."

The real Martha Toolin looked thoughtful. She nodded slowly. "She could be all of those things, and more. And then she could be spiteful and angry and aggressive. The thing was, she could turn on a sixpence. You never quite knew what you were going to get. I don't think she knew either. I suspect it was out of her control. Nowadays of course she'd probably be diagnosed with borderline personality disorder or some such. I don't hold much truck with all of these psychological analyses, this need to put labels on everybody."

"Gran." Toby's voice was gently reproving. "A lot more is understood about the human mind now, you know that. Sometimes this 'labelling', as you call it, can be really useful in getting people the right kind of help."

"And sometimes, Toby, all it means is that people get off too lightly. You have to take responsibility for your own actions. You know that as well as I do, and this girl never did, no matter what allowances people made for her."

"You said she stole your identity," Mike said, feeling the need to change the direction of the conversation. "That she used your name?"

"She did indeed. She stole documents from my house which enabled her to open a bank account in my name. Of course, it was easier to do that back then. She then stole a cheque from a very dear friend, forged her signature and paid that cheque, made out for a considerable sum of money, into the account. It was some time before I realised what had happened — it was only when the friend noticed that this money had gone out of her bank account and we managed eventually to track it down. But as you can imagine, it took a lot of dealing with, a lot of keeping quiet, and in the meantime Anne Hargreaves had been spending money left, right and centre, and signing up for credit agreements she couldn't possibly hope to repay."

"Why not just report it?" Jude asked.

Martha Toolin's look was frosty. "Because, my dear, I did not want my friend's name dragged through the courts. We used our contacts to hush things up, I suppose you'd say. You do not drag respectable people with respectable names through the mud just because some young wastrel has taken advantage of them."

Mike could see that Jude was itching to say more but he didn't think it would be helpful, so he quickly said, "And that was your last contact with her?"

Martha Toolin pursed her lips. "Not quite. She suddenly turned up one day, out of the blue. Toby was five years old at the time. My housekeeper opened the door and Anne, or Julia, or whatever she was calling herself by then, just marched in. She took Toby by the hand and declared that she had come to collect her child."

"*Her* child?" Mike and Jude said in unison.

"Her *stolen* child — or so she said. Absurd, of course, on so many levels. Least of all that her child was a girl and was born years before Toby. Anyway, we did call the police then and she was sectioned shortly afterwards, I believe. That is the last time I had any dealings with her."

"She must have been grieving for her own baby," Jude said quietly.

"That woman would have been a totally unfit mother," Martha Toolin declared. "What could she have offered a child? As it was, her baby at least had a chance." She sighed and shook her head, "Though blood will out, as they say."

"I'm not sure I understand," Mike said. "Did something happen to her daughter?"

"To the child that she had given up for adoption, you mean? Sadly, yes, which just goes to show you can do everything in your power and still . . ."

"My grandmother stayed in touch with the adoptive family," Toby explained. "They were known to our family, you see, so she knew how Emily was doing and what happened, and I happen to think it's deeply sad." His reproving tone was aimed at his grandmother, who huffed irritably.

"Emily Dawson killed herself when she was seventeen," she said coldly. "The family gave her everything they could, did everything for her, sent her to therapy or whatever you call it and spent a small fortune trying to put things right, but in the end there was nothing they could do."

"Emily was anorexic," Toby said. "She spent some time as an inpatient and seemed to be making progress. She was allowed home for a weekend, but at some point she left the house, walked to a nearby railway bridge and threw herself off in front of an oncoming train."

Jude gasped. "Oh my God! Poor little thing."

"Her family were devastated," Toby said. "They had tried everything, and they really did love her." He shook his head sadly. "Teenagers can be so impulsive. Everything is felt so acutely, isn't it, when you are that age, and sometimes a decision taken in a moment can be enough. Caroline, Emily's adoptive mother, still blames herself. She keeps asking what would've happened if she had noticed a few minutes sooner that Emily had gone. Emily had been sitting with the family, watching television and laughing at some comedy. She went to the kitchen to get a glass of water, and it could only have been five minutes or so before they realised that she had gone. But by that time it was too late. It was only a ten-minute walk to the bridge."

They sat in silence for a few moments, not quite knowing what to say, until eventually Mike said, "Did Emily know she had been adopted?"

"She did, yes," Martha Toolin said. "She and her siblings had all been adopted. She had two brothers, one older and one younger, and they had all been told as soon as they were old enough to understand."

"You didn't approve?" Mike asked.

She shook her head. "I thought they had been told too young."

"Inspector, I don't think that was a factor, if that's what you're driving at," Toby said. "The children always knew and, frankly, it wouldn't have taken much working out. They looked nothing like either parent, and nothing like one another. No one believes that had anything to do with what happened to Emily. I've spent my life working with young people and sometimes—"

"What do you do?" Jude asked him.

"I'm a paediatric psychologist," he said.

Jude nodded. Mike sensed that she was not as impressed as Toby hoped she'd be.

"Anne — Julia — knew that her daughter had been called Emily Dawson, yet she was convinced Emily Dawson was a granddaughter. Does that make any sense to you?" Mike asked.

"How would it make any sense to me?" Martha sounded impatient. "I haven't seen the woman since, what, 1985? I don't know how she got hold of the name because none of *us* would have told her. There was certainly no grandchild. Poor little Emily was certainly not pregnant when she died in 1989. All I can think is that this was part of the same obsession, this same psychosis that made her believe that Toby was her child."

"But how would she have found out the name?" Mike asked.

Martha and Toby looked at one another and then back at Mike. "We've asked ourselves that same question many times," Toby said. "All we can think is that because it was a private adoption and, as we told you, my mother knew the family . . . perhaps she found out enough to make the connection."

"Was there anything to suggest that she had made contact?"

"If she did, then that's a secret Emily took with her to the grave," Martha said. "She left no note, she didn't keep a diary, she left her family with no explanation. The only thing she left behind was grief."

There seemed very little more to say after that. Mike left his card in case either of them remembered anything else, and he and Jude drove away. Mike felt oddly sullied by the experience. Criminals he could deal with. Self-righteous octogenarians were a little more difficult. Still, he knew that people became more set in their ideas over time, and he had no doubt that the *real* Martha Toolin fervently believed that her actions had all been right at the time — and, Mike supposed, in the context of the times she lived in, it could be argued that they had.

Jude was a little more direct in her observation. "Bitch. I wonder how many other lives she ruined?"

* * *

That evening, Mike and Jude briefed the team on what they had learned from the real Martha Toolin. It did nothing to lighten the mood or lift the sense of frustration engendered by the loss of Jason Matthews as a suspect.

"Toby Merrifield, the grandson, has provided us with some paperwork pertaining to the adoption and the mother and baby home, now long gone of course. And there are some news clippings both about the Anne Hargreaves criminal cases and also about young Emily Dawson's suicide." The train driver, Mike had learned, had never recovered, never returned to work.

"So, if she'd lived and had a kid, I mean back when she was seventeen, then her kid would have been about the same age as Tom Pollard," Terry Gleeson commented.

Mike nodded. "And?"

"OK, look, this is going to sound like a stretch so feel free to rubbish it, but this woman, what are we calling her, by the way?"

"We've decided to stick to Anne Hargreaves," Jude told him, "seeing as that's the earliest name we've got."

"Right, so this Anne Hargreaves finds out the name her kid was given. She seems to have had a bit of an obsession about losing her child — which is why she tried to take Toby, I suppose. However you look at it, she was having mental health issues here and there, right?"

"She was certainly sectioned on at least one occasion," Mike said. He had been given a contact number for the hospital in which she had been confined.

"So . . . her daughter is adopted, Anne Hargreaves misses her kid, later she manages to find out who adopted her or at

235

least what she was called after the adoption. Somewhere in her head this gets mixed up. She invents a grandkid, she gives her the name of her own daughter, she then spends time and effort trying to track down this kid that doesn't exist. Given that she's had problems in the past, what if something triggered her more recently? Some anniversary we don't know about but which was important to the dead woman?"

"Tom Pollard told me she'd befriended him about eighteen months ago. *After* which she decided that her lost grandchild was actually a daughter."

"So she conflated the facts," Jude said thoughtfully. "Actually, it wasn't the first time she'd been confused about basic facts, was it? She came to claim Toby, saying she'd come for her own kid, while we know for a fact that her own child was female and much older than him. Maybe she was heading for some kind of breakdown again?"

"And yet she appeared rational. Her thinking was organised, at least on the surface. John Tynan noticed nothing wrong, neither did the Beals or anyone else in direct contact with her," Mike objected.

Jude shrugged. "I'm no expert, but . . ."

But, Mike thought. It was all ifs and buts, wasn't it?

The CSI had examined Tom Pollard's car but apart from the list Jude already had, there was little of use to add. Tom seemed to have been sleeping in his car, which wasn't surprising.

"And our man in the black jacket?" Mike asked.

One of the constables took the floor, looking rather pleased with himself. "Tracked him down, sir. He'd played a bit fast and loose, given us the right street but the wrong property number. But I went house to house and I found him. His real name is Gordon Spence — he'd told us it was Graham Spencer. Anyway, he rents a little office above a shop and," Mike could almost hear the drum roll, "he's registered as a private investigator, specialising in insurance fraud and messy divorces."

Mike closed his eyes. Katie Matthews. Had Katie hired him to catch her husband? No one had yet managed to speak to Spence, but they now also had a home address, so that would be the first job the following morning.

It was at least some small progress. Though in what direction Mike was not yet sure.

* * *

"So, could that happen?" Mike asked Maria later that evening. "That someone could have major mental health issues but still appear to have total control in everyday situations?"

Maria uncurled, turned over and lifted herself onto an elbow. "And what kind of question is that, Mr Detective? People do just that all of the time. The soldier suffering from PTSD who still walks his dog, takes his kids to school, has a barbeque with family at the weekend; the functioning alcoholic or weekend drug user who still turns up for work on a Monday morning and never misses a deadline. The bereaved who still manage to do the weekly shop, catch the right bus, have a conversation, even though half of their brain is overwhelmed by grief. The father who kills himself and whose family all assert that he was a good dad and loving husband and no one realised he was even depressed.

"Human beings compartmentalise, it's how we survive. Sometimes that ability breaks down. It's like . . . like the sea defences on that beach in Happisburgh. Most of the time they hold, they break up the tide, but it only takes one big storm and that's another great chunk of coastline gone."

Mike nodded, chastened. He knew all of this but sometimes he needed someone else to point things out.

Maria settled at his side, her arm across his chest, and he listened as her breathing slowed and she eased into sleep. She was right, of course. After his son had been killed he'd been granted compassionate leave. He and his then wife had handled the funeral arrangements, comforted relatives, chosen flowers, paid bills . . . Eventually he had returned to work and he could recall how it had been with shocking, Technicolour clarity. He had read a report and thought 'my son is dead.' He had accepted the offer of coffee and thought 'my son is dead.' Had laughed at a friend's lame joke and thought 'my son is dead.' He had functioned, relying at first on social niceties, on habits, on the expectations of colleagues to get him through the day, but every thought, every action, every sentence had been punctuated by the thought 'my son is dead. My son is dead.'

Tears still threatened when he remembered those first days and weeks. Months, if he was honest. And then the anniversaries when the whole tsunami of grief crashed about him, dragging him under and leaving him gasping with the force of it, and knowing that his now estranged wife must, in her own way, be suffering the same, and knowing also that there was nothing either of them could do to stop the other from drowning.

CHAPTER 37

The exhumation of the little grave took place early in the morning. John had watched exhumations before but this one was different. For one thing, the grave was tiny, small enough for one man with a spade to strip off the turf, probing gently and then proceeding to open up space around what he thought was a wooden box. The second thing that was different, of course, was that John had almost convinced himself that he remembered the burial. What he definitely did remember was standing there with his mother on that rainy winter's day, a young child not really understanding what was going on.

His cousin Billy had come over to be with him and John was oddly grateful that it was not Maria standing beside him, or Mike. His relationship with them was different somehow, and he'd have found it hard to deal with their concern and sympathy. Billy was pragmatic, practical, and, John realised, he was not nearly as close to his cousin as he was to these two friends. On an occasion like this, John thought, that was a good thing.

"There's definitely something here," the gravedigger announced. He was on his hands and knees now, trying to find the edges of the box, conscious that he might smash what was probably quite fragile and half rotten. Representatives of the police and the church stood around, drinking coffee from a large urn that had arrived with the vicar — the odd nip of something stronger added to certain individuals' mugs. John reflected that most people present seem to have a hip flask with them.

"Strange business, this," Billy pronounced. "You really think it's one of ours in there?"

John was saved the bother of answering by the sound of wood splintering with a loud crack.

"Bugger," the gravedigger said, and then apologised for the mild expletive. "It's going to come out in bits, nothing I can do about it."

A white sheet was laid beside the grave and onto this was placed a selection of splintered planks followed by tiny bones. John caught his breath and moved closer, Billy shadowing him. Now the mood had changed. Before, the expectation had been that *something* would be in this little grave, but it still hadn't felt quite real. Now there was no doubt. Buried in what looked like a rough wooden crate, with mismatched planks of wood laid on top, were the bones of a tiny child. They saw a skull and arm bone, and what looked like a couple of little ribs. The bones were so old and so fragile that it was likely most would have simply rotted away. John could see that what was laid out on the sheet was in really poor condition.

"Poor little sod," Billy said. "I don't know about you, lad, but I think I've seen enough."

John Tynan nodded, reflecting absently that it was a long time since either he or Billy had been lads. Billy wandered back to the car. John paused for a quick word with the solicitor and the vicar, and then followed him. The assembled team would be quite some time at the graveside, the excavation would be slow and careful, continuing until they were sure they had extracted everything that could be extracted, so for John there was nothing more to be done.

Billy drove and John was glad of that. "We need a pub," Billy announced. "One that serves grub and a decent pint. I fancy a pint and a bowl of stew with swimmers. But I doubt anywhere will do that these days, so I'll settle for fish and chips."

John was about to object that it was a bit early for that but instead he nodded. "Head out towards the coast. The tourist pubs will be open already, and by the time we get there they'll be serving lunch." Swimmers, he thought with a smile, a local type of dumpling that floated on top of a thick stew. Grace used to cook them, so did his mother. He'd not eaten that particular meal in years.

He was profoundly saddened by what he had seen, but strangely he also felt relieved. At least now the child could be reburied with a name on a headstone, and it might be possible to find out what had happened to cause her death — though from the state of the bones, John doubted that. Whatever evidence there had been on the little body was long gone by now.

* * *

Mike and Constable Terry Gleeson had spent the morning interviewing Gordon Spence, a.k.a. Graham Spencer, the PI who now admitted to having been employed by Katie Matthews to follow her husband.

"She suspected him of having an affair. She said she didn't care whether or not he spotted me. I think really she wanted him to know that she was onto him."

"Was he having an affair?" Mike asked.

"*Is* having an affair," Spence said. "Her name is Amanda Levinson. I have an address for her."

Mike exchanged a glance with Terry. This was the woman who had come and offered Jason Matthews an alibi. No great surprise there.

Spence, seemingly keen to oblige now, was going through his records and writing down an address for Amanda Levinson. Mike didn't like to say he already had it.

"And that's not all. Regular little Lothario, is Jason Matthews." Spence seemed almost gleeful now. It must be a lonely life, Mike thought, gathering evidence for divorce cases. You couldn't exactly confide in anybody else or celebrate your cleverness in tracking down scandal.

"There were other women?" he asked.

"*Are*. At least two others." Spence scribbled something else on his pad, tore the page out and handed it over to Mike. "He had several *meetings* with the woman who was murdered at the Two Bells."

"Meetings?" Terry picked up on the emphasis. "We know they met, but that doesn't mean she was having an affair with him."

Spence delved back into his folders and this time produced photographs. He laid them down on the coffee table between them and picked up his coffee mug with a triumphant air. "That looks like more than talking to me," he said, stabbing a finger at one of the photographs. Jason Matthews and the woman who had once been known as Anne Hargreaves stood very close together, and in the next shot they were definitely kissing. Mike recognised the beach and the breakwater. "You have a date for this?"

Spence pointed at the printed numbers that Mike had not at first noticed. "I timestamp everything," he said, "and, yes, before you ask, I make sure my dates and times are accurate."

"Two days before she died," Terry observed.

Mike nodded. "I want copies of everything you have," he said to Spence.

Spence looked a little taken aback but then nodded. "Of course. It might take me some time to—"

"We can have another coffee while we're waiting," Terry told him cheerfully. "I'll see to it, shall I? Got any bikkies?"

Knowing himself to be well and truly railroaded, Spence set about making the copies while Mike watched.

"And the other woman?" Mike asked.

"Name of Louise Thompson. She's a student, just turned twenty. Studying clinical psychology, currently on a work placement. He's been seeing her for about a month.

I don't think it's serious. She looks a lot like his wife did when she was younger, so I figure he's trying to recapture his lost youth." Spence laughed uneasily. "You realise I'm only telling you any of this because I have Mrs Matthews's permission."

"And you realise I could easily get a warrant," Mike said. "This way no one loses face, do they?"

"So Mrs Matthews knew we'd be over to talk to you?" Terry asked him.

"She assumed you would at some point. After you searched their house and everything."

Terry, about to pour more water on the really not very good instant coffee, glanced over at his boss. Mike nodded slightly, knowing what he was thinking: that Katie Matthews had not volunteered the information that she had hired a private investigator to check up on her husband.

Terry gestured with a spoon towards the coffee whitener, and Mike shook his head. Terry added a generous amount to his own mug and that of Gordon Spence and came back to the table. He rifled through the photographs of Anne Hargreaves and Jason Matthews. Mike could see he was frowning and raised an eyebrow. Terry, using the cover of the noise made by the photocopier, leaned towards his boss. "Don't know about you, guv, but these look staged to me," he said quietly. "Like they both knew. Like they wanted to give this fella something to talk about."

Mike examined the photographs more closely and then nodded, sensing that Terry was probably right and making a mental note to show them to Jude when he got back to the office. Something else to talk to Jason Matthews about, something else that neither Jason Matthews nor his wife had chosen to mention.

More documents and photographs were dumped on the coffee table and Mike looked at the images of a much younger woman, Louise Thompson. There were a few pages of background information which told Mike that she was in her second year at uni, was hoping to stay on to do an MA and was currently on a placement in a private clinic. The name of the clinic, Ormond Park, rang a bell but it took him a moment or so to remember that this was where Toby Merrifield worked, grandson of the original Martha Toolin. Interesting. Everything seemed to circle back to that woman.

"And this Amanda Levinson, when did the affair begin?"

"When did the affair begin *again* is a better question," Spence said. "Jason Matthews and Amanda Levinson were engaged to be married when he met Katie Edwards, as his wife was then. They'd been together for almost four years, and then Amanda decided to take a job in Scotland and, since Jason wasn't prepared to go with her, she broke it off. She came back seven or eight months ago and it seems they picked up where they left off."

"And you have been employed by Mrs Matthews since?"

"Mrs Matthews came to me with her suspicions six months ago. I discovered very quickly that her misgivings had justification and gathered the usual evidence in preparation for divorce proceedings." He gave a short laugh. "Far more evidence than anyone would ever need, but she seemed to want to make certain."

"And yet those proceedings have not yet started. According to your evidence, her husband has been running around with at least three women. Mrs Matthews must have known about all of this, and yet she seems to have done nothing."

Spence shrugged. "Sometimes people use such evidence to attempt a fresh start. Sometimes it even works. Some use it as emotional blackmail, I suppose. I think Mrs Matthews wanted them to stay together for the sake of the children."

Mike almost sighed. Since when had that worked out for the best?

The photocopier went silent and Spence came over with a sheaf of papers and laid them on the table with the rest. "There." He sounded almost triumphant, as though he had achieved something important, and Mike wondered what Katie Matthews had really given him permission to reveal. Was she trying to build evidence against her husband, so that the police would look at him more closely? Was she simply out for revenge? If so, why not tell Mike that she was having her husband followed and investigated?

Everyone and his dog was playing games here. Mike set his execrable coffee aside and gathered the paperwork together, taking his time, aware that Graham Spence now wanted them gone. He was checking his watch, glancing out the window and almost dancing with impatience.

"You have somewhere to be?" Mike asked.

"I'm not just working for Mrs Matthews, you know," Gordon Spence said importantly. "I am a very busy man."

Mike tapped the pile of paperwork. "And this must all have been very time-consuming. According to Jason Matthews, you've followed him around practically 24/7 for the last few weeks. Katie Matthews must have been paying you well, that's all I can say."

Graham Spence was a pale man, but now two bright spots of colour appeared on his cheeks and his washed-out eyes flashed with annoyance. "I have cooperated fully, Inspector. As my client requested."

"I hope so," Mike told him. "Though there's one question you've still not answered. Why did you come to my incident room with a report that you saw the murdered woman in what we now know to be Tom Pollard's car? Tom Pollard, who is also now deceased. You reported this giving a false name, Mr Spence. And that begs two questions. The first is, why conceal your identity? And the second is how did you come to see the dead woman in Tom Pollard's car?"

Spence looked embarrassed. "I felt that, as I was working a case, I should be discreet."

"Or did you just fancy being a man of mystery?" Terry asked, a grin spreading across his freckled face.

"I . . ."

"OK, we'll put that aside," Mike said. "Where and when did you see the woman you knew as Julia Matthews, or was it Martha Toolin, in Pollard's car? What had Mrs Matthews told you about her?"

"Nothing. I mean she wasn't my main focus of interest, you understand. She came up on my radar because I was investigating Mr Matthews's infidelities. I just happened to see her in the car one day when that kid dropped her off to meet him."

"To meet Jason Matthews?"

"Yes."

"And where was this?"

"At the café. The Beach café, near the Two Bells. She must have been out somewhere with the kid because I followed Jason Matthews out to the coast later that afternoon. He parked up near the café and stood leaning against his car. I'd parked down the road and walked up, but then the little brown Fiat or whatever it was came trundling up the track and I saw her in the passenger seat. So I watched while her and the boy got out. They all stood talking for a minute or so, and then the kid got back in the car and drove away."

So Tom Pollard was definitely known to Jason Matthews. Yet he had denied recognising him.

"I took pictures. They're in with all that stuff I've copied for you."

"But you had no direct contact with Tom Pollard?"

"Well, no. I'd probably have got around to doing some background on him but the woman was killed a couple of days later, and then the kid was washed up dead on the beach so . . ."

"Washed up dead on the beach," Mike repeated. "That wasn't quite how the papers reported it."

Spence had the grace to look awkward. "I happened to be in the vicinity that morning. I saw the activity on the beach and just assumed . . ."

"And you were in the vicinity doing what?"

Spence looked annoyed. "Look, I've cooperated fully. I'm often out that way, especially lately. Jason Matthews had been with Amanda Levinson that night . . ."

So she said, Mike thought.

"I followed him after he left her place but when I spotted the police cars, I thought . . ."

"It looked more fun than tailing a chap who was likely just going to work," Terry put in.

Spence glowered. "Now, if we're done here?"

Mike took a card from his pocket and laid it squarely on the table. "I'll leave my card in case you suddenly feel that your cooperation has not been as full and frank as it might have been. Or that your client's interests and your — professional — interests are perhaps not as closely aligned as you might like to think. Good morning, Mr Spence."

They carried the paperwork back to the car and set it down on the back seat. Terry glared at it. "More bits of dead tree to shuffle. Like we've not got enough already, most of it leading nowhere." He settled in the passenger seat and tugged impatiently at his seatbelt. "You get the feeling, don't you, that everybody is laying down a trail of breadcrumbs, leading us off everywhere but where we *should* be looking. Every bugger has his own agenda."

Mike found he was unable to disagree with him.

* * *

From his office window, Graham Spence watched the policemen drive away. He held his mobile in his hand, but only when he was sure they had gone did he call Katie Matthews. He told her that the police had been and that he had given them everything she had requested him to.

"I expect that you will be the next port of call, Mrs Matthews," he said. "They wanted to know why you had not informed them that you'd hired me. Pardon me for saying, but you should have said. They *are* conducting a murder enquiry and they take a dim view of withholding evidence."

He grimaced at the reply. "Of course. As you wish."

She ended the call and Graham Spence tossed his phone onto a nearby chair. The sense of unease that had been germinating at the back of his mind over the last few weeks had now flowered into something that made him very uncomfortable indeed.

CHAPTER 38

Back at the incident room, Mike found that there had been some developments. A forensic accounting team had been going through Jason Matthews's financials and discovered some interesting activity.

"You know the new company that Jason was supposed to be going to work for," Jude said. "Well, it looks like he's been receiving regular but concealed payments from them over the last couple of years. Payments for information about his father-in-law's company, maybe?"

"Show me," Mike said.

Jude sat down beside him and opened the folder. "OK. You're going to have to get a proper briefing from the experts later, but I talked to them on the phone this morning and got the basics. See here." She pointed at a payment from something called South Port Holdings. "That's a shell company, based in Holland, and it seems to be responsible for a variety of financial transactions for a number of other companies — financial transactions that don't go through the books. The fraud squad has come across South Port Holdings before and is sufficiently cognisant of the way that they work, so they've backtracked and found that they are responsible for operating shell companies for Jacobs and Johnson, among others. That's the company that is going to be employing Jason Matthews — though I don't recall him telling us what his new job title was going to be."

"So Jason Matthews has been trading financially sensitive information about his father-in-law's company," Mike said. "But what sort of information? Have they any idea?"

"Well, they've only just started digging and you can imagine how complicated this lot gets, but it seems that a couple of years ago a deal brokered by Gavin Edwards — that's Jason's father-in-law — which would have allowed him to build on a number of brownfield sites just north of London fell through at the last minute. The way it was explained to me was that he got gazumped. The deal was all ready to sign when, literally just as he was entering the building to sign off on it, another offer came in. What happened next is fairly well documented because he complained to the Ombudsman but," she shrugged, "no dice. He lost out. The thing was, no one was supposed to know the purchase had even been proposed. It was being executed as a land transfer rather than a property purchase. The fees were for services, and weren't on the books as being for the land itself. The actual cash had been run through a variety of shell companies, so the money transfer came from about three different sources and the individual amounts were not big enough to arouse anybody's suspicions because it wasn't an amount that would have covered the purchase of these brownfield sites. I'm not explaining it very well, but I hope you get the drift. The whole deal and the amounts involved were considered commercially sensitive and therefore—"

"Someone found out at the last minute and put in a higher bid," Mike finished.

"And it's not the only time this happened. There are three separate instances of dubious manoeuvres, all of which led to him losing a big deal or a lot of money. Gavin Edwards's business might look healthy on the surface, but only because he's sold off holdings, pulled back on his purchasing, got rid of staff and generally consolidated over the last six months or so. All of this has been done really quietly. Few of the redundancies have been from the same part of the company, everything has been well spread out, but he's really had to pull his horns in. And each time something has gone wrong for his father-in-law, Jason Matthews has received another big bonus."

"Sounds risky."

"Not really. Jason and Katie Matthews have a joint account, but the only thing that gets paid into it is his wages. The money passing through the account covers direct debits, spending money for Katie, housekeeping and all the stuff you'd expect, plus there's an allowance from Daddy that is still coming in, despite the fact that she's married. I've no doubt that Katie Matthews knows how much Daddy is paying Hubby, but I'm sure she has no idea at all about what else he's into. It looks like Jason's allocated spending money from their joint finances to a separate account and then there are these amounts going in each month. See?"

Mike thought for a moment and then he said, "So, Anne Hargreaves. It would be no good her trying to blackmail Matthews about affairs that his wife already knew about. This, however . . ."

"She couldn't have known the scale of it," Jude said. "If she had, she'd have demanded a hell of a lot more money."

"Or maybe she was just probing, seeing how much she could push for. You know, start small, and then put the pressure on."

Mike asked how much money they were talking about.

"Over three hundred grand this year alone," Jude said.

"How do you keep that from the taxman?"

"Looks like the same shell company that deals with his payments from Jacobs and Johnson takes care of that side of it too. Jason Matthews Associates is also registered in the Netherlands, which pays dividends to said Jason Matthews, which accounts for the other amounts going into his personal account. Essentially, it acts a bit like a limited company only with better tax breaks. No need for the public record at Companies Court. Look." She laid the bank statements alongside the other financial information. "These are dividends from Jason Matthews Associates. Smallish amounts, paid monthly, and on which he *does* pay tax, but the capital is held in an offshore account. Katie Matthews would have a hard time getting her hands on it if she divorced him, but he'd be well set up for the future."

Mike shuffled the papers around on the desk. It would take him a while to get his head around all of this, but it was potentially the best motive they had so far, at least for the murder of Anne Hargreaves. The death of Tom Pollard — well, they were no nearer to understanding that.

"And has Mr Edwards been apprised of his son-in-law's duplicity?"

Jude grinned. "Not yet, no. I've no doubt we will enjoy giving him the good news."

Mike brought her up to speed on what they had learned from Gordon Spence. He asked her to check that his memory was correct, and that Louise Thompson was in fact working at the same clinic as Toby Merrifield. She was.

The first results of the TIE interviews had come in, those with whom Hargreaves, a.k.a. Martha Toolin and whatever other identities she had used, had contact. Those who felt their aged relatives had been conned into leaving money to this relative stranger, or who felt that she had interfered in the natural distribution of legacies. Trace, interview, eliminate. TIE. So far there was very little of interest in terms of the murder enquiry, though Mike could feel the anger and frustration of the relatives pouring off the pages of their statements. At a quick glance, only two looked worth following up, as they had no alibis for the night of the murder and had also been actively pursuing this woman through the courts. Anne Hargreaves seemed to have left a legacy of mistrust, anger and broken families in her wake, to say nothing of disappointed expectations.

* * *

Katie Matthews returned to her father's house to find three missed calls on the home phone, matching the half dozen that had come through to her mobile. Detective Inspector Croft and ds Jude Burnett. Katie had deliberately ignored all attempts at contact since Spence had phoned her. She definitely had no wish to speak to any police officers, nor anybody else, really. Understanding this, her parents had agreed to pick the girls up from school and take them swimming and then for a pizza, to give her some time alone. Katie really didn't know what she'd have done without her mum and dad. Lately the girls had suffered both from her bad temper and their father's obvious absences, so they needed a bit of spoiling. It would have been clear to anyone with half a brain that their dad simply didn't want to be around them — or her — and the girls certainly had more than half a brain. She was proud of the way they were coping with all the upset.

Katie thought about phoning Spence but wasn't sure she could deal with the PI right now. The man was efficient enough but she wasn't keen on his slimy manner. It had really got on her nerves. No, she'd run a bath with plenty of bubbles, pour herself a glass of wine even though it was really too early to be indulging, and have a bit of a soak.

Katie had moved back into her old room. After she moved out, her parents had used it as a guestroom complete with en suite, but now that she had come back it was hers again. It was almost as though she had never left. The girls shared a room next to hers, smaller than the one they had at home but they didn't seem to mind. Already it was filled with toys and games. They had used this room before when they had stayed overnight with their grandparents, so it was familiar and friendly and they had settled well, only once asking when they were going home. It helped, Katie thought, that they were still going to their old school every day, seeing friends and having play dates, doing all of the stuff they usually did. All in all, they were handling the breakup better than she was, so Katie was content to let her father and the solicitor do the rest.

Life was going to work out. Perhaps everything happens for the best after all.

* * *

John Tynan and his cousin Billy had spent a moochy sort of day, wandering along the coast and not doing anything very much. Billy had his pint with his lunch, but no more than that as he was driving. It was, John thought, probably the longest the two of them had spent alone in years and it had taken a while to settle back into natural and easy conversation — Billy's wife, Caroline, usually being the one who took charge and kept conversation flowing — but in the end it had been pleasant, despite the day's traumatic beginning.

Billy had booked himself into a hotel with a restaurant for the night and the two of them were to meet up with Mike and Maria for a leisurely dinner. As it happened, only Maria turned up, Mike being held up at work.

"Hopefully that means they are finally getting somewhere," Maria joked. "It's never good news for a case when he gets home on time."

John told her how the exhumation had gone but clearly didn't want to talk about it much, so conversation moved on to other things and inevitably to the latest sightings of the black dog which Billy had noticed in the evening papers.

"Jerry was obsessed with the damn thing," he commented.

"Really?" John asked. "I mean, we found a lot of cuttings and stuff but I hadn't even realised that he was interested until then."

"Well," Billy conceded, "I suppose obsessed is a bit of a strong word. He was interested in local history, I know that, and he collected all sorts of bits and bobs, even talked about writing a book at one stage."

John raised an eyebrow. Another thing he had been unaware of.

"It never came to anything, of course. I think a lot of us think about writing a book and maybe get to about the fifth page before we realise just how much hard work it is. I thought about producing something on car restoration. Still might. It's a darn sight easier than it was, what with all this self-publishing lark. We've got this young apprentice, he's all fired up with computers and Lord knows what, built the new website for us and is now talking about all the stuff we know being too good to lose."

"He has a point," Maria said.

"Yes, but that implies I won't be around to impart it, and frankly I don't like thinking about that." Billy laughed. "But what he has started doing is writing stuff down. We photograph every stage of a job, and we're thinking about putting something together, self-publishing it. I'm too old and not rich enough to take on another apprentice, so it's going to be up to the lad whether he continues with the business or not after I've gone. And he's right, we've built up a lot of experience over the years and it would be a shame if it was all lost. One brain, even two brains, can't remember everything."

A waiter arrived and took their orders.

"So Jerry liked myths and legends." Maria brought the subject back.

"He did. And he seemed to have a bit of an interest in family history, but Black Dog, well, he loved those stories. He reckoned he saw it, did you know that?"

Something at the back of John's mind caused him to nod. "I remember him saying something, but I was just a boy at the time and probably didn't take a lot of notice. Just the one sighting, was it? I know that's enough for me."

"Oh, aye, you spotted something, didn't you?"

"I spotted a big black dog with big sharp teeth and a big bad attitude," John confirmed. "Whether it was *the* big black dog I have no idea, but it was definitely flesh and blood and I'd not be keen to renew the acquaintance. Where did Jerry reckon he had seen it?"

"Well, there's the thing. He reckoned he'd seen it once when he was a boy, running along the beach. I don't recall which beach. The second time was at the old house, your grandfather's place, padding around the yard, he said, just after your grandmother's funeral. But here's the funny thing, he reckoned he and your grandfather stood in the upstairs window and they both saw the same thing."

"Black dogs are not exactly uncommon," Maria said. "Every farmer and his boy seems to have a Black Lab crossbreed of some sort."

"I did not see a Black Lab cross," John objected. "This was big and definitely not imbued with the Labrador temperament. What was the third time?"

"Well, that would have been just a few weeks before he died," Billy said. "He reckoned it was a harbinger of some kind. I don't think it frightened him, but he did decide it was time to make sure all his affairs were in order, I know that."

"It's not that uncommon," Maria said, "for a family to have a tradition of seeing something specific before someone dies — or to remember it that way, anyway. As you say, it was a fair few weeks before he died. So it wasn't like an instant harbinger of death or anything, it may be it just fitted in with what he already believed about these things. You know, focused his mind on what he knew already, that he had to get his affairs sorted out."

Billy viewed her with amusement. "Yes, Doctor. But even you have to agree there's been an unusual number of sightings this summer."

"There have," Maria agreed. "But the thing is, when one person sees something, a phenomenon that is already connected to myth or folklore, everybody else starts looking. What would normally be the sighting of, say, a Black Labrador cross, suddenly acquires significance."

"Like when someone buys a new car and suddenly all they ever seem to see is that particular model," John added. "Isn't there a specific bit of the brain involved?"

"Mostly it's the reticular activating system," Maria said. "That's the bit that selects and matches — among other things — and draws our attention when it finds a match."

The food arrived and drew their attention for a while, until Billy said, "OK, but to turn your argument on its head, if these things are always there, these phenomena like Black Dog, but people take notice of them only because something has already drawn their attention to them, like you said, then maybe it's *what* has drawn their attention that matters. Some sense of something being off, you know? Like most of the time we just accept what's a bit weird and odd or coincidental as part of the scenery, we don't even notice, beyond maybe the odd remark about something being a funny coincidence. But when we're unsettled or worried about other things, then—"

"Then *everything* assumes significance," Maria said. "In the worst cases, this can be part of a psychotic experience, where everything is an omen or part of a broader pattern that only the person experiencing it can perceive. And you're right, that is a recognised behaviour. Do you think that Jerry was particularly worried about things in the weeks before he died, that his response to the black dog was part of his more general anxiety?"

Billy thought about it for a moment and then shook his head. "If anything, I'd have said he'd made peace with the world. He was calm in those final weeks, didn't seem worried about anything. It might be just hindsight, but we both got the feeling, Caroline and me, we both felt that everything had fallen into place for him. Like he had accepted that the end was near and that there was nothing he could do about it, and he wasn't particularly upset and certainly not frightened by the fact. He seemed happy and he had no pain, we were so glad of that, he wasn't even particularly ill, just very old. He died in his sleep — a good way to go, I reckon."

"And did he talk much about the black dog after he said he'd seen it?"

"Not so I remember. Of course we didn't see him every day, not like the nursing home staff. They might recall, of course. But no one mentioned that he seemed upset about anything, or that he was obsessing or anything like that. I know it was what made him call in the solicitor to check over his will, that sort of thing. And he added a few little gifts to staff and friends, which was when he decided to leave the picture frame to that woman. Sorry, John, I know you liked her but she's not exactly proved to be sound, has she?"

John merely lifted his glass and took a sip. No, she had not proved to be sound — and for that matter neither had his own judgement.

"If this was a sheepy area, chances are our Black Dog would have been shot by now," Maria said.

"A *sheepy* area." Billy chuckled. "No, I suppose it isn't. It's mostly potatoes and lavender. Not so many sheep to worry about or to worry, should you be that kind of dog. Though I suppose that would have given us a bit of useful physical evidence, wouldn't it? If you find a sheep with its throat torn out, then it's more likely to be a flesh-and-blood dog than some kind of semi-mystical hound."

"I never claimed that what I saw was anything but flesh and blood," John said.

"Anyway, it has to be a bit of both, flesh and blood *and* people misinterpreting because of the legends. Maybe even a genuine spectral dog, for all we know. Well, think about it," Maria suggested. "You can't have just the one dog, not considering the geographical spread of sightings. You ask me, there's one big and probably vicious dog that's covering a fair bit of ground and the rest is a good bit of collective hysteria, based on a well-established set of myths and legends."

"And not enough sheep to prove it either way," Billy added.

* * *

Mike had had to miss dinner in order to sit in on an interview. Jason Matthews had been brought in for interrogation under caution, but this time not directly as part of the murder enquiry. Katie hadn't spoken to her father that afternoon and was therefore in ignorance of what her husband was suspected of doing, but Gavin Edwards had been furious when he'd received a call from one of Mike's team. A corporate council now joined the serried ranks of divorce lawyers ranged against Jason Matthews.

From a police perspective, the investigation was in its early stages. Jason had been brought in for interview by a specialist team, on suspicion of fraud, money laundering and possible other offences. Mike knew that they were still putting their case together, so he would have preferred to wait until they had a more solid package of evidence, rather than embark on what was in effect a fishing expedition. Jason was certainly guilty of wrongdoing in the eyes of his father-in-law, but how much of what he had done was actually illegal and how much of that could be proved?

Mike was aware that this preliminary interview was as much to get the measure of Jason Matthews as it was an attempt to prefer charges. Just how clever had he been?

From Mike's point of view, there was only one thing he really wanted to ask, and he finally got his opportunity two hours in — two hours of Jason Matthews replying with variations on 'no comment.' He had nothing to say to the questions about his financial dealings, insider trading and the selling of confidential information to rival businesses.

Collins, now formally acting for Jason Matthews, had, on the other hand been busy, making notes and casting the occasional curious glance at his client. Mike got the impression that he didn't actually know him very well despite their work connections.

Eventually the DCI in charge of the interview leaned back in his chair and gave the questioning over to Mike.

"Did you know your wife had hired a private investigator, Mr Matthews?" Mike said.

Jason stared at Mike, the sudden change of direction appearing to take him by surprise. "I knew," he said. "He wasn't exactly subtle."

"Apparently she had told him that," Mike consulted his notes, "she didn't care whether you knew or not. Maybe she hoped that the shock of being followed would bring you back in line?"

Jason Matthews laughed. "Back in line. That was it, wasn't it? Always. I was always expected to toe the line. To be grateful. Well, fuck the lot of them, that's all I've got to say."

Mike nodded. "You implied that Julia Matthews, as you knew her — the woman we now know was called Anne Hargreaves — tried to blackmail you and that the blackmail was about your affairs. But, Mr Matthews, your wife was all too aware of those affairs. So why did you pay her? Was it because she'd found out about your rather complex business dealings? That you were potentially trying to ruin your father-in-law's business?"

"I must object," Jason's lawyer began. Jason waved the objection away. "Nothing to say."

"So, Julia — Anne — found out that you were doing the dirty, both in your personal life and your business dealings. My guess is that she was still trying to put it all together. The amounts she tried to blackmail you for were not massive, were they, Mr Matthews? Substantial enough if she was just threatening to tell your wife about the affairs, but if she was beginning to uncover the rest . . . well, you'd know that the demands she'd made so far would be just the tip of the iceberg, wouldn't they? You'd be paying her to keep her mouth shut for how long? A woman like that, you think she'd ever go away, Mr Matthews?"

"Nothing to say," Jason Matthews said, but Mike could see he was rattled.

"So, the temptation to get her out of the way once and for all must have been—"

"I never laid a hand on her. I've got an alibi. We've already established that. I've got a frigging alibi." Jason got to his feet and his solicitor, startled, scraped his notes together and also stood.

"And for the night Tom Pollard died?" Mike said.

"Are we done here?" Jason said.

"This is an interview under caution, Mr Matthews. You've not yet been charged. I can't prevent you from leaving," he exchanged a glance with DCI Clarke, who nodded, "but if I could just return to the subject of the woman you knew as Julia Matthews for a moment." He opened the folder on the table in front of him and passed some photographs over to Jason and his lawyer. These were the photographs Spence had given him, of Julia and Jason in what looked like a very passionate embrace. "It seems you were a little more intimately involved than you told us, Mr Matthews."

Jason Matthews laughed, as though the whole idea was absurd. "I told you before. The woman had a screw loose. She just grabbed me one day, and kissed me like that. Maybe she and this private eye were in cahoots, how the hell should I know?"

"It doesn't look as though you objected too much, Mr Matthews."

"Christ's sake, she was a nutcase. She took me by surprise."

"What's more, I doubt you'd be making a comment like that if the roles were reversed," Jason's solicitor commented. "It smacks a little too much of the 'she was asking for it' line of questioning, don't you think?"

Mike regarded the man in mild surprise. It was the first full sentence he had produced since the introductions. Mike supposed he had a point.

His client rather ruined the moment by adding, "And besides, she was hardly my type. I do have some pride."

"You prefer your women younger, that right?" Mike said. "Like Amanda Levinson who is, what, a couple of years your junior? Or even younger than that, perhaps. Like Louise Thompson?"

"Aw come on . . ." Jason began.

The solicitor coughed. "As I understand it, Mr Matthews was brought in for questioning regarding his business dealings. His personal life is irrelevant."

Mike said nothing. Jason Matthews was not a man who was good with silences.

And lo and behold, Jason had to fill it. "Lou was fun, but I only saw her two, maybe three times. Nothing much in common, truth be told." He turned to his legal counsel. "Going now, are we? I don't know about you, but I'm bored with all this. If my father-in-law wants his pound of flesh, then so be it. But he should remember that I know where all his bodies are buried — metaphorically speaking."

Mike and DCI Clark exchanged a glance. "I don't think you understand, Mr Matthews," Clarke said. "Your father-in-law's wishes are of no account here. This is a police investigation. Maybe you should remember that."

Jason's mouth tightened, while his solicitor once again gathered his papers and prepared to leave.

"No doubt we'll be seeing you again, Mr Matthews," Mike told him.

CHAPTER 39

Mike was trying to get a timeline clear in his mind. Anne Hargreaves had been born in 1957 and would have been seventeen when her daughter was born in 1974. That daughter had been adopted, subsequently becoming Emily Dawson. It had been a private adoption organised by the real Martha with a family she had known.

Back in 1989, when Toby, Martha Toolin's grandson, was four or five and Emily Dawson must have been fourteen, Anne Hargreaves had turned up, demanding the return of her baby. She had tried to take Toby, despite the fact that he was the wrong sex and wrong age ever to have been her child.

"So," Mike said to Jude, who was driving, "that was the first time she was sectioned. It does not seem to have been the last, but for the last twelve years she seems to have either been healthy or completely dropped off the radar."

"And that grandson, who is now all grown up, seems to have followed the family tradition and become a psychiatrist or whatever."

"Paediatric psychologist," Mike said. "I get the feeling he could only have become that, or a High Court judge."

"Whatever. But he currently happens to be working at the very clinic where Louise Thompson was doing her work experience, or whatever you call it."

"And Jason Matthews just happens to have been seeing this Louise Thompson. I don't care if it was just two or three times, it seems awfully convenient."

"And according to the interview our colleagues conducted with said Louise Thompson, she broke it off with Jason Matthews because he was putting pressure on her to look in confidential files and give him information."

The young woman had been very upset by all of this and had in fact gone to her boss. As she had done nothing wrong, she had continued with her work placement, but the matter had been reported to the police and Louise Thompson had been interviewed. It had only been when Jude had started to ask questions at the clinic that this piece of information had come to light. They were now on their way to speak to her.

"I managed to speak to that social worker yesterday," Jude said, with a flourish, it seemed to Mike, like that of a magician preparing to produce a rabbit from a hat. "You remember Mrs Green, the social worker?"

"I'm guessing you got further than I did."

"Um, well, you could say that, but the most important thing to come out of the conversation was that Tom Pollard saw a counsellor. Not Toby Merrifield, but it was at the same place."

"Really? And when was this?"

"About two years ago. He'd been suffering from depression and a lot of anxiety about leaving the care system. They do all they can, but it's going to be a big shock, isn't it? The counsellor he was seeing has moved on, but with the help of the social worker that you so offended, I managed to speak to her on the phone. According to her, in the last couple of sessions Tom was feeling a lot happier because he'd found a long-lost relative who was helping him out."

"And we all know who that was," Mike said.

"So how does this all tie together?" Jude asked. "This Anne Hargreaves gives up her child for adoption, a decision that she probably regretted later, and one which seems to have coloured her whole life. Several years later she has some kind of psychotic episode, and tries to claim a child that is definitely not hers — our Toby Merrifield."

"She's sectioned," Mike continued, "and spends about six months being treated. Now we know that she also had a criminal record, and that she spent a good deal of her time conning, persuading or beguiling various old people into leaving her money, including three houses and a quarter of a million in cash."

"That's a lot of beguiling," Jude commented.

"And a little silver picture frame," Mike added, "from John Tynan's uncle Jerry."

"I'm not being funny," Jude said, "but what did Mr Tynan have to offer her? I mean, he's a really nice guy, but she did seem like someone who just made friends for the sake of what she could get, if you see what I mean. What did she think she could get out of John Tynan? What did Jerry tell her that made her target him?"

Mike frowned. He'd never really thought about it that way. John's place in this had always seemed like something of a side issue. "The house?" he said. "I've never seen it but from the sound of it, it's big, occupying two or three acres. From what John said there were developers interested in knocking the old place down and building a whole clutch of houses on the land, but Jerry wouldn't have it, so they lost interest."

"And I wondered who the developers were," Jude added. "Could there have been a connection with Jason Matthews, or his father-in-law's company? His job was smoothing logistical problems on the development side, wasn't it?"

"You could be onto something there," Mike said. "But if she was hoping for a close relationship with John Tynan, and then that he would eventually die and leave everything to her, that would have been a very, very long con indeed.

Not to mention the fact that she seemed to be chary of close personal involvement."

"Unless she hoped to come up with an heir. She was very interested in the family history," Jude said.

Mike frowned, then his face cleared. "That seems rather too convoluted. But I suppose it's possible she saw an opportunity. How about this? Maybe she knew that if an heir wasn't found, John would end up inheriting a potentially very valuable piece of real estate. Maybe she'd hoped to persuade him to sell, or to make some kind of deal that she could profit from? Especially if Jason Matthews was involved."

"Which would suggest that her relationship with Matthews was far deeper and more important than we had assumed," Jude said. "But that's certainly possible, isn't it? I wonder if Jerry told her about baby Silvia. I mean, the gift of a silver photo frame is one thing but to give it with such a precious photograph still in it? Odd, wouldn't you say?"

"It would have been, had he given it to her while he was still alive," Mike argued. "But Jerry Matthews was dead when the frame was handed over. I doubt that anyone else would have seen the significance. No one in the family seems to have known about Silvia."

"True, but what if Jerry had intended for her to give the photo and the story to Mr Tynan? Once he knew the story, he'd be bound to try and find the baby — just as he is now," Jude said.

Mike laughed. "Now you really are speculating. And if that was the intention, why didn't he give John the photo and tell him the story long ago?"

Jude shrugged.

Mike thought he might have the answer. "Maybe for the same reason, whatever it was, that made Jerry insist that the solicitor was not to start the search for Silvia until he knew he didn't have long to live. Jerry insisted that, should the solicitor strike lucky and find Silvia or her family, nothing would be done until after he was dead and gone."

"That's strange," Jude said. "Sad, too. Almost like he thought she'd just reject him and he didn't want to have to face that."

Or he knew Silvia would never be found, and he was just going through the motions to salve his conscience in some way. Mike would have been surprised if the same thought had not occurred to John. Even more surprised if John were to ever tell anyone what he thought — even him.

Jude pulled up in front of a smart little semi-detached house, part of a newish estate of smart little houses, all with clipped lawns. This was where Louise Thompson still lived with her parents when she wasn't at university. The door opened as they got out of the car and a middle-aged woman peered at them suspiciously. The mother, Mike guessed.

"It's all right, Mum, they're the police, they're not going to kidnap me." A young woman stepped out into the hallway and beckoned them inside. "Come on through. Though I don't know what I can tell you that I haven't already said to the other officers."

Mike recognised her from the photographs — small, blonde and pretty, but there was an intelligent gleam in her eyes that hadn't been apparent in the images Spencer had captured. She led them into a small front room, its neutral colours causing Mike to wonder if the family had changed anything since they had moved in, and if in fact this had been the show home. It had that bland, inoffensive and vaguely stylish look to it. She bade them sit down and her mother announced that she would go and make some coffee.

"She worries," Louise said. "I told her Jason was a mistake, and that it was only two or three dates before I found out what he really wanted. All she was worried about was that he wanted to get into my knickers. I kind of wish it had been that simple. I mean, I could deal with that."

Jude laughed. "So he wanted you to look at confidential files. Can you remember exactly what they were about?"

"I told the other officer — a kid called Tom Pollard. I wrote everything down at the time and then I went to see

Mrs Mehan, that's the boss, and I told her all about it. She phoned the police and helped me make a statement. I was in a right state, I can tell you."

She picked up a notebook from the arm of the chair, opened it, extracted a few sheets of folded paper and handed these and the notebook to Jude. "That's a copy of the statement I made for Mrs Mehan and the one I made to the police. You've probably already got it, but Mrs Mehan recorded it and then had it typed up, just so we had our own record of everything. I can't tell you how worried I was. I mean, I'm only just starting out. I hadn't even graduated at that point and my career could have been finished if anyone suspected I'd done something wrong."

"You obviously acted very properly," Mike told her. "And the information Jason wanted, was it just about Tom Pollard?"

"Yes. I've put it all down in the statement and the notes I made at the time. Just take it all with you. I've got copies."

The mother came in with a tray and set it down on a low table with another suspicious glare at Mike. She seemed to dislike Jude less, but in Mike's experience that was often the case.

"And how many times had you been out with him when he asked you to do this?" He raised a hand to fend off the inevitable comment. "I know it's in the notes, but if you can just tell me."

Louise sighed. "I met him in a nightclub. He came over and asked if I wanted a drink. I was with friends and I said OK, why not? I asked for a bottle of lager and watched while the barman removed the top and handed it straight to me. You have to be careful these days. I only accept a drink from strangers if I see it poured, or it's in a bottle that they can't tamper with."

"Sensible," Jude commented. "And then you got to know him a bit better?"

Louise glanced uncomfortably at her mother but nodded. "I figured he was either married or divorced, or whatever.

He was older than the usual crowd, and he wasn't with anyone, which often means they're one of those. But he was kind of fun, so when he asked if he could see me again I said yes, why not? He told me he was getting divorced and that he had two kids. Frankly, I didn't see it going anywhere. I thought it might be fun to have another night out but I really didn't want to get involved with someone who was getting divorced and had two kids, if you get what I mean. Anyway, the second time we met up we went out for a meal. It was just pizza but we chatted a lot. We got on fine, and he seemed really interested in what I was doing my degree in and where I was working. I didn't think anything about it at the time. The third time, he said we should meet for something to eat and then go on to a nightclub — the one where we met. That was fine with me because I was going to meet friends there later anyway. Then all of a sudden he's put this envelope of cash on the table and he says he knows how hard up students are. Then he says that he's got a friend who really, really needs some information about a kid that was adopted, or fostered, and ended up in care, because she thinks they might be a relative. So I ask him why this friend doesn't just go to social services and ask them. Then he gets really cagey and pushes the money towards me, and he says maybe I could just have a quick look at one of the files. And then he unfolds a bit of paper with a name on it and says this is the name, this is the boy they want the information about."

"And she immediately told him where he could go," Louise's mother said.

"Mum! Anyway, I left him sitting there and came home and told Mum about it, and then I phoned my boss. She was so concerned that she said to come right over, and so I did, and we phoned the police. I made a statement and I've never seen him again."

"Did he say what, precisely, he wanted you to look for?" Jude asked.

"I didn't let him get that far. The police said that his story sort of stood up. He'd said he was acting on behalf of a friend. He swore he was just trying to do everyone a favour, and they told Mrs Mehan that they couldn't prove otherwise, so it was unlikely to," she frowned, "reach a threshold? Is that right?"

"Unlikely to reach the threshold of evidence where the CPS would recommend a charge be brought," Mike said. "The Crown Prosecution Service have to pick their battles these days. They have to be convinced that there is a real possibility of getting a conviction." He extracted a photograph of Anne Hargreaves from his pocket and laid it on the table. "Have you ever seen this woman?"

"I'm not sure. She looks kind of familiar but I can't place her. Sorry."

They departed shortly after that, Jude having left her card on the off chance that Louise would remember where she had seen Anne Hargreaves, a.k.a. Julia or Martha, before.

"It sounds as though Jason Matthews definitely had a much closer relationship with the woman previously known as Anne Hargreaves than he's letting on," Jude commented as she drove away.

"So it would seem," Mike said. "It doesn't alter the fact that he has an alibi for the night she died, and the more we probe that alibi the more witnesses seem to come forward to confirm it."

"It's a bit of a bugger, that. Do you think that she might have been blackmailing him for more than money? Maybe she offered to leave him alone in exchange for information? Or even said, OK, I won't make you pay but I need you to . . . oh, I don't know. And why would he or they want to see a confidential file about Tom Pollard anyway? Tom seems to have been open enough about his history. "

"That, I don't know," Mike said. "We're going to bring Matthews back in, that's for sure. And in the meantime, we keep prodding away at that alibi."

* * *

The next visit promised to be a difficult one. The adoptive parents of Emily Dawson also lived in a semi-detached house but theirs was much older and grander, and two cars were parked in the driveway. Mike was not really surprised to find that Toby Merrifield was also to be present. The Dawsons, it seemed, had requested it.

There were photographs of Emily Dawson on the mantelpiece — a pretty, dark-haired and rather shy-looking teenager. A giggling toddler. A tiny baby dressed in a pink hat and matinee coat. An adolescent, standing between two boys that Mike guessed must be her brothers.

Emily Dawson's adoptive mother sat on a sofa, next to her husband. They held hands, and Mike could see from their faces, drained of colour, that they still grieved. "We loved her," Priscilla Dawson said. "She knew that, but this awful thing that took over her mind meant that all the love in the world could never be enough. There was nothing we could do, but that doesn't mean I forgive myself for not doing something more."

Mike shifted uncomfortably in his seat. "I lost my son," he offered. "He was killed in a hit-and-run accident when he was only ten years old. I won't say that I understand what you went through, but I do know what it's like to lose a child."

He could sense both Toby and Jude staring at him. He rarely talked about Stevie with people he didn't know. Jude, at least, must have known what it cost him to do so.

"She was a lovely girl, beautiful and talented and lively, but when she got to be fifteen everything seemed to fall apart for her. Suddenly she wasn't going out with her friends any more, she was doing badly at school and she became faddy about what she ate. At first we thought it was just a phase, and then we slowly realised that she was losing weight, that it wasn't just being fussy but something was seriously wrong. We got her the best help we could, I want you to know that."

"Of course you did," Toby said soothingly. "The inspector knows that."

"I know this is difficult," Mike said, "but did the birth mother ever get in touch with you? Do you think she ever contacted Emily?"

"How could she? She didn't know who had adopted Emily. Surely there was no way she could have found out?"

She looked inquiringly at Toby, who shook his head. "The agreement was confidential," he confirmed.

"The agreement might have been confidential," Jude said, playing the gentle but insistent devil's advocate, "but the fact is, you were known to Mrs Toolin, and she was the one who arranged the adoption. Anne Hargreaves might well have known that Mrs Toolin had had Emily placed with friends, or at least people who were known to her. Mrs Toolin might even have told her so, to reassure her. If that was the case, then maybe it wouldn't have taken a lot of working out. A bit of investigation, a bit of nosing around in Mrs Toolin's wider social circle to find out who'd had a baby, or who had adopted a baby at the right time, and—"

"My grandmother was always very careful." Toby sounded defensive.

"I'm sure she was," Mike said, "but I doubt she envisaged anything like this happening. Anne Hargreaves grew into a very determined, extremely persuasive woman, who was capable of extracting information from people — we know this from what we've been able to find out about her life in recent years. It's well within the bounds of possibility that she worked out who had adopted her daughter."

"*Our* daughter." Priscilla sounded angry.

"Your daughter," Mike agreed.

"And yet she came to my mother's house and tried to kidnap me," Toby reminded them.

"She did. She was already very unwell, and she tried to take away a child that in her confusion she imagined was hers, despite the fact that she knew she had not given birth to a little boy and that her own child would have been in her teens by then. I doubt she was rational at that point. It's even possible that she came to your mother's house looking for help and just happened to see the child. The psychosis did the rest. I'm no expert, but I think that is a possible scenario," Mike said.

Toby grimaced but didn't contradict him.

"Do you think she approached our daughter?" The husband spoke for the first time, and there was almost a hopefulness in his tone. Maybe there was a reason after all.

"Emily never mentioned anything that led you to believe someone other than your normal friends and acquaintances had been talking to her?" Mike asked.

"Not specifically, no," he said.

"Not specifically?" Jude asked.

The Dawsons looked awkward. "You've got to understand. Emily was angry about everyone and everything," Mrs Dawson said. "There were times when she was completely irrational, violent and furious, and then she would swear that she hated us, hated herself, hated everything. Sometimes she said she should never have been born, or that she wished she'd never been given to us."

"That must have been very hurtful," Jude said.

"On one occasion she said she knew who her mother was, her real mother, as she put it. We didn't take a lot of notice at the time because she was saying a lot of dreadful things, and I suppose so were we. When you look back, you realise there is no point in not being honest with yourself. Sometimes I was so angry with her—"

"We had no experience of anything like it," Mr Dawson said. "Her older brother was the total opposite — calm and placid, totally at home in his own skin. We thought Emily was the same until suddenly everything fell apart around her and around us too, because frankly, we didn't know what to do. Her younger brother was terribly upset by it all and we worried about the effect it was having on him. Emily didn't want to be at home, and then she blamed us because she thought we'd shut her away. We hadn't. She was taken into hospital after she collapsed one day. If we could have had her back home and treated her here, then we would have, but . . ."

Mike knew that in real terms it didn't matter. He knew that there was nothing he or anybody else could prove about a possible contact with Anne Hargreaves, but he asked anyway. "Looking back, do you wonder if she did meet her birth mother? If Anne Hargreaves had made contact with her?"

Priscilla nodded. "It would make sense in some ways."

In some ways it might ease your pain, Mike thought sadly.

* * *

Katie Matthews and her children were back from the school run by the time Mike and Jude got to them. Both he and Jude were feeling totally wrung out by then. It was one thing to interrogate a suspect, but it was quite another to deal with raw pain, even if that pain was decades old.

Katie Matthews stood at the kitchen door, watching the children play. "So that's what he was up to," she said. "Trying to screw my father out of his business, even after everything Dad did for him. Dad treated Jason like a son, a proper flesh-and-blood son, and this is how he repaid him."

"I take it your dad's at work," Jude said.

"Yeah, he's with the accountants. Mum's there too. She used to work in the accounts department. I think she just wants to be there so she can help out in any way she can. They just can't believe Jason did that to them."

"The private investigator, Spence, says he showed you some recent photographs of your husband with other women."

"He did. The kid, that young girl, I can understand. At least she was young and pretty. But that other one . . . I mean, my God, she was my mother's age. It's disgusting."

"You mentioned that this Anne Hargreaves, the woman your husband knew as Julia Matthews, approached you on more than one occasion. Have you told us everything about what happened then? What she said?"

Katie Matthews shrugged. "Nothing else to tell. I sent her away with a flea in her ear."

"Mrs Matthews, can I ask you where you were on the night that Anne Hargreaves was killed?"

Katie frowned. "I already said. Jason was out at a business meeting — or so he said — and I was at home with the kids. Don't you lot remember anything people tell you?"

"I don't think I was there when you were asked before," Jude said gently. "I just couldn't recall what was in your statement. I know it's tiresome when you keep being asked the same thing over and over, but we need to know where *everybody* was and when, so that we can build up a timeline for that night. You know, get the whole picture. The more information we have, the more we can discount certain things and focus our attention on the essentials. If your mum and dad were here I'd be asking them the same question. If you wouldn't mind passing that message on, we'd be really grateful if they could just give us a call when they come home."

"Oh, I see." Katie looked somewhat mollified. "I suppose you can't be expected to know everything." But she glared at Mike, as though he was at fault for not informing Jude.

Mike raised an eyebrow. Smooth. But he wondered where the question had come from. Jude would have read the notes and she, of all people, would remember what Katie Matthews had said. She'd been quiet on their drive here, thoughts obviously fermenting in her mind. Mike's had most likely followed a similar direction. What if Katie Matthews had much more of an idea than she let on about what her husband was up to — not just with the other women but what he was doing to her beloved father?

"Anyway," Katie reiterated, "I was at home with the kids. Where else would I be? I'm always at home with the kids. Unless I can get a sitter, I'm always bloody home." She paused. "I might nip next door to see Linda, but if I do that I take the baby alarm with me so I can hear if the kids wake up."

"And did you do that on the night Anne Hargreaves was killed?" Mike asked.

She shrugged. "I don't think so. Linda might remember, I suppose, or one of the old women who always seem to be looking out of their bloody net curtains, no matter what time of day or night it is. You know what nosy gits they are in this close. If I did go next door, somebody would have seen, wouldn't they?

"She has a point," Jude said as they drove off. "There are an awful lot of curtain twitchers, and the neighbourhood watch is very active. But—"

"Maybe we should go and take another look," Mike finished for her. "Perhaps there is some way that Katie Matthews could have left and no one seen her. Even if that meant leaving the girls on their own."

* * *

Linda Brooks, Katie Matthews's next-door neighbour, was reluctant at first to even admit that Katie left the children on their own, but under Jude's gentle but persistent questioning, she eventually caved.

"It was only next door. She always brought their baby monitor with her, and it's not like they're little babies anymore."

"No, they're not," Jude agreed. "And I'm sure they were fine. As you say, Linda, she was only next door, and I suppose the girls knew where to find her if anything was wrong."

A tiny flicker of unease in Linda's expression. Mike spotted it too but Jude was on it in an instant. "It *was* only next door, wasn't it? She only ever left them to come and visit you?"

"Was it more than that?" Mike asked. "Linda, you're not in any trouble and neither is Katie. We're just trying to establish some facts here."

"We know her marriage was in trouble," Jude added, "and that she was unhappy. Could it have got too much for her sometimes?"

Linda looked from one to the other of them. She nodded. "You're right. She *is* unhappy. Jason is a pig of a man.

275

She knew perfectly well that he was always running after some woman or other, but he'd just say she was imagining things or that she was jealous and a bit, you know?" She touched her forehead and twirled fingers in the air.

"Neurotic?" Jude offered.

Linda nodded enthusiastically. Mike doubted that Jason had ever used that phrase, but apparently it was acceptable to Katie's friend.

"She told me . . . she told me all about him and how she'd just like to prove it, once and for all. Maybe follow him and get some pictures . . . ?" She trailed off, clearly embarrassed. "We'd sometimes have a glass or two, you know, and then she really let rip."

Mike controlled his impulse to ask the next question. Jude had eye contact with Linda, who had turned to face her, the conversation suddenly almost confidential. "And did she do that?" Jude asked, wide-eyed and sounding slightly awed, as though she considered this a daring strategy.

Linda nodded. "She did. God, she did it so often I got scared for her. I told her she'd have to stop. She'd leave the baby monitor with me, and the door key, just in case, and she'd let herself out of my back gate. You can get into James Road from there. She'd leave the car out there . . ." She hesitated. "Actually, she'd usually take mine. I park out back most of the time. It's easier if I've got the babies and the shopping. The cul-de-sac gets a bit tight." She broke off, clearly wondering suddenly what this was really all about. "Did she find anything out? I mean, I know she followed him. I know she said he was definitely cheating . . ." She looked at Jude.

She was not to be enlightened. Jude and Mike left shortly afterwards, Linda watching them from the living room window, her face now a picture of puzzlement and doubt.

"How long before she's on the phone to Katie?" Mike said.

Jude grinned. "She'll give us until we reach the end of the road. Just in case we do a Columbo and go back to ask 'just one more thing.'"

"You think Katie Matthews killed Anne Hargreaves?" Mike asked.

"I think it's becoming more and more likely," Jude said.

* * *

Mike called in to see John Tynan on the way home, taking with him photocopies of the contents of the blue book that had been found in Tom Pollard's car, together with a copy of the photograph of Silvia and her mother.

"The original has been processed, but it's being kept as evidence," Mike told John. "And we've just had word from King's Lynn. The search teams have found about a dozen more notebooks concealed beneath the floorboards."

John skimmed through the pages Mike had given him. "This is all about Jerry," he said. "Jerry and the family and . . . and about me."

"The other notebooks contain similar information," Mike said, "but pertaining to other old people whose friendship she cultivated. Other families she researched — well I suppose you could call it research. She was thorough."

John was outraged. "Some of this looks like transcripts of conversations."

"We think she probably used her phone or a digital recorder to capture conversations and transcribed anything she thought might be useful. It was elaborate and time-consuming but when you look at the properties and the money she acquired as a result of it, I suppose it could be said to be profitable. It seems that Anne Hargreaves certainly thought so."

"I feel like such an idiot," John said bitterly.

"Never that. But what we'd like you to do is pick out what information she got from you and Jerry that she deemed important. Then we can see how it all fitted together. You spent time with her, John. You stand more chance of making sense of this than an outsider might."

John pushed the pages aside and picked up his tea, drinking in great gulps as though to wash a sour taste from his mouth. "No fool like an old fool," he said at last. "Well, I was certainly taken for a fool, and right now I feel bloody old."

Mike laughed. "So get your detective brain into gear and help us figure out what this woman wanted from you and Jerry."

"Any closer to getting who killed her?"

"I think so, yes. Tom Pollard is more of a mystery, though — and I know it's unprofessional, but his death bothers me more. He seems to have been an innocent caught up in her machinations. Just a kid looking for a home. No one should die just because they want somewhere to belong."

* * *

John listened to the sound of Mike's car fading away, then picked up the photograph and studied it intently. The crease where it had been folded into the frame was a black line across the copy. Ever so gently, John touched the woman's face. The baby was small and delicate, snuggled close in her mother's arms. Baby Silvia.

It was no wonder the solicitor had failed to track down either Silvia Jones or her mother, Isobel. Jerry must have known he was sending them on a wild goose chase, paying good money to find a woman who had never existed. Or at least not under that name. But John recognised her now, and he thought he might be able to guess the rest of the story.

CHAPTER 40

Having visited the Two Bells the previous evening, Terry Gleeson told the assembled company at the morning briefing that Mr Beal had recognised Katie Matthews. She'd turned up with another woman on a quiz night, but they had been unable to persuade the two of them to make up a team. From the description of her companion, Mike guessed it was most probably Linda.

The Beals both recognised Gordon Spence as the man who'd been hanging around in the car park with the 'other journalists.' Terry hadn't disabused them of the notion.

"Thing is," Terry said," Mrs Beal is almost certain she saw him talking to Tom Pollard a day or so before the kid was killed."

"Did she hear what they were saying?"

Terry shook his head. "No, but she said Tom seemed upset or annoyed. Of course, that might just have been her interpretation, but it's interesting all the same."

It was, Mike agreed. "Did Jason Matthews come up with a reason for asking Louise Thompson to sneak a look at Tom Pollard's records?" he asked. He had arranged for Terry and Amit Jacobs to speak to Matthews while he and Jude went to see Linda Brooks.

"He insists that it was Julia Matthews — our Anne Hargreaves — who required the information. She wanted to know if Tom Pollard was telling the truth about his past — or so he says." Amit nodded towards Terry. "We both think he's dissembling, but he's sticking to his story."

"Actually, I think he's a bloody liar," Terry said. "But dissembling looks better in the report."

A brief burst of laughter broke the tension in the room.

Leaving Jude to bring the team up to speed on the notebooks found in the King's Lynn search, Mike beckoned to Terry and Amit and sent them off to see Gordon Spence.

* * *

The private investigator let them in with bad grace.

"Yes, I spoke to the boy," he said. "I told him I was sorry about what happened to his friend."

"And this was at the Two Bells," Amit said.

"Outside. I think he bought something from the burger van. Looked like a lost soul, poor lad. I don't know what that woman was to him but it must have been a real shock, her getting killed like that."

"And then he ends up dead too," Terry observed.

"And? I mean, yes, it's tragic, but I fail to see what it has to do with me."

"And who were you following that day?" Terry wanted to know. "Was Jason Matthews skipping off work again? You couldn't have been watching Anne Hargreaves because she was dead, so was our Jason out that way again?"

Spence looked both discomfited and annoyed. "I'd have to check my records. But it's quite possible it was unrelated to that investigation. As I told you before, I do have other clients, and if you can't give me a precise day or time, then how am I supposed to help you?"

* * *

Once the police had left, Spence made a phone call. "I saw you that evening, on the beach," he said. "Sooner or later I'm going to have to mention that fact."

He paused. Listened.

"No, I'm not threatening you, just telling you honestly that it will come out. That boy is dead, that woman is dead and . . . yes, yes, all right. Two o'clock. Yes, I can manage that. The usual coffee shop."

Spence rang off and stood for a moment, considering. He almost decided to call Mike Croft. Almost. He would raise the matter when he met his client, try and persuade her that honesty was the best policy. After all, she was only *talking* to the young man when he saw her that night, her hooded jumper pulled up against the cold that had suddenly rolled in as the wind changed and blew off the sea. He had spotted her from the clifftop, surprised first to see her there and then even more surprised to see her speaking to the boy.

"Keep an eye on him for me," Katie had said. "I don't want him thinking he can just pick up where that bitch left off."

CHAPTER 41

Katie Matthews was not an impulsive woman but she was used to making swift decisions. She made one now. Spence was not to be trusted. Damn the man, he was supposed to be working for her! Some sense of loyalty he had.

She checked her watch. Just a little after ten. Her parents would be out all day, still dealing with the legal team and the accountants and her girls would be at school until three, so there was plenty of time. She opened the cutlery drawer and removed one of the old-fashioned wooden handled steak knives her parents had had since they were first married. She slipped it into her handbag, checked she had her keys and phone and drove off to Spence's home.

* * *

John received a phone call from the diocesan office mid-morning. A preliminary report on the bones suggested they belonged to a baby no more than three months old and probably somewhat younger. The bones were in a very poor state, so it was unlikely that DNA would be found or be viable even if it could be extracted. The wooden box in which the tiny body had been buried had decayed but it seemed that her coffin had been improvised from packaging for motorcycle parts.

"But she had been wrapped in a blanket or shawl," John was told. "There are fragments of textile."

She. The tiny infant they assumed was Silvia.

"And there's one more thing. She was buried with a toy, a tiny little thing, but it looks like a dog. One of the team suggested it might be a Britains toy, you know, the people who made lead soldiers and that sort of thing. Apparently they made animals as well."

There was a pause while John absorbed this. A dog. Had it been a black dog? The thought almost made him laugh.

"It suggests that someone cared. The shawl, the toy, the fact that she was buried in a churchyard. It all indicates that she was loved."

Oh, Silvia was loved. But it didn't alter the fact that John still didn't know how she died. The bones were too fragile and too few to reveal the answer.

* * *

Spence was surprised to open the door to his flat and see Katie Matthews standing there.

"I thought we were meeting this afternoon," he said.

"Change of plan."

She walked ahead of him into the flat, and Spence was left with no option but to follow her. They stood in his living room, facing each other. "Look," he said. "I've no intention of making trouble for you. I reckon you've got enough to deal with right now. But the fact is, other people will have reported seeing someone talking to young Tom Pollard and—"

"And the only one who can tell the police it was me happens to be you."

"Well, I suppose so, but what does that matter? You must have connected the boy to the woman Jason was seeing. What could be more natural than that you took the opportunity to . . . Katie, Mrs Matthews, what are you doing?"

He backed away.

As though it was the most natural thing in the world, Katie Matthews had taken the steak knife from her bag and pointed it at Gordon Spence. She sighed. "It worked once, so let's see if I can get it right a second time, shall we?"

Gordon had backed up about as far as he could go. She had him pinned, between table and wall. He tried to make a run for it, push her out of the way, but Katie Matthews was a woman on a mission. The knife entered his body. Graham Spence screamed and fell.

Katie turned on her heel and walked away.

Once in her car she glanced at her watch. Too early to go back home and much too early to go and wait for Gordon Spence to meet her at the coffee shop. She checked her clothes for blood, relieved to see only a trace on her sleeve. She rolled her sleeves up and decided that maybe her time would best be spent buying something to replace the shirt. There was plenty of time before two o'clock. She planned to keep her appointment with Graham Spence, knowing that he'd probably noted it in his diary or even mentioned it to someone. It would, Katie thought, look suspicious if she didn't turn up.

Katie started her car and drove away.

CHAPTER 42

They arrested Katie Matthews at the coffee shop. She was drinking a cappuccino, supposedly waiting for Graham Spence, when Mike and Jude entered and sat down opposite her. Uniformed officers had been stationed at the exits.

"Graham Spence is currently in surgery," Mike said. "He'll probably live."

"Shame," Katie said. "Mind if I finish my coffee?"

"No, I don't mind."

With a steady hand, she drained her cup and set it squarely on the saucer. "I've made a right pig's ear of things, haven't I?"

"You have," Mike said.

"I thought the second one was supposed to be easier. The first time I was just so bloody angry. Spence had brought me those photographs and all I could think was that Jason had betrayed me with . . . that! Then I found out what she was really up to. My dad's a good man. He was good to us, good to Jason. He didn't deserve what Jason did to him."

"But it was the woman you attacked, not your husband." Mike was curious now. "Look," he added, "I can't exactly do the interview here, can I?"

"I suppose not," Katie agreed. "Why did I go after her and not Jason? Because it was her that told my idiot of a husband just what to do and how to do it. Jason couldn't have worked it all out, he hasn't two brain cells to rub together."

"We should go now," Jude said quietly. "You can tell us all about it at the station. You need to do it properly, you know."

Katie made no fuss and gave them no trouble. Mike watched the uniformed officers lead her away. "She seems shocked," he said. "Like she almost doesn't believe what she's done."

"And she only spoke of a second time," Jude added. "So what about Tom Pollard? What happened to him?"

CHAPTER 43

Maria was packing when John Tynan arrived that evening.

"So, you finally get to take Mike to see the new baby."

"We'll be leaving first thing tomorrow. Stick the kettle on, I'll just put these in before I forget." She had a selection of toiletries in her hands. Small packs, made for travelling. Not like Martha. To him, Anne Hargreaves would always be Martha.

Mike was cooking.

"So, it was the wife," John said, filling the kettle and switching it on.

"It was the wife," Mike confirmed. "For what it's worth, I don't think she initially intended to do anything more than confront Martha . . . I need to get used to calling her Anne, I suppose. But things got out of hand, and once she'd embarked on that particular journey, she couldn't turn back."

* * *

Mike had seen to it that Katie was taken into the less formal of the interview rooms. One more usually reserved for witnesses and victims than for the accused. Her father had arranged for a solicitor and it was clear, from the way he greeted Katie, that he was also a family friend.

"You don't have to say anything, Katie," he'd told her. "You don't have to."

"Yes I do," she told him. "It's all right. I need to. I want to."

She'd taken a deep breath, wrapped both hands around her coffee cup. Mike started the tape, listed those present, and then she had begun.

"I knew what room she was staying in. I'd planned to wait for her there, and then I realised there was no one staying in the room across the hall, so I hid in there. I'd only gone to talk to her, you know, try and warn her off, and I almost changed my mind and went home but the pub got busy and I knew I'd be seen. So I had to wait it out." Katie had looked at Mike, as though checking that he understood.

"Go on," he'd told her, gently. He kept having to remind himself that she was a murderer. She seemed suddenly very fragile and uncertain, all brash and bluster had disappeared.

"I heard her go into the bathroom and then Mrs Beal came up the stairs and told her there'd been a phone call for her earlier, and then I heard her running a bath and shutting the door and then someone else coming up the stairs. I looked out through a crack in the door and I saw Jason. He went into her room like he was used to doing it, you know? So I waited. I wanted to catch the pair of them together, confirm what Spence had told me." She paused. Grimaced.

"You know what? My pride was hurt more than anything else. I wanted to catch them in the act. Confront the pair of them."

"But you didn't," Mike said.

She shook her head. "I heard her come out of the bathroom and I was just about to follow her into the room but she must have opened the door and seen him." Katie laughed. "She wasn't pleased. She said something like 'what the hell are you doing here? I told you to stay away,' and so I waited to hear what would happen next. I kind of realised that this was something else. Not just sex."

"Do you know what time this was?"

"Midnight, just after. I'd left Linda in charge but I was still worried about getting back to the kids. They don't usually wake up, but . . ."

"And what did you hear?"

For the first time, Katie seemed genuinely upset. She had learned to deal with her husband's affairs, after a fashion, but not this. "Jason said he thought my dad was on to him. He'd been asking awkward questions about some contract that was due to be signed off the following week. It had all been fine but now the CEO of the other company was being difficult, trying to delay matters. Anyway, I listened and I realised . . . realised this wasn't an affair, it was a business arrangement. The pair of them were screwing my dad over. And after all he'd done for Jason. After all he'd done."

Katie fell silent.

"And what happened then?" Mike prompted gently.

"Jason was leaving. He'd been there maybe an hour. I heard him go downstairs and then she went into the bathroom again. I followed Jason. I saw him unlock the door and I was going to follow him out when I thought . . . I thought, why should that fucking woman get away with it? Jason would never have done any of that on his own. He just isn't that frigging bright. And then . . . and then I thought it might be dangerous, you know? So I went over to the cutlery tray and I took the knife."

For the first time, he sensed, she had strayed from the truth. Katie Matthews had not been frightened at all. She had been vengeful.

Mike held his peace. "Go on," he said. "You took the knife and . . . . . ?"

"And I went back up the stairs. I opened the door, she turned to face me and I stabbed her. Drove the knife right in, up to the handle." She looked almost apologetic. "Like I keep telling the kids, you never know what you're capable of until you try. Or you're really up against it. She fell back and straight away, I knew she was dead."

"And then?"

"I thought she'd probably have Jason's number in her phone and I didn't want anything linking her to him." She paused. "I never thought about the bloody dog hairs."

"So you took the phone."

"It was in her bag. I took that and a little address book thing. I don't know if he was in either but I wanted to make sure."

She paused, took a sip of coffee and seemed to gather her thoughts.

"And you left the way you'd seen Jason go out?"

"Yeah. And I kept an eye open for where the security lights were. I'd parked up the road away from the pub and I was heading back to my car when I saw the boy."

"Tom Pollard."

"If that's his name. He was walking down towards the Bells. I didn't think he'd seen me but . . . Anyway, I dodged into the field and stayed there until I thought he'd gone and then I thought of the phone and the book. If I took them home, well. Part of me wanted to take them back and confront Jason, but then he'd know what I'd done. I didn't want to risk taking them into my house. It was like . . . like they were contaminated, you know?"

"So you . . . ?"

"Rabbit holes. I nearly twisted my ankle stepping in one. I keep a tiny little torch on my key ring. I found a rabbit hole, smashed the phone and shoved the whole lot in."

"The address book as well?"

Katie nodded. "I pushed everything down as far as I could, and chucked the SIM card and memory card out of the car window on the way home. I read somewhere that you can trace a SIM but not a phone."

She slumped back in her chair, her face grey with exhaustion. She had clearly finished.

But Mike wasn't done yet.

"And Tom Pollard? Did you kill him?"

Katie Matthews laughed. "No. Why would I do that? I didn't kill Jason either, did I? Look." She leaned forward with sudden energy. "The way I see it, some people are manipulative and other people are born to be manipulated. To be taken for every ride going. Jason is like that. I figured this kid must be too. I was certain he'd not seen me but . . . Anyway, Spence let me know where he usually parked that little car of his and I drove over a time or two, just on the off-chance. Got Spence to keep an eye out. He called me that night to say the kid was on the beach, chucking stones into the water and drinking, and did I want him to see what he could find out. I told him no. It didn't matter anymore."

"But you went out there yourself."

Katie nodded. "Tom Pollard was too drunk to see straight. I talked to him for a bit but he was making no sense, he kept pointing at me and laughing and saying, 'I know about you. You're the wife. You're the poor bloody wife.'"

"That must have hurt."

"Pissed me off. Anyway, what happened. I didn't kill him. He fell. He was up on one of the breakwaters, fooling about trying to balance. I told him he'd fall. He was standing up there, looking down at me with that expression on his face. That contemptuous expression like I was just shit on his shoe. 'You're the wife. You're the poor bloody wife.' I just made a swipe at him. Didn't even touch him. But he kind of wobbled and lost his balance, and then he fell. Hit his head."

* * *

"Do you believe her?" John asked when Mike had finished his account.

"His blood-alcohol level was high. He could have fallen. She could well have assisted gravity. Chances are we'll never know. It's the two little girls I feel sorry for."

"It's always the children who suffer," John said.

"Any more news on the baby?"

John shook his head. "Silvia Jones could well have died of natural causes. This was a year before the NHS was established. Families couldn't always afford medical care. Babies die now. I imagine more died then."

"Then why not arrange a proper burial?" Mike asked. "If she was your uncle Jerry's child?"

"If she was. I've come to doubt that, Mike."

"Was there something in Anne Hargreaves's blue book?"

"That, and other papers," John said. "Little clues here and there. If you don't mind, I'm not ready to talk about it yet."

And so the subject was left alone. They ate a meal and chatted about nothing. John admired the latest baby photos Maria had on her phone.

As he drove home, John allowed his thoughts to return to the little burial. To the family into which the child had been born, the brute of a man who had fathered her and the son who had tried to protect the mother and the baby, not knowing that the child was already dead.

Transcripts from the book kept by the woman he had known as Martha Toolin, of conversations she'd had with Jerry. She'd obviously recorded what he'd said and then written it in her book. "*He said if I wanted the girl to be left in peace then I'd better give the child my name. And I'd better go back and live with him. Take care of him in his old age. My Lord, the girl was just fifteen. Poor little chick, what could she do to protect herself from a man like him? Mean he was, with the drink in him. Mean as hell.*"

Issy, the girl who'd come with her mother to clean and cook for his grandfather. Issy, who'd come alone to the big house when her mother was ill. Little Issy who had died only weeks after her baby had been born. John had recognised her in the photograph that Jerry had kept for all those years and which had finally come into Martha's possession. He had thereby come to know how she had died because he now knew where to look for her death certificate. What name to look for. Isabel Manch. Suicide. She had hanged herself when she had left the home for unwed mothers and her family had refused to take her back. And John now recognised the voice of the other woman in his grandfather's house — Isobel's mother, bringing the baby to the house of the man who'd fathered her and expecting him to accept responsibility.

"As if," John said to himself. "As if he ever would or could."

So what had happened to baby Silvia after that night? How had she ended up buried secretly in that tiny grave? One thing was certain, John's mother had known, but she had now taken the secret with her to her own grave. Jerry had spent his life living with a man he hated and, if Martha's transcript was to be believed, had done so to protect the reputation of an innocent girl and her child.

Or had he got it all wrong? Had Jerry in fact returned to prevent his father from doing further harm? Ernest Matthews had raped a child, fathered another, maybe even killed that baby — at any rate, his actions had driven that poor young mother to suicide. That, and the rejection by her own kin.

Had Jerry been gaoler rather than victim? That made far more sense. And had Jerry known that Silvia was dead? The more John thought about it the more he thought that Jerry probably had, that the wild goose chase he had sent the solicitor on was to keep the woman he had known as Martha from getting to the truth. This woman that they knew was capable of blackmail.

Was Jerry still trying to protect the family name? To protect John? It was an odd thought. "That *is* a rum 'un," John muttered to himself. More than rum, but it would do for now. Rum was manageable.

Feeling lighter than he had in days, John pulled up in front of his own little cottage, switched off the engine and sat in the silence.

So Ernest Matthews's house would soon be his after all. John had already decided what to do with it. The whole damned pile should be burned to the ground, and John was more than happy to light the bonfire.

Slowly, John got out of his car and wandered up the path to his small front door. He paused, key in hand. Somewhere in the distance, a dog was howling.

THE END

ALSO BY JANE ADAMS

FREE KINDLE BOOKS

Please join our mailing list for free Kindle books and new releases, including crime thrillers, mysteries, romance and more.

www.joffebooks.com

Thank you for reading this book. If you enjoyed it please leave feedback on Amazon or Goodreads, and if there is anything we missed or you have a question about then please get in touch. The author and publishing team appreciate your feedback and time reading this book.

We're very grateful to eagle-eyed readers who take the time to contact us. Please send any errors you find to corrections@joffebooks.com

Printed in Great Britain
by Amazon